What the critics are saying…

"Recommended Read/ *5 Angels*" ~ *Fallen Angel Reviews*

"*5 Stars*" ~ *JERR*

"*5 Cups*" ~ Coffee Time Romance

Rhyannon Byrd

A Bite of Magick

MAGICK MEN II

ELLORA'S CAVE
ROMANTICA PUBLISHING

An Ellora's Cave Romantica Publication

www.ellorascave.com

Magick Men II: A Bite of Magick

ISBN # 1419952110
ALL RIGHTS RESERVED.
A Bite of Magick Copyright© 2004 Rhyannon Byrd
Edited by: Pamela Campbell
Cover art by: Syneca

Electronic book Publication: November, 2004
Trade paperback Publication: August, 2005

Excerpt from *Against the Wall* Copyright © Rhyannon Byrd, 2004

Warning:

The following material contains graphic sexual content meant for mature readers. *Magick Men II: A Bite of Magick* has been rated *E-rotic* by a minimum of three independent reviewers.

Ellora's Cave Publishing offers three levels of Romantica™ reading entertainment: S (S-ensuous), E (E-rotic), and X (X-treme).

S-*ensuous* love scenes are explicit and leave nothing to the imagination.

E-*rotic* love scenes are explicit, leave nothing to the imagination, and are high in volume per the overall word count. In addition, some E-rated titles might contain fantasy material that some readers find objectionable, such as bondage, submission, same sex encounters, forced seductions, etc. E-rated titles are the most graphic titles we carry; it is common, for instance, for an author to use words such as "fucking", "cock", "pussy", etc., within their work of literature.

X-*treme* titles differ from E-rated titles only in plot premise and storyline execution. Unlike E-rated titles, stories designated with the letter X tend to contain controversial subject matter not for the faint of heart.

Also by Rhyannon Byrd:

A Bite of Magick
Magick Men II

Trademarks Acknowledgement

The author acknowledges the trademarked status and trademark owners of the following wordmarks mentioned in this work of fiction:

Levi's: Levi Strauss & Co. Corporation

Pottery Barn: International Designers Group, Inc. Corporation

Betsey Johnson: B. J. Vines, Inc. Corporation

Jaguar: Jaguar Cars Limited Corporation United Kingdom

Land Rover: Rover Company Limited, The Corporation

The Sopranos: Time Warner Entertainment Company, L.P. American Television and Communications Corporation (DE Corp.); Warner Communications Inc. (DE Corp.) Limited Partnership

Bewitched: Screen Gems, Inc. Corporation

The Man Show: Funhouse Productions, Inc. Corporation

McEwans (Scottish Ale): Scottish & Newcastle Brewiers PLC Corporation United Kingdom

Playgirl: Playgirl Key Club, Inc.

The Man Show: Funhouse Productions, INC

Harry Potter: Time Warner Entertainment Company, L.P. American Television and Communications Corporation

Prologue

Susie MacIntyre was a wicked little Witch, and Kieran McKendrick was about to ride her hard and long.

It'd been one hell of a week, what with his cousin's Binding Ceremony and obvious bliss. Not that Kieran wasn't happy as hell for the man he loved like his own brother — but the enviable glow of pleasure Lach wore these days was wearing him thin. He hated to admit it, but he was losing the battle against the darkness within his soul. Bit by bit, it was rooting beneath his carefree surface, tunneling under his skin, making his bitterness all the more frustrating.

Bitterness he'd done well to shield from even those who knew him best.

And though he struggled to deny it, Kieran could feel the hard edge of its power, steady with intent, digging its claws into his heart until he felt as if the burdensome organ would shatter from the mounting pressure.

In short, it was a living, breathing nightmare, and he was going to do what he did best to forget about it — if only for a few moments — and screw the hell out of a hot little *Cailleach*.

Susie lay back on her lavish, satin-covered bed, her smile wantonly sly as she spread her smooth, pale thighs, letting him see just how wet and ready she was for him.

He stared with his dark-as-midnight eyes, trying to work up some hunger for it — for her. Damn, even a flicker of interest would've been a relief, but about the only bloody response he could manage was the hard-on slowly taking shape within his pants.

Thankfully, it was more than impressive enough to blind her to the fact that he was having to work really hard to get "up" the enthusiasm to nail her.

Saephus, what the hell was his problem? Women didn't get better looking than Susie, even if she had the personality of a pit bull, which was being damn unfair to the breed. She was tall and lean with a drenched pussy and pink-tipped breasts like melons. He should've been drooling like a randy dog, instead of mulling over the fact that Lach had found love.

Damn it, he was genuinely happy for the man. So why was he so pissed off? Why was he so damn restless?

Maybe because he understood his own turn was coming—and he knew only too well there wasn't another Evan Hayes waiting just around the corner for him.

Not that he wanted his cousin's pretty little mortal wife. Oh, he'd have fucked her in a heartbeat if she weren't already taken by his best friend, but he held no love for her beyond that of family.

She was Lach's now. That was it. End of story.

No—it was the connection they shared. Kieran marveled at it—chewed on it during the long Scottish nights, trying to get a handle on it.

It was an age-old question. How did a man know when he had the right woman? Or Witch, in his case, as he avoided the *gnach* whenever possible. And he sure as hell never screwed them.

But what was the sign for that kind of love? What did it feel like? And where in the name of Saephus' sacred battleground was he going to find a woman who could accept him as he was, thorns and all?

He snorted to himself, thinking "thorns" was probably putting it a little lightly—spreading it a little thin. He'd managed to contain that primitive side of his soul for so long, but he could feel his control weakening, like precious oil slipping between his fingers as he tried to trap it within his palm. And when that tenuous hold was finally lost, Kieran knew there'd be hell to pay.

Damn it, he should have heeded his father's advice long ago and embraced his birth curse, rather than battle the beast for absolute dominance. His resistance had steadily become a weakness...a distraction...a vulnerability—dangerous liabilities he simply couldn't afford these days.

Things he could never afford, damn it, but certainly not *now*. Not with a pain-in-the-ass mating curse just waiting to knock him on his ass.

Before him, Susie spread her legs farther, raising her knees higher, eyeing the bulge of his cock behind the fly of his black jeans like it was gonna be her friggin' dessert. She licked her lips, and not even the sight of her pink little tongue had his blood racing. Man, he must be dead inside. That—or bored outta his ever-loving mind. Since when had nailing a gorgeous Witch become such a bloody chore for the McKendrick cousin known to fuck for days on end when the hunger was riding him hard?

He nearly laughed at the thought, thinking that he and his cousins were *all* pretty much known for their outrageous sex drives. They caught quite a bit of flack for it, too, but had learned to take the good-natured ribbing in stride—except for Dugan, who was just the sort that one didn't comfortably tease. Something about those dark green eyes, their intent expression of constant alertness, combined with the title of Enforcer, tended to make him the kind of *Magick* that most steered clear from. All, that is, except for his cousins, who took an almost painful joy in pushing his buttons.

Susie gave a throaty moan, jerking his attention back to the moment, though he was beginning to wish he'd never bothered coming here in the first place. She was beautiful, aye, but somehow...not what he wanted. Though what he did want, he wasn't even sure he could say. Just...*not this*.

He watched as she eased back on her elbows atop the black satin sheets, a lascivious pose meant to entice, and he tried like hell to play along. The gods only knew he'd played the game enough times to go through the motions, even if his heart wasn't in it.

Huh—and wasn't that the crux of the issue right there? Wasn't he waiting for his own turn to be cursed by the Council…simply because his heart had *never* been in it?

"Come here, Kieran," Susie purred in a seductive murmur, demanding his attention as she trailed her blood-red fingernails down the sides of her voluptuous breasts. "I've got something that'll make you feel all better."

His black brow rose at the trite words. "Who says I'm no' feeling fine, Suse?"

Her rouged lips lifted at the corners, ice blue eyes moving over the shoulder-length black silk of his hair, across the wide breadth of his T-shirt-covered chest, before settling on the firm, sensual line of his mouth. "You look like someone just stole your best friend. Pouting that Lach'll never go tomcatting around with you again, big guy? Because I've seen the way he looks at his little wife, and that man's cock has been staked for good. It's sad really. I used to enjoy fucking my way through the McKendrick boys. You're an impressive group, if I do say so myself."

"I'll be sure to pass on the compliment," he drawled in a sardonic tone that was clearly lost on her, and crossed the distance to her bed in a long, lazy stride that spoke of power and masculine grace, if not a subtle touch of danger. He kept his black eyes glued to her cunt, watching the way it breathed, dripping with cream the closer he came. Feeling the sudden need to get the whole damn thing over and done with, he ripped open his fly and took his still growing erection into the firm, biting grip of his fist. He gritted his teeth, and a few violent pumps of his shaft had the wide, round head wet and purple.

Through narrowed eyes, he watched how Susie eyed his cock with rapt fascination while he dug a rubber out of his back pocket, ripped it open with his teeth, and slipped the thin latex over the burning length of skin. He pumped again, feeling his blood surge beneath his fingers, the ever-thickening root transforming into an impossibly long, massive rod of steel-like flesh.

True to the name McKendrick, his size went beyond that which was normally considered "well-endowed" — and he could feel the little Witch's lust for every single vein-ridged inch of his impressive equipment. Too bad he'd grown bored with "impressing" wicked little Witches ages ago.

She moaned up at him while her heart-shaped face flushed with heat and hunger, perfect teeth biting into her blood-red lip. Kieran grabbed her beneath her knees, shoved them back against her chest, and drove straight into her, giving her every brutal inch with his first digging thrust.

A raw, carnal sound of ecstasy and surprise shot past her lips as she fell back against the bed from the force of the powerful impact, her perfect features warped into a twisted mask of pain and pleasure beneath him. He'd screwed her enough times to know how rough she liked it — to know her limits...or lack thereof. He could ride her as hard as he dared, his massive cock pounding her with a driving, savage force, and she'd only beg him for more.

There'd been a time when he'd found her insatiable, bloodthirsty sex drive a refreshing change from the restraint he'd normally been forced to use, even with the most experienced *Cailleachs*, the only women who could truly hope to enjoy his size — but now it just bored him.

Hell, these days, everything bored him...including mindless fucking.

No two ways about it, he was in some serious shit. Susie's juice-soaked cunt gave way too easily around him, and the boredom settled heavily into his balls, dragging them down like weights. Ah, hell, his mind was already wandering...drifting away.

Shit, man, focus! Focus!

He pulled back, drove deeper, changed his angle and then rammed even harder, staring down at her with sightless eyes as he desperately tried to lose himself within her accommodating depths. He felt a moment's remorse that he could use her so coldly, until the painful raking of her nails down his shirt-covered back reminded him that she was only looking for the fuck his monstrous cock could provide. She held no interest in the man himself—or his demons.

Saephus, what am I doing here? he thought with an inner snarl directed solely at himself. He forced his hips to work harder, desperate for the release that would leave her wrung out with pleasure and afford him his immediate escape. He had to get away—be alone—and get his bloody head together. He pumped his hips in firm circles, pulsing against Susie's swollen clit, and she finally broke, writhing around the buried root of his throbbing dick like the cock-hungry little Witch that she was.

"*Yes,*" he snarled through his teeth, finally feeling a hot surge of cum blast through the core of his cock. It exploded from the sensitive organ, pumping like blistering lava from the nestled slit in the wide head, and for that one shattering moment, he felt a second of calm—a cool, motionless pool that quieted the raging in his head, offering him one uninterrupted instant of blissful peace.

The calm before the thundering storm.

Susie had already fallen thankfully quiet, but his ears were still ringing from the keening pitch of her screams as they continued to echo through the stillness of the night. He sighed, eyes stinging with sweat as it dripped from his head in streaming rivulets, the physical hungers of his body momentarily sated, if not completely satisfied. Arms straight, his hands fisted in the bedding at her shoulders, he was careful not to touch her anywhere but the warm, wet place where his cock impaled her cum-soaked pussy. Blinking her into focus, he saw her eyes were now closed, as if she already slept, and he grunted in relief, pleased to know he'd fucked her into a sound enough sleep that he could easily get away.

He tightened his muscles, preparing to carefully pull back his hips, when he felt the tingling at the base of his spine, spreading up over his nape, pounding within his temples—and Kieran knew he'd just landed in hell.

"*No!*" he roared, plunging involuntarily deeper, waking Susie with his murderous bellow and burgeoning cock, pressing her into the giving mattress as his body came down heavily against her own. "*Oh shit! Not now! Not now—*"

He tried to pull out, but Susie's strong legs wrapped around him, pulling him deeper, another wave of clenching release instantly firing through her quivering sex. She writhed beneath him, eyes open and passion-glazed, unaware of the danger driving into her greedy depths, and Kieran grasped at the shreds of his control as he struggled not to give over. Their hair flew around their flushed faces, the rumpled bedsheets thrashing in the strong blasts of air as his power broke free, whipping the inside of her immaculate bedroom into a stormy frenzy. His teeth gnashed, jaw aching—but the second the wide head of his cock rammed against her womb, forcing another sharp scream from her throat, Kieran felt the inevitable change coming over him.

Chapter One
Three Months Later

He was in a bad way—so fucking bad it felt as if a noose were cinched around his neck, the world going black from his growing lack of faith that this nightmare would ever be over. For the past three months, he'd searched from one end of the British Isles to the other and found nothing.

No one.

Not a single goddamn woman who tempted him.

No escape.

And here he thought he'd been prepared for his father and uncles, after the hell he'd watched Lach go through, but the crafty old bastards had struck straight at his Achilles' heel.

They hadn't cursed him—they'd cursed his bloody beast. That part of himself which he struggled against the hardest—that he fought to contain—and here they'd gone and released it with no care whatsoever for the outcome. It was open season on his soul, and Kieran very much feared that once the cursed creature escaped again, once it got another taste of the carnal pleasures of sex, he'd never be able to fully rein it back in.

Saephus only knew it'd been hard enough to do with Susie, and he hadn't changed until *after* he'd fucked her.

From the time of his birth, he'd been marked with a black curse upon his blood, thanks to the ancient Witch Serena the Sable. A curse that he had always struggled to control, no matter how strongly the Council tried to convince him to do otherwise. He knew the dangers of refusing to embrace what he was, thanks to his mother's bloodline, but what they couldn't understand was that he had no choice. To give in would have been far more dangerous than the battle.

For in truth, he enjoyed the beast's power far more than his own *Magick*.

And it scared the ever-loving hell out of him.

His father and uncles knew this—knew he feared the animal's dominance over him, though he'd kept the creature's increasing restlessness to himself as it grew over the recent years—and yet, still, they had placed the mating curse upon him in a way that left him completely at its mercy. That was the most disturbing thought of all, because it meant that as much as they wanted little ones to bounce upon their knees and to fill the family halls with laughter, there was a greater purpose behind their dangerous meddling than mere procreation.

A purpose the Council had as yet kept to themselves. Saephus, there had to be. Nothing else could even begin to justify them taking these blasted curses to such diabolical lengths.

Something had to be coming—a danger brewing that would be a threat to them all. It was the only justification Kieran could conceive of that would push them to such extremes.

The Council obviously wanted to ensure that the family was not only assured of a future generation in the form of bonny little McKendricks, but they wanted to see the current generation in prime condition to handle whatever might be headed their way. It was the worst form of coercion, but clearly, their logical conclusion was to see the whole bloody lot of them mated. For only through a Binding Ceremony based upon true, everlasting love, could a Warlock ever hope to gain a definitive knowledge and understanding of his power in its absolute entirety.

Not that he gained greater, or even extra *Magick* through the union with his *bith-bhuan gra*, his soul mate, but the perfect balance that having her by his side provided within his soul opened a doorway into his ability to access that power—to harness his *Magick* for the purposes of protecting his loved ones.

Yin and yang. The chalice and the blade. The concept was nothing new — the knowledge that two parts could produce one perfect union. And from that perfection was born the understanding of all that one's *Magick* could accomplish.

It was a subject looked upon gravely by the Council, for they had learned their lessons the hard way. Believing themselves invincible, they had arrogantly refused to be mated and bonded to the Witches who bore their sons, leaving their fledgling families vulnerable to attack. One by one, they had lost their chances at everlasting happiness as they lost their lovers — which is why Kieran suspected they were now willing to take such warped measures to see his cousins and him successfully bonded for all eternity.

His father and uncles knew firsthand the agony and repercussions of their mistakes. And with a little help from their clever mating curses, they intended to see those same mistakes were not repeated by their sons and nephews.

And the boon of their endeavors — they got the grandchildren they had so desperately been waiting for.

For such a powerful force of *Magick*, they were still a group of old softies at the end of the day.

Nosey old softies who had seen fit to play havoc with his and his cousins' lives with the cunning of the devil himself.

And their insufferable plan was working.

So far, only Lachlan had been bonded, but already his abilities were increasing at an exponential rate. Whereas before he could control the wind with no more than a flick of his wrist, Kieran knew that he could now call a thunderous hurricane on little more than a whim. And though Lach's skill as a warrior had always been fierce, there was no denying that he now possessed such mastery over his powers, it was difficult for others to spar with him. Not without ending up on their asses, their bodies aching and sore for days on end.

These powers which he and his family shared — the power to control the elements and beyond — were not to be used lightly, a fact which only worried Kieran all the more. If he found his mate—his *bith-bhuan gra*—and his already incredible abilities grew in strength and intensity, how would he continue to control the feral side of his nature? Would it too feel the heady increase of power? And how would he keep that primitive side of himself from abusing such power?

It was enough to drive a man—a Warlock even—mad in the way the worry could spiral upon itself in his mind, weaving deeper and deeper into his soul like an insidious sickness.

And to top it all, he was hornier than hell. So randy he hurt from his soles to his scalp, his body one throbbing pulse of sexual agony. A first-class case of blue balls that would have made a normal man break down and cry, begging for absolution. It was a disgusting thought, though there were times when Kieran feared he wasn't far from it.

He hadn't fucked in months. Months! And this from a man—well, Warlock—who never went more than a day or so without a hot, willing Witch to satisfy his physical needs. And pumping himself did no good. Just as Lach had been unable to drive himself to orgasm with the clench of his fist, neither could Kieran. All it did was increase the agony of having a dick in dire need of a serious distraction. Saephus, his cock was so fucking primed, he felt as if he'd blow his load at the first sight of slick, wet pussy—but he hadn't let himself be tempted to try.

The consequences were too damn dangerous. He'd barely escaped with Susie. Would have failed to, in fact, if not for her quick thinking and vicious temper. Not that he blamed her. Hell, he'd thank her for saving them both, were it not for the vow she'd taken to see him dead before ever speaking to him again.

And to think he'd thought Lach had had it bad. Hell, having a cursed cock was nothing compared to this.

As if he could read his mind, his cousin's auburn brow rose above his clear green eyes. Lach stared at him from across their corner table in The Wicked Brew, a knowing grin breaking across his rugged face. "I told ya I'd be smiling like a jackass. And before you start in with your complainin', let's just remember who said he'd no' have any objections when his own turn came along."

A low, beastly growl rumbled from Kieran's throat, his big hands fisting and releasing in his lap, dark eyes bright with fury. The tips of his fingers tingled with the power of the *beithíoch*— the beast—a fact he refused to even dignify with acknowledgement. "It isna the bloody same and you know it. At least you had a choice! I canna even *try* to bed a lass unless I want to see myself bloody mated to her for all eternity. Look what almost happened with Suse!"

At the mention of the name, Lach winced. Kieran wished his reaction could be as simple. Instead, the memory of that night flooded him with bone-chilling terror. After all, that was the night he'd almost found himself mated to a bitch of a Witch for all eternity.

Saephus save him. He shuddered, and the jackass' smile fell back into place. "What you need, Cousin, is a new outlook on life."

Kieran snorted. "And why do I get the feeling this is another one of your bloody ideas that I'm no' going to like the sound of?"

The gods only knew there'd been enough of them over the years—like the time when they were randy teens and Lach had convinced him that sneaking into Katie Green's bedroom for a midnight visit (after the pretty little seventeen-year-old had spent the entire day making eyes at him during her sister's Binding Ceremony) was a sound idea. With Lach waiting on the lawn below, Kieran had used his power over the wind to elevate himself to the girl's second-story balcony, snuck into the darkened room, and created a flickering sphere of flame upon his palm to help him locate the busty, beautiful Miss Green within her bed—hoping to find her waiting for him.

Aye, it'd been a sound plan—right up to the point where he'd found himself standing face-to-face not with the blushing little brunette, but Angus Green, the girl's Neanderthal father, who'd obviously known a hell of a lot more about protecting his daughter than they'd known about planning seductions. It'd taken Angus but moments to convince Kieran that the bonny Katie was not to be pursued by what he called "those hound dog McKendricks", and then he'd been promptly tossed right back out the bloody window.

Hell, to this day Kieran could still remember how sore his backside was after landing on his blasted cousin, taking them both crashing down to the dew-covered lawn. He'd been too stunned to remember to use his power to soften the fall—a fact Lach had teased him about until his hotheaded temper had gotten the better of him. Before he knew it, he and Lach had been brawling across that cold, wet grass, laughing nearly as hard as they were hitting, until Angus had finally had enough of them and called the Council to come and collect them. But by that time, they'd already turned the man's immaculate garden into a thundering, sopping mess as their powers broke free and rained down upon their brawling bodies—all in the name of good-natured fun.

Of course, neither of them had thought it was *fun* when they'd been forced to spend the next two weeks of their winter break putting everything back to rights—without the use of their *Magick*. It'd been a lesson that the Council had struggled to make them all understand as they grew into men—to control one's *Magick* and never carelessly leak it out upon the lives of others.

"Why do you get that feeling?" Lach repeated with a low chuckle, suddenly snagging Kieran's attention back to the present. "Maybe because you know me so well?"

Kieran couldn't help it. His cousin's look of marital enchantment was pissing him off, and he knew better than most that when he was mad, he was dangerous. It was just one of the many things that made him so good at what he did, protecting other *Magicks* from those who would cause his kind harm. He was well-trained and an expert soldier. Damn it, he should've been able to handle Lach's teasing, but the bloody bastard had been grinning for months now, while all he wanted to do was rage at the blasted futility of his situation. "I'm going to have to tell Evan to stop loving you so well," he all but snarled. "I swear you're no' fit to live with anymore."

Lach shook his head, his eyes sparking with mischief despite Kieran's threatening tone. "If I dinna know better, I'd say you sound just a mite jealous."

Well, hell. That stung. But what Warlock in his right mind wouldn't want what Lach had found? The kind of connection that went deeper than fantastic sex — that made you practically glow no matter if you were talking or screwing? And to have found it with a woman like Evan Hayes, McKendrick now, seemed more good fortune than a Warlock could ever hope for — no matter that the lass was mortal. Certainly more than Kieran could ever dream of having. What woman in her right mind would tie herself to him for all eternity? Hell, even Susie had been horrified by the idea.

The night he'd spent in her bed — in her body — thundered through his mind again, and he wondered if he'd ever forget the horror of feeling so out of control. Thank Saephus her *Magick* had been powerful enough to stop him when he'd been in such a weakened state, the unexpected change having momentarily sapped his strength, because Kieran wasn't entirely certain he'd have had the presence of mind to hold back. The beast had controlled him, and he'd been utterly at the mercy of its wants…its hungers.

He couldn't believe what they'd done to him, though it hadn't taken a genius to figure out the finer details of the Council's curse. Of course, he hadn't been in the frame of mind to reason out his shoelaces, much less a bloody nightmare come to life. His hands settled around his thick mug with a grimace, his mind replaying the events after he'd shifted, his tattered clothes blown through her room, and Susie blasting him to perdition with her virulent rage. He recalled how he'd leapt off her balcony and raced through the shadows to Lach. He'd been thankfully concealed in the blanketing darkness of the night, hidden from the eyes of the *gnach*, though their dogs had howled from one end of Edinburgh to the other.

When he'd finally made his way to Lach and Evan's rear garden, he'd tossed stones up to the second-story bedroom window, until the man had eventually opened it. His cousin's skin had been flushed, his auburn hair sweaty around his strong features, as if he'd been reluctantly pulled away from the Sybaritic pleasures of his marriage bed.

Kieran would have never believed his cousin's absolute devotion to one woman unless he'd seen it with his own eyes—and it was now a fact he witnessed every day of his life. As Susie had said, "...that man's cock has been staked for good." And it had.

What cosmic ass the man had kissed to get such an incredible woman, Kieran would have loved to know. Hell, he'd probably be the first in line with his lips puckered up, ready to lay one on.

That night, Lach had looked down to the pacing...*monster* trampling his wife's daffodils, and immediately rushed downstairs. By the time he'd walked into the unearthly stillness of the garden, Kieran was already retaking his original shape, shivering and cold, thankful for the clothes and blanket his cousin had thought to bring along...and desperate for answers.

He should have been able to figure it out on his own, but he'd had one hell of a night, and the changing always left him disorientated and somewhat dizzy. Thankfully his cousin had been more capable of reasoning than he.

Lach had brought him into the warm, cozy kitchen and put on some much needed coffee. Then, at his suggestion, Kieran had explained the events in Susie's bedroom with rough, short bursts of words spoken between his laboring breaths.

Wearing nothing more than a well-worn pair of Levi's, Lach had taken a moment to talk with Evan on the intercom, poured two steaming cups of the daily blend from The Wicked Brew, all the while going over the events Kieran had relayed in graphic detail. Settling his big body back in one of several wide oak chairs situated around the rectangular breakfast table, he'd finally sighed and said, "It must be the bite."

Kieran's normally black eyes had still shone like liquid silver over the rim of his dark blue mug, the thick pottery betraying the slight shaking of his hands. "The bite?" he'd grunted, struggling to follow his cousin's thinking through the sluggish, dizzying mess of his mind.

Lach had nodded, rubbing one large palm against the rough auburn stubble covering his cheeks and chin. "Aye, the bite. You said yourself that the moment you changed you wanted to mark her. That's never happened before."

Kieran had snorted. "True, but I've never been riding a lass when I changed before either. And it isna bloody likely I would've ever gone around trying to mark someone in the heat of battle, which is the only time I've ever made the change, now is it?"

"Aye, but I know of others with Serena's Lupine Blood Curse, and they manage to fuck without marking every *Cailleach* they come across, no pun intended. I'd say your desire to bite…to mark her, was definitely the Council's doing."

"There's just one flaw with your theory," he'd snarled, his voice lowering to a coarse tangle of sound, "and it's pretty easy to see, even to someone as scramble-headed as I am right now. No matter how you look at it, there's no fucking chance in hell that Susie MacIntyre is my *bith-bhuan gra*! So why in the hell would I want to mark her as my mate—*a life mate*, for Saephus' sake? I'd rather be bonded to a bloody collie!"

A small twitch had twisted the corners of Lach's mouth, but to his credit, he hadn't smiled. A fact that had most likely saved him from a black eye…or two, so fierce had Kieran's temper raged. Instead, Lach had taken a slow sip of his coffee, using his *Magick* to warm the mug between his palms as the drink began to cool, and explained his theory. "You're assuming that the curse merely consists of a bite to your mate, but there has to be more to it than that. I think the Council has outdone itself on this one, knowing how hard we tried to break my own."

"So then they've upped the stakes, is what you're saying. Lucky me."

"Well, they've sure as hell made it more complicated," Lach had murmured, his sharp mind obviously working its way around a conclusion.

"Something tells me I'm no' going to like hearing this, but by all means, enlighten me." Kieran had leaned forward, bracing his elbows on the gleaming surface of the table, his eyes so hot Lach had been amazed when he didn't singe. "And then I'm going to track down those crazy old bastards and bloody well kill them, starting with my Da!"

Lach had ignored the heated threat, recognizing its source all too well, and continued with his explanation. "We know that the curse calls upon your already existing Lupine one."

Kieran had slumped back in his chair with a heavy thud. "Yay for me."

"Sarcasm is going to get you nowhere, Cousin."

Laying his black head back on the chair, he'd blown out a long breath of frustration. "Neither is fucking, apparently."

"Yeah, and thanks to the curse, you're going to shift when you fuck, whether you want to or not. That's the first part. The second, no doubt deals with the bite. In your Lupine shape, you're going to be compelled...driven...to bite the woman beneath you, whoever she may be, marking her for life."

"So what the bloody hell does this have to do with my soul mate? Shit, I nearly marked Suse!"

Lach had shaken his head. "No...I dinna think it would have come to that. Suse was, in a way, just a warning. I wouldna be surprised if they chose to introduce the curse tonight with her, knowing her *Magick* would be strong enough to fight you off long enough to allow her escape. Did Iain know you were going to see her tonight?"

Kieran's look had been so hostile, it would have cowered a lesser Warlock. "Aye, he knew. The miserable, cock-sucking asshole!"

A slow smile had lifted Lach's lips. "That's no way to be talking about your own father."

"Then cover your ears, Cousin, because it's about to get worse."

"Och, you've time to curse him plenty later. Right now, you need to think about the one element of this situation you've yet to figure out."

Kieran's shoulders had slumped. "Considering the rest of it, I dinna think I want to know."

"You already do."

Kieran had lifted a questioning brow.

"You said it yourself, Suse is no' the one."

"Aye," Kieran had slowly replied, wondering where his cousin was going with this.

"So, man, the logical conclusion is that you've got to find her."

"Her?"

Lach had leaned forward. "Before you sink back inside a woman, you sure as hell better make sure you've got the right one."

"So then this whole fucking curse nonsense is just a way to ensure I dinna fuck anyone until I find her? I've got to be bloody faithful to a woman I dinna even know?"

"Not yet anyway, but I think that's the gist of it. They're probably hoping that the break in your endless line of meaningless affairs will give you the chance to notice her once you finally find her."

"Shit."

"And there's still one more thing you've yet to think about."

"Christ, what's that?"

The corner of Lach's mouth had twitched again. "When you find her, you sure as hell better hope she likes her men with fangs and fur."

At his cousin's words, Kieran had deflated in his chair once more, looking as if the world had just been pulled out from beneath his feet. "Well, hell."

"Aye, cousin. I imagine it will be."

That was how he found himself here, three months later, cursing the miserable day he'd been born. And it was all such a depressing, useless waste of time. Whatever his family's hopes, Kieran knew there was going to be no happily ever after waiting around the corner for him. Not unless it had four legs and peed in the woods.

A sudden, surprising chuckle escaped his lips, and he shook his head of black hair, wondering how he could find humor in such a morbid situation. Hell, maybe Lach was right. Maybe he really was stark raving mad. At this point, it wouldn't surprise him.

Shit, nothing would surprise him.

Or so he thought, until he caught a scent in the air that had his head spinning, the blood in his veins suddenly pumping in a hot, heavy rhythm, like the sensual beat of a heavy jungle drum. *Boom. Boom. Boom.* The air in his lungs felt thick as well, as if he breathed through a veil of fog, and he could have sworn mist formed around the edges of his vision. His skin burned, alive with sensation, and he shivered as beads of sweat snaked down his spine.

What...the...fuck...was...that?

He turned, and it felt as if the bottom of his world fell out, only to be replaced with something so spellbinding, it hurt just to look at it. Through the haze in his mind, he could hear Lach talking to him, but the words were nothing more than an unwanted commotion—a graffiti of sound that threatened to shatter the pure perfection of the moment.

"Shut up," he growled, and Lach's sharp laugh echoed back in response.

"You might want to shut your mouth before you start panting," his cousin drawled behind him, clearly amused by the situation. "It's generally considered impolite to drool on women—unless, of course, you're in the midst of something that requires a bit of skilled drooling."

"I'm no' bloody drooling on her," he managed to grunt, completely unable to drag his black gaze away from the vision on the other side of the bustling café.

The door had only just pulled shut behind her, its heavy weight ensuring that it never remained open to allow the warm heat to escape from within the cozy confines of the store.

"Ah…it's hard when it hits you, isn't it?"

"What?"

"Kinda like running headfirst into a brick wall." At Kieran's fierce expression, Lach's smile only broadened, spreading across his face with devilish delight. "Trust me, I know. It was the same way when I found Evan. Damn near knocked me on my ass."

"I dinna know what the hell you're talking about."

"No?" Lach laughed, easing back in his chair. "Then I guess you willna mind when I ask Blu to show the lass around town while Evan and I are busy with the reconstruction here. I'd tell Evan to just go ahead and leave it to me, but you know how well the woman listens," he ended with a pained sigh.

Evan's working status had become a point of contention between the couple since they were bonded…and they still argued constantly that she no longer *needed* to work. According to Evan, Lach might own her soul and her heart, but they couldn't spend every second of every day boinking like bunnies, though Kieran strongly suspected Lach would have liked nothing more. So they were now, in addition to Lach's training studio, the proud owners of The Wicked Brew, with enough new staff that Evan could afford to come and go as she pleased. The refurbishing, however, she demanded to oversee herself.

Which still didn't explain what any of this had to do with the little bundle of pink he was seriously considering throwing over his shoulder and running back to his house with, hard and fast…and desperate, until he could rip her clothes off and introduce himself while he introduced her sweet cunt to his throbbing cock.

Kieran leaned forward, muscles bulging. "You let Blu anywhere near her and I'll—wait, what the hell makes you think that *gnach* would let one of us anywhere near her?"

Lach's brow rose over wickedly gleaming, pale green eyes. "Well, one does tend to trust *family*."

Kieran stiffened. "That woman's no McKendrick." They had cousins from one corner of the Isles to the other, and he'd sure as hell never lusted after one of his own before.

"Aye, she's no McKendrick. Not yet, at any rate," Lach drawled, seriously pissing him off. "And no' by blood. Hell, man, stop looking with your cock and use your bloody eyes."

Oh, he was using his eyes all right, devouring every sweet inch of her, from her sneaker-covered feet to the fuzzy pink cashmere of her sweater. Hell, he was afraid to friggin' blink, in case she disappeared on him.

"What in the hell makes you think that woman would trust a McKendrick?" he muttered. It was true that in the world of the *Magick*, they were considered the finest catches around, but mortals tended to be somewhat leery of their size and dominating presence—not to mention their aura, which scared the hell out of them, though they had no way of knowing what it was. They simply recognized the danger of something different from themselves, and their first instinct was usually to stay clear of anything more than casual contact. Strange, how that had never bothered Kieran until this moment.

Most *gnach* could go bugger themselves for all he cared, but this one he wanted to get close to. As close as humanly possible. And considering he was far from human...even closer.

His cousin's smile was slow and easy and once again total jackass, tempting Kieran to knock it away with his fist. "What makes me think she'll trust a McKendrick?" Lach drawled, clearly enjoying himself. "Probably because her sister is married to one."

Chapter Two

Kieran whipped back around so fast his chair nearly toppled. "The hell you say. That's no'...I mean—it canna be..."

"Aye, it is." Lach leaned forward once more, preparing to rise as the woman began trying to weave her way through the long line of customers waiting to place their orders. "Though from the look of her, I'd say she's been through a bit of it lately."

Well, hell, that was putting it pretty lightly. The picture he'd seen of Bronté Hayes was of a cute, curvy little pixie with a short cap of titian-colored hair and a shy smile. The vision walking toward the counter—and a vision she was, looked worlds apart from the image he'd kept of this woman in his mind.

Even as an adorable imp, he'd been...*intrigued* by Evan's little sister. There was something in those luscious lips and luminous eyes that had always pulled at him, causing his breath to hitch with the oddest sensation. But he'd never, not in a thousand lifetimes, expected to feel like *this* when he finally saw her in the flesh, face-to-face.

What the hell had happened to her? She looked like she'd been honed down, streamlined into a compact version of the charmingly cute girl she'd been. This new version of Té, as Evan called her, was all lean lines and toned muscles. Even the delicate bones of her pretty face shone more prominently, the cheekbones strikingly strong above a now sharp little chin.

He honestly hadn't recognized her, she'd changed that much from the small snapshot he'd seen in Evan's wallet. From the first moment he'd set eyes on it, a strange seed of possessiveness had taken root, though he'd never really been able to put a name to it. He'd always assumed it was wrapped up in casual attraction and familial protection. McKendricks looked out for McKendricks, and even though she might not bear the last name, they all considered her a part of the fold. But sitting here, watching her, seeing her for the first time, there was no mistaking it for exactly what it was.

A primitive, primal, archaic sense of ownership.

His, though he didn't have a clue where that was coming from, but it was pounding through his veins, whispering through his mind…and making the nether regions of his body decidedly uncomfortable, feeling far too contained within the worn denim of his jeans.

Here was *the one* who belonged to him. He didn't know how he knew it. He just did. Hell, maybe he always had, and just hadn't wanted to admit it—but there was no denying it now that she was *here*, in the same room with him, and her lush, tender scent of promises and something darker…something edgier with need was making its way to him over the muddied smells of the mortal world.

He wanted to wrap himself around her and force away the weary shadows in her eyes. She'd obviously been through hell. No one changed that drastically, that quickly, without some sort of life-altering experience.

The woman before him now was but a shadow of the voluptuous girl he'd seen in that picture—a snapshot of two sisters smiling into the camera. He knew it was from Té's college graduation, and she'd been achingly sweet in her blue gown and goofy graduation hat. Charming and cute, with the obvious Hayes' good looks.

But whereas Evan was gray-eyed and golden-haired, Bronté had been blessed with magnificent eyes the color of a deep, dark sky when it was at its most blue, and a luxurious veil of hair that shone like a blaze of flame, from dark red to shimmering gold, falling just beneath her sharp chin. Her neck was a slender column, begging for his mark, lean shoulders leading into graceful arms with fragile wrists and delicate hands. Small earlobes from which sparkling little hoops of silver could be seen reflecting the café's light, and a new, decidedly sexy arc of silver gleaming at the tip of her left eyebrow. And those firm, full, lush breasts that begged for the teasing drag of his teeth, the suctioning, suckling heat of his mouth as he ate at the plump, giving flesh.

But his favorite feature was the one that hadn't changed at all—that subtle, sexy little mole at the top of her right cheekbone, just beneath the far edge of her right eye. He wanted to press his lips to that perfect little spot. To run the rough scrape of his tongue across it, and then trail down to the moist, succulent cavern of her mouth, lower to the delicate tips of her breasts, and finally lower, to where he could settle into a long, luscious tongue-fuck that had him eating his fill of her juicy, pink-fleshed little cunt. It would be warm and soft, like the tempting, syrupy sweetness of an exotic fruit, moist beneath his lips, vulnerable to his hunger...and entirely addictive.

He'd liked the girl, but the woman damn near killed him, blindsiding him with a sudden, biting, overwhelming urge to get inside of her and stay there for as long as she'd let him. He felt it in every cell of his body, as if his chemistry were changing...altering...recognizing a necessary component for life that he had never before even realized was missing.

"How did you know?" It rankled to admit he'd been unable to recognize her, especially when Lach so obviously had.

"Well, it's easy to see, if you're no' staring at her chest."

Kieran swallowed, trying to lift his eyes off the soft, gentle, tantalizing sway of her plump breasts, but damn, it wasn't easy.

He should have met her by now, but she'd missed the Binding Ceremony, and no one was really sure why that was exactly. Her excuses had been vague...and hardly satisfying. Evan had tried not to worry, but they had all noticed how her sister's continued absence had begun to take its toll. After all, there'd been nothing more than a few scattered postcards in the last few months, providing barely adequate explanations for why she couldn't accept their repeated offers of a ticket to

Scotland. Lach had wanted to take the situation into his own hands, and Kieran agreed, but Evan wouldn't have it.

When her sister was ready, she would come, and that had been Evan's final word on the subject.

All they knew was that Bronté Hayes had up and left her job in Chicago three months ago, right about the time of the Binding, and taken off for the coastal town of Xoetché in Mexico, teaching English to the village schoolchildren. That was it. No personal address, just a PO Box number in Chicago that was being forwarded her mail...and nothing else. No phone. Not even a bloody email address.

Lach had kept him updated on Evan's growing concern that something definitely wasn't right, but so far, she hadn't wanted to press. According to the independent Evan, Té was a twenty-five-year-old woman who had the right to go anywhere she damn well pleased, no matter how the McKendrick men might look at it. After all, just because Té was a female didn't mean she couldn't handle herself. Hell, Evan had even gone so far as to call them archaic Neanderthals a time or two while they argued the point, though Kieran strongly suspected she actually liked Lach's "caveman" routine—at least in the bedroom. But when it came to her sister, the woman was steadfast in her determination. It may have been driving her crazy, but so long as Té said she was fine, they had to accept it as the truth.

None of it sat well with Kieran, though he'd had little time to spend worrying over it himself with the way his life had been lately. But it was always there, brewing in the back of his mind—that subtle suspicion that there was something he *should* be doing, damn it, such as tracking down the little *gnach* and dragging her stubborn ass to Scotland where they could all keep an eye on her.

Then again, considering the circumstances, maybe the whole thing had been for the best. It was true that most mortals had trouble accepting them as easily as Evan had, and Binding Ceremonies were a *Magickal*, mystical affair. If she'd come, it might have been more than she could handle. Though, from the look of her, Kieran had a sudden feeling that there wasn't much the little spitfire couldn't get a grip on.

And damn it, just the thought of what he'd like to give her to *grip* was enough to make his throat tight, and his dick throb with an uncomfortable, growing knot of desire.

He watched as she finally bypassed the long line of customers waiting to place their orders, choosing instead to walk to the far end of the counter, near the service aisle. She still hadn't completely looked their way, but then her eyes seemed to be scanning the area behind the pastry display cases, obviously searching for her sister.

She stood in their direct line of vision now, with her back to them as she faced forward, and he wanted nothing more than to howl at the sight of her luscious ass wrapped up in delectable little blue jeans. Damn, did she have to look as edible from the back as she did from the front? He'd always been a sucker for a nice ass, but this was ridiculous. He hadn't even seen it bared to his hot eyes, and already he felt the urge to drool over it. But then it looked finer than any he'd ever seen. Round, pert, the twin globes perfect for his large palms to fondle and knead, long fingers digging into her resilient flesh.

A low growl vibrated in the back of his throat, and beside him Lach laughed, clasping him on the shoulder. "Shall we go welcome the lovely lady, Cousin?"

Should they? If by welcoming, Lach meant him throwing her over his shoulder and hightailing it to the nearest place where he could fuck her hard and deep, for hours...*days* on end, then Kieran was in full agreement. But if he meant to play nice, Kieran wasn't so sure he could do it.

And his dick knew for damn sure he couldn't.

With his lips pressed into a grim line, he shook his head. "I think maybe I should just...go."

Lach arched his brow, his look challenging, and Kieran gritted his teeth. "You're no' afraid, are ya, man? After all, she's family."

A muscle began to twitch annoyingly in his cheek. "Damn it, stop saying that! She's no' my bloody family!"

"She's not?"

"No' to my dick, she isn't! And you're pushing it, Lach. Keep pissing me off and Evan willna be thinking you're so pretty if I decide to rearrange the location of your nose."

Lach snorted. "I'd like to see you try."

"Dinna tempt me."

"Stop being so temperamental and come introduce yourself…if you're no' too afraid," Lach teased, his light green eyes gleaming with mischief.

Afraid? Hell, he was fucking terrified.

And Saephus help her if he wasn't right about what she could handle, because she was about to have a whole new world dropped right into her pretty little lap.

* * * * *

"Hey, beautiful."

"Oh my friggin' God!" Evan shrieked as she spun around, the tray of glass pastry plates topped with a variety of fresh cheesecakes wobbling in her arms. She stared at her sister, gray eyes huge in her beautiful face. "Crap, Té, you shocked the hell out of me! What are you doing here?"

Té flashed a cheeky grin. "Thought I'd surprise you."

"Hah," Evan muttered with narrowed eyes. "You could've surprised me three months ago, when I was getting *married*."

"I'm sorry I wasn't here," she said around a wince. "I didn't mean to let you down."

Evan's look was pointed, demanding an answer. "Where the hell have you been?"

Té lifted her brows. "I told you I was with Jamie. She'd been asking me to come down and help out at that school for ages. Didn't you get the postcards?"

"Yeah, I got them. And I've written you back at that damn post office box address, as you well know, asking you to call. I mean it, Té, I've been worried sick about you. Just look at you! Jesus, I hardly recognized you."

She blew out a tense breath, having known this was coming. "Evan, I'm not a child. I'm sorry you were worried, but I had some things I had to take care of that couldn't be put off. I told you I'd get here as soon as I could."

"Yeah, well, you can make it up to me by promising to stick around for as long as possible, and I just might think about forgiving you."

A slow grin curved the corners of her gloss-covered lips. "As gracious as always, I see."

"You bet your ass I am," Evan mumbled, still juggling the tray in her arms, looking around for a place to set it down, but finding none. "I really have been worried sick about you, and I will get the whole story, in teeny tiny detail."

Té shrugged her shoulder, letting her heavy backpack slide down her arm until it snagged on her wrist. Feeling the ache of sitting for so many hours on the plane twist through her body, she lifted her arm to rub her hand across the back of her neck, kneading the tired muscles. "I know. I know. Just not now, okay. I'm feeling pretty beat."

Beat, jetlagged, and ready to grab some much needed rest. She looked around the lovely, thriving café, and for the first time in months, she felt the heavy comfort of safety wrap around her. In that moment, she wanted nothing more than to crawl into the nearest bed and crash for a year.

"You look like hell," Evan muttered, her gaze intense as she studied her sister's weary face, able to see the strain she'd been carrying for far too long.

Té smiled, knowing Evan was only worried and didn't mean it the way it sounded. "And you look gorgeous. Just like a happily married woman."

Evan grinned back. "You bet your ass I am."

"So…where's the lucky groom?" She lifted her brows. "Is he really as fine as you said in your letters?"

Evan gave her a mischievous wink as she slid the display case open, realizing the only way she was going to get her arms free so she could give her sister a hug was to put the damn cakes away. "Even better, if you can believe it. And you can see for yourself, because he's right over there," she said, nodding her head toward Lach and Kieran as they worked their way through the bustling, early morning crowd of patrons.

Té's eyes went wide as she looked over her shoulder, unable to do anything but stare at the two intimidating giants quickly closing in on them. "Jesus," she whispered around a sudden lump in her throat. "Which one is he?"

Evan gave a dreamy smile, clearly besotted. "The auburn-haired hunk."

"Nice," she replied with a low whistle.

"Yeah, I think so, too."

"And the black-haired one?"

"His cousin, Kieran."

"Does he always look so…intense?"

Evan cocked her head in consideration. "Nowadays, yeah, though I've never seen that particular expression before. He looks like he wants to eat you alive."

"What?" Té sputtered, turning back to Evan, trying not to appear as shaken as she felt. Her belly was doing a strange little dance of excitement, her palms going embarrassingly damp.

"Mmm…he definitely looks interested. Oh man—you're so in for it now," Evan laughed around a dangerous grin.

"Evan…what are you talking about?" she demanded under her breath, rubbing her hands on the front of her jeans. "So help me God…if you try to set me up or force me on that poor man, I swear I'll make you pay."

"Sheesh, where's the trust, I ask you?"

"Hah! I know you too well."

Her sister's face took on a dramatic, pained look of hurt. "And just when have I ever steered you wrong before?"

Té's words were forcefully blunt, though her lips quirked up at one corner in a little half-smile. "J.D. Worthy."

Evan groaned. "Not fair, Té. How was I supposed to know he was a sniveling little sleazebag? He was valedictorian, for crying out loud. I thought he'd be a little saint!"

Té clucked her tongue. "You should've done your research before you weaseled him into taking me to the prom."

"You were excited," Evan insisted, setting a decadent piece of chocolate fudge cheesecake on the top shelf of the refrigerated case.

"I was stupid!"

Evan blew out an exasperated breath. "It wasn't that bad."

"How would you know?" she laughed, bracing her elbows on the counter. "You didn't have to listen to him go on about how much he wanted to *cultivate* my love flower."

Evan was choking on a giggle when Kieran and Lach reached the counter. Sensing them at her back, Té turned and damn near did some choking of her own. Christ almighty, they were even more gorgeous up close. Six-foot plus inches of rock-hard, solid, mouthwatering male, the testosterone-based energy pouring off of them broadsiding her like a roaring, towering wave, sucking her under as the powerful force retreated once more into the raging, volatile sea.

She felt her face go pink, and knew she was blushing like a schoolgirl as the auburn-haired one smiled at her, while the black-haired beauty did, indeed, appear to be eating her up with his intense, smoldering gaze. Her body went hot, and she felt a tiny trickle of moisture dance down her spine beneath the soft cashmere of her sweater, another sliding between her lace-covered breasts. God have mercy, she'd never seen anything like them.

"Té," Evan wheezed around a fading chuckle. "Allow me to introduce you to my husband, Lachlan."

"It's a pleasure, lass," the handsome Scot drawled, engulfing her little hand within his wonderfully warm, large grip.

She smiled, feeling her face flush with heat, but unable to do anything about it. Thank God she'd managed to acquire a nice golden tan down in Mexico, or she knew she'd probably be blinding them with the hot color on her normally fair skin. "It's so nice to finally meet you," she replied, lips feeling tight, her gaze darting repeatedly to the dark, dangerous man standing at Lach's side. She knew it was rude to stare, but God, she couldn't tear her eyes away from him. Not that Lachlan McKendrick wasn't a fine specimen. Damn, Evie hadn't been joking when she'd said her husband was drop-dead gorgeous. But there was something about the other man that...*enthralled* her. It was the only word she could think of to explain the bizarre reaction pumping through her system, setting her on a keen, simmering burn of anticipation.

"And this brute is his cousin, Kieran."

The man opened his mouth as if he'd say something, but then his beautiful lips pressed together in a hard line and he gave her a curt nod instead. He did, however, reach for her hand, and the sudden heat of his rough skin against her own damn near made her melt. That, and the intense force of raw, masculine energy zinging through the point of contact between their palms. It was such an innocuous touch, and yet, it felt inexplicably seductive, as if he were actually rubbing the tender, aching folds between her legs.

She had a sudden mental image of her laid out naked, thighs opened wide with utter abandon while that deliciously male palm held her possessively, those tantalizing calluses teasing her swollen, humid flesh. She blinked up at him, eyes going glassy, and nervously licked her lips. His midnight gaze narrowed and he opened his hand with an almost audible hiss, as if he'd been burned, and she could've sworn she heard him groan beneath his breath, but then Lach said, "So what brings you to us now, Bronté? It's the truth we've all been anxious to have you here."

She struggled to pull herself together and smiled up at the tall Scot, then sent a questioning look at her sister. "What makes you guys think I'm not just here for a friendly visit?"

"Because we're not stupid," Evan drawled. "We've been asking you to come for three months, and then you just suddenly show up out of the blue."

Té watched her sister as she shifted the tray of glass plates, rebalanced the precarious load on her other arm, and began arranging them again in the display case. "Well…"

"Out with it, Té."

She played with a stray strand of red-gold hair, tucking it behind her ear, and stroked the silver hoop in her brow, all obvious signs of nervousness. After shooting a quick glance at the two studs standing to her left, she narrowed her gaze back on Evan. Her sister's determined expression said she wasn't giving up anytime soon. "Oh hell, fine." She took a deep breath, and then said one word. "*Palo.*"

Evan squealed and jerked her arm, which sent the tray crashing to the wooden floor in a splintering sound of shattering glass and bouncing metal.

"Shit!" they all four exclaimed at the same time, every eye in the café zeroing in on them.

"Oh crud," Evan sighed, looking up from the floor behind the counter to her husband. "Um, babe, now promise you're not going to freak out."

Lach arched one brow in an amused expression. "Because you're a klutz, sweetheart?" He started around the corner of the display case. "I'll help you get it cleaned up. I dinna want you cutting yourself on that glass." But he stopped when Evan held up her hand, halting him.

Her smile looked strained, and Lach's own smile fell. "What is it?"

She looked down, swallowed, and then quickly looked back up, her complexion going strangely pale. "I'm afraid I'm an even bigger klutz than you thought. And I really should've worn my jeans today."

"What the hell's going on?" he grunted, rushing around the counter, drawing up short when he saw the blood beginning to pool beneath Evan's left ankle, the fragile skin having been sliced open by a sharp shard of broken glass. Her plaid miniskirt and Mary Janes had been absolutely no protection against the flying glass as it bounced off the floor. "Oh fuck. Bloody fucking hell."

Kieran and Té leaned over the counter as Lach dropped to his knees, getting a closer look at the wound.

"Oh my God!" Té yelped, while Kieran said, "Aw, Evie. What did you do to yourself, lass?"

Lach looked around for a clean cloth to staunch the steady flow of blood. He found a neat stack of white towels on the shelf to his left, and immediately pressed a soft strip of terrycloth to the raw wound, cursing beneath his breath the entire time, his hands none too steady.

Evan smoothed her hands through his thick hair, trying to soothe him, and Té said, "She's going to need stitches in that."

Lach looked up at his wife, his green eyes burning bright with purpose. "Nae. I'll be handling this myself."

Chapter Three

Té's eyes rounded with surprise. "You can help her?"

Lach nodded, his strong hands incredibly gentle as he lifted Evan in his arms and carried her to their back office. Evan smiled at the two employees working the front counter, calling out that she was fine as Kieran and Té followed them.

The stylish office looked like something right out of the pages of a Pottery Barn catalog, and Té looked around with a warm appreciation while Lach set Evan down gently on the modern little black leather loveseat placed beneath a large window. Kieran handed him another clean towel, one he'd picked up on their way back, and Lach began cleaning the edges of the seeping wound.

Té looked over her brother-in-law's wide shoulder, relieved to see the bleeding was beginning to slow. "You said you'll take care of this yourself. You're a doctor, then?"

Kieran gave a soft chuckle beside her, the only sound she'd heard the beautiful man make other than his sympathetic words to Evan, but Lach only said, "No' really."

"An EMT?"

"Uh...no."

Té was starting to get suspicious. "A nurse?" she asked hopefully.

He looked up at her from beneath his dark auburn brows, and his look said it all. No, definitely not a nurse, and beginning to get irritated with her questions.

Too damn bad.

"Then how are you going to help her? It's not that deep, but it's definitely going to need stitching."

He returned his attention to the gash, pressing a clean part of the cloth to the wound, but Té could see the sensual line of his mouth go thin. "Evan?" he groaned, seeming to be at a loss as to what he should say.

Despite the fact that she must be in pain, her sister smiled at his put-out tone and winked at her. "He wants to use his *Magick* to heal me, but he's worried about your reaction." She paused, giving her husband a very direct look. "Not that I'll let him use it."

There was a strange silence for several beats. Finally Té frowned and said, "So you're a magician?"

Lach's hand jerked so suddenly that Evan yelped, socking him in his wide shoulder. "Fuck no!" he muttered, clearly insulted.

"Sheesh, okay...I'm sorry."

"No need to apologize," Evan explained with another smile, this one tight as she glowered at her husband. "He's normally not so grumpy, but I think the sight of my blood has the poor thing feeling a bit on edge."

Lach growled something under his breath that Té figured she was better off not hearing. The man definitely seemed upset.

Hmm...this was getting stranger and stranger. She looked to the one named Kieran, but his expression seemed trapped somewhere between amusement and dread, those black eyes guarded as he watched her.

What in the hell was going on here?

"Okay, then, I give up."

Evan sighed. "I was going to explain this better tonight, when we could be alone, but he wants to use his *power*, Té."

"His power," she repeated slowly, watching as Lach rose to stand beside her. He was as tall as Kieran, towering over her rather average five-foot-five frame like a freaking giant.

A small smile hovered around the edges of his mouth. "That's right," he drawled, "and I'm sorry for barking at you, lass." He looked down at Evan's injured ankle. "It's the truth I'm a bit...*upset* at seeing her hurt."

Té shot a questioning look at Evan. "I'm sorry, but I just don't get it."

"Aunt Ellie," Evan said with a wry twist of her lips, as if that would explain everything. "Believe it or not, I guess some of those crazy things she used to tell us really *are* true."

Big, dark blue eyes blinked in fascination. "You can't be serious."

"Oh, but I am."

Té's jaw dropped. "*Leprechauns?*"

Both of the men made an odd sputtering sound, and Evan turned beet red, shaking her head. "Uh, no...the *other* one."

Kieran's shoulders were trembling, his fingers pinching the bridge of his nose as he looked down at the hardwood floor. Té had a sudden sneaking suspicion that he was trying very hard not to laugh at her. "Your aunt believes in leprechauns?" he wheezed in his deep voice, still not looking her in the eye.

"*Believed* in leprechauns," Evan corrected him. "Actually, she believed in lots of stuff. But her two favorites were leprechauns and," she looked back to her sister, "something else."

"Honestly?" Té whispered, leaning closer.

"On Peter Erickson for a prom date," Evan teased, using their favorite "promise keeper" as crushed-out teens who would dream of being asked out by the drool-worthy Pete, star of the varsity football team.

Té felt as if she'd been poleaxed between the eyes, the import of what her sister was claiming registering in her system like a heavy, stunning jolt of caffeine, while Lach grunted, "Who the hell is Peter Erickson?"

"No one important, babe," Evan evaded, which had him muttering under his breath something that sounded like "stubborn woman" and "judge of that" along with some rather choice curses.

"Holy shit," Té breathed, using both hands to brush her hair back from her flushed face. "Honest to God *Magicks*?"

"In the flesh," Evan drawled.

Her eyes found them again, narrowing, dark blue gaze piercing, as if she'd see right through them, beneath their rugged clothes and tanned skin and well-defined muscles, down to what really made them tick. The kind of look a schoolteacher could use to wring a confession out of the most recalcitrant five-year-old bully. It would have made Kieran smile, except that there were things there…hungers inside of himself that he didn't want her to see.

He swallowed, feeling the ridiculous urge to fidget, unsure how she'd take the information, or if she'd even believe it. His cheekbones went hot beneath her intense examination, and he wondered for about the hundredth time in the last ten minutes what it was about this woman that so utterly sent his world reeling out of orbit. She was fine, no doubt about it. More than fine, in fact, but he'd had beautiful women since he'd first been old enough to appreciate them, and none had ever made him feel like…*this*. Like she could make or break him. As if she alone held the key to not only his happiness, but his soul.

And as exhilarating as it was, he felt an instinctual need to rage against it, knowing that with the promise of ecstasy came the reciprocal threat of pain. It always did. Anything worth having was always something that could be taken away from you. It was one of the fundamental facts of life, for mortals and *Magicks* alike.

Though he had a feeling he wanted little Té Hayes bad enough that he just might be crazy enough to risk it.

And he really, really wanted a *taste* of her. Just wanted to spread her open and let his tongue feast like a cat given its favorite bowl of satisfying, decadent cream. Lap her up, drop by delicious drop.

It was a nice fantasy—a great one actually—though they were racking up pretty quickly right about now. Fantasies about him and the little *gnach*, of hot bodies and savage hunger, of sweat and uncontrollable passion as they rolled across his tangled sheets, their flesh burning with ravenous need, desperate to get as much of the other as they possibly could.

There was just one damn problem, and no way to get around it. She may, by some miracle of her upbringing and this crazy Aunt Ellie, be able to believe he was *Magick*, but no way in hell was this pretty little *gnach* ever going to lie down, spread her legs, and let a Lupine sink his tongue, his cock...or his bloody teeth into her.

And that, more than anything, meant that he couldn't have her—*ever*—whether he wanted her or not.

Too bad his cock, and his soul didn't appear to give a damn.

Finally she laughed, those magnificent eyes sparkling and clear, like a window into her soul. It was strange, but for all her secrets, she seemed a remarkably direct, refreshingly honest, utterly spellbinding woman.

"You'd think I'd be more surprised," she admitted with a slow smile, "but looking at you two, it somehow seems to make perfect sense."

Evan shot a smug smile at the men. "I told you she'd believe me."

Kieran looked at Lach, his black brow arched in humor. "She is taking it rather well, wouldn't you say?"

Lach shrugged his wide shoulders. "I'll admit I was a bit worried, but Evie told me she'd no' have any trouble accepting the way of things."

"Still a bit strange, though," Kieran replied thoughtfully, rubbing his chin.

Té set her hands on her hips, blowing out a frustrated breath as her humor quickly faded into irritation. "Don't you two know it's rude to talk about someone as if they aren't in the room, when clearly they are?" She frowned at Kieran, wondering why she couldn't get over her fascination with the man. God, she just wanted to keep staring at him…*forever*. "And I'm not strange."

He shot her an amused smirk, towering over her petite height. "Aren't ya now?" he drawled, black eyes shining with what looked oddly like pleasure, and maybe a tad bit of relief.

Her smile felt brittle. "No, I'm not."

"So you truly believe what Evan says?" he murmured, walking slowly toward her as she back-stepped to keep the distance between them, his movements speaking of mouthwatering power and strength and masculine grace. "Even though you've had no proof?"

She snorted—a delicate, feminine little sound that made him want to keep smiling. "Of course I do. I was raised to be open-minded about the world we live in. Only an idiot assumes they have all the answers."

"Wise words for a mortal," he murmured softly, his expression one of clear, seductive intent.

Her lids lowered. "You know, I don't think I care for the way you said that."

His smile flashed, white and charmingly sexy. "Then I'll have to be more careful, won't I?"

"You'll have to be something," she mumbled, wondering why bantering with him was getting her more excited than the foreplay she'd enjoyed beneath the hands of other men. Granted, she hadn't had *that* many lovers, but certainly there was someone in the short list who should've been able to compete with a sexy Scottish devil. She racked her brain, but came up with nothing. Not even Lexi, and despite the fact he was a spineless bastard, he'd been the best lover she'd ever had.

Still, he'd never gotten her juices flowing even close to the way Kieran McKendrick's wicked, knowing gaze did.

She shivered, her trembling body going hot and cold, and his sinful smile became an even sexier grin, her traitorous knees going weak at the sight. Christ, he even had a dimple in his left cheek—a perfect, sexy little indent that she very much wanted to explore with the tip of her tongue.

And holy hell, where on earth was this stuff coming from?

He moved closer, her eyes all but devouring him as they began an inspection that started at his scuffed boots, traveled up the long length of his lean, muscled, powerful body, and didn't stop until she reached the sparking fire of his midnight gaze.

"What happened to your glasses?" he drawled, low voice no more than a smoky rasp of sound.

"Um, contacts. I got contacts."

Kieran nodded, feeling his muscles clench with keen anticipation, his skin itching to get the feel of her against him—beneath him—as soon as humanly possible.

He gave a silent laugh at the expression, wishing for the first time ever that it were possible. If he were but a man, something told him that he'd already have Té Hayes on her back, those sweet thighs forced incredibly wide, his cock hammering into her delicate cunt, spearing her with pleasure until she was hoarse from the screams spilling past those glossy, fuckable pink lips.

"Yeah, you *must* be *Magick*," she said with a soft, sudden laugh, tilting her head to the side as she studied him. "I mean really, how could you possibly be anything else?"

"Good question," he agreed, reaching out to run his finger along the curve of her jaw, unable to resist the need to discover if she was as soft as she looked. He could tell his touch, as innocent as it was, unnerved her, but he could no more stop the caress of his fingers than he could control the erratic pounding of his heart. She was calling to the beast in him—and the beast very much wanted a chance to get out and play...to touch and taste and consume.

The man simply wanted to get those lush limbs wrapped around his body at the nearest possible moment, for the longest possible time, and fuck her ever-loving brains out.

And hell, it looked like he was back to that again already.

"So you're a Witch?" she asked into the heavy pause, voice haltingly breathless.

A lopsided grin played at one corner of his mouth. "Uh…Warlock, actually. *Cailleachs*, Witches, are female."

She stared up at him, her eyes blinking slowly against the soft morning light streaming in through the window. "I've never actually met a Warlock before. What exactly is it that you can do?"

He took a step closer, the warm scent of virile male and rich leather surrounding her, touching her body like a sexual mist that could easily seep into her pores. A sensual cloud of erotic seduction and sin. He was a perfect mix of beauty and danger, something she knew she should run from while at the same time wanting to melt into him, tempting fate.

For the first time in her life, she felt an impossible urge to press herself against a man with full, utter abandon, flesh-to-flesh, heat-to-heat, and beg…actually *beg* him into her body. Not just for sex, though the sex she definitely wanted. But something that went beyond the mere physical union. A deeper, more primitive hunger and need for connection, as if she'd be taking him into her soul. How odd that this would happen with a virtual stranger. Not even Lexi had affected her like this, and Lexi had damn near made her head spin, albeit in a way that had been uncomfortably frightening, as if her will had not been her own.

"What do you need?" Kieran drawled in answer to her question, and the wicked sound of his deep burr stole into her body, seeking out her tender core until it had settled itself in for a hot, molten burn. Oh Lord, he was actually flirting with her, and her body liked it…a lot. She shifted, just to feel her thighs rub together, and his smile widened, impossibly wicked, outrageously seductive, as if he knew just how needy she was between her trembling legs. She licked her lips, strangely aware that she was losing her footing here, knowing that was a mistake she couldn't afford to make. Not with this man. Not with any man—damn it—but sure as hell not with this one. He was too much…too much everything.

But God, wouldn't she love to be able to take him for a test ride. Just throw him to the ground, rip those faded jeans off that gorgeous body, and sink down onto what would surely have to be the most impressive erection she had ever seen. And considering Carly Simpson's secret collection of *Playgirl* back in high school, she'd "seen" quite a few. None, however, that she thought could compare to the bulge behind Kieran McKendrick's fly.

It was with a little shock of awareness that she realized she was staring at his fly.

Yep, right at his crotch.

And, for some inexplicable reason completely unbeknownst to her, she wasn't stopping.

How odd.

Oh hell, was she really just going to stand here and keep ogling the man's magnificent jeans-covered penis? She tried to look away, she really did, but her eyes had ideas of their own, so it looked as if she were going to keep on staring.

That being the case, she seriously hoped she didn't start to drool.

Yeah, drooling would definitely be bad.

So would touching, come to think of it, but if she didn't look away soon, she was fairly certain her lust was going to get the better of her and she'd find herself reaching out to touch someone.

Hmm…grabbing an arrogant Warlock's cock…now that was something she sure as hell didn't do everyday. Maybe she was more beat from the flight than she'd thought. Huh—and she should probably stop, starting right about now, before she did something she was really going to regret. It was a fabulous idea, if only someone would explain the finer points of it to her greedy eyes…and even needier sex organs.

She swallowed the lump of Kieran-flavored lust clogging her throat, mesmerized by the way the heavy bulge was beginning to grow—thickening within the soft denim—right before her eyes, and then the spell was broken as he reached out to tip her face up, his strong fingers warm beneath her chin.

His deep burr was a rough stroke of sound, gritty with suppressed need, and his eyes blazed, the opalescent black swirling around the nearly invisible pupils as he stared down at her. "You'd best be careful, because you're playin' with fire, lass."

She held his stare, surprised by the husky sound of her own voice as she all but croaked, "I don't play with men." She had the strangest compulsion to keep challenging him, though for the life of her she couldn't explain why. But it was a burning impulse in her gut, and one she had no power to deny.

He broke their staring match, his black eyes dropping a scant distance to settle on the pouting lower lip she was suddenly trying very hard to keep from trembling. "So it's like that, is it?"

"From where I stand, *it's* not particularly like anything."

"It could be like anything you wanted it to be," he promised in a silky rasp, moving closer still, until her aroused nipples were nearly grazing the soft leather of his jacket. Kieran didn't know why he was pushing her, except that it infuriated a place deep within that she was trying to act *uninterested* in him. God knew he couldn't do anything about his outrageous attraction to her, but he was damned if he was going to let her act as if it didn't bloody exist!

One look at her and he'd been ready to take her. Hell, he'd been rock-hard and ready at the first whiff of her lush, intoxicating scent. It'd called to him, even though there was something elusive about it—something buried within that triggered his internal alarm. Something that wasn't quite mortal, and yet, not entirely *Magick*. And the animal in him wanted it gone. Wanted to obliterate what smelled like the lingering scent of another man and replace it entirely with his own.

And he was ready to do just that. Ready to simply slam her up against the nearest wall and bury his aching dick as far up into her as he could possibly get it. He wanted her tender cunt open and wet, the sleek muscles kissing the heavy head of his cock, milking his blunt tip, begging to have him speared into her, crammed deep until he'd nailed her to the wall and hammered her into an endless stream of orgasms that coated him in her cum and made him feel like a part of her.

He wanted it—*all of it*—every single sight, sound, and taste so bad he could practically feel the need shaking through his starved system, like he'd been craving her for years instead of mere minutes.

And he couldn't fucking have it.

It was so wonderfully ironic, after the way he'd manipulated the situation between Lach and Evan. Not that it wouldn't have eventually happened on its own, but he'd been so certain they were meant to be that he'd taken it upon himself to make it happen, giving Evan his cousin's address and sending her after the stubborn ass. From the devilish look he'd seen in Lach's light green gaze since Té's arrival, Kieran could only guess at what he was planning, but this was different. Saephus, how he wished it weren't, but there was no denying the danger he now posed to *Magick* and *gnach* alike.

As much as he wanted the little spitfire standing before him, he couldn't fucking have her.

"Powers," she finally managed to murmur, her chest rising and falling in an agitated rhythm, though she tried to keep her expression calm. "I was asking about what you can do with your *powers*. I assume you have them."

"Aye, but you know what they say about assuming things, lass."

"Yeah, but from what I can see, you're already an ass."

He smiled, telling himself to keep his damn eager hands off of her, but he couldn't help but trace the feminine curve of her cheekbone, noting the incredibly silky texture of her skin, the way she flushed…trembled, at his touch. "And here I thought you didn't know me at all."

She would have responded, but the argument between her sister and new brother–in–law suddenly erupted, snagging their attention. It'd have worried her, if not for Kieran's lazy smile as his cousin exploded with frustration.

"Och, it's a simple power, woman. You trust me with your heart, why canna you trust me in this?"

Evan smiled sweetly from her sprawled position on the leather loveseat, completely unfazed by the threatening note of aggravation in her husband's deep burr. "No."

"Damn it, I dinna want some man putting his bloody hands on what's mine," Lach gritted through his teeth. "Especially when I can heal you better than he can."

His wife rolled her sparkling gray eyes. "You know, I seriously doubt the doctor will get a hard-on looking at my ankles, no matter how Scottish he is."

Lach snorted with derision. "Yeah, well, I get hard looking at them. Why the hell wouldn't he?"

"You get hard when the wind blows!"

Té was trying very hard not to strangle on a swallowed laugh when the man nodded his head, as if confirming her sister's accusation. "Aye, if it carries your sweet scent, you can bet your little ass I do. But only for you. I dinna get hard for anyone but *my wife*, and I damn well dinna want some other man putting his hands on what's *mine!*"

Evan's silvery gray gaze narrowed and Té recognized the look. Oh man, her gorgeous brother-in-law was in trouble now.

"You keep referring to a *him*. Are you implying that a woman couldn't do the job, McKendrick?"

Lach stiffened, clearly understanding the blatant fact that he was suddenly treading on some dangerous, shaky ground. Té assumed he'd be smart enough to play it safe and backpedal…fast, till she heard him mutter, "No bloody doctor is laying his hands on *my* woman."

Té shook her head sadly. Poor guy. Maybe he wasn't as bright as he looked. Then again, it didn't really matter how intelligent they were—sometimes they could just slip into pure idiot mode as involuntarily as they breathed. It was one of those male things that women would never be able to comprehend, like beer for breakfast and *The Man Show*.

She watched with a small grin as Evan poked a delicate finger into her husband's broad chest. "Don't sound like such a chauvinist, Lach! I'm sure there are female doctors at that hospital just as talented and as highly qualified as the male ones—if not more so."

He growled in the back of his throat, and Té couldn't help but stare in fascination. These McKendrick men were a marvel of arrogance and beauty and mesmerizing dominance. And her sister obviously had this one wrapped so tightly around her little finger, it couldn't help but make Té proud.

"You know what I mean, Evan," he muttered. "This is a simple skill—"

"Well, I'm not buying it," she huffed, the tone of her voice warning that she meant business. "You don't go fixing your own injuries with your hocus-pocus, damn it. If it's so freaking simple, then why did you have stitches in your leg when we first—"

Evan broke off as her eyes cut to Kieran's and Té's engrossed expressions, the two of them clearly enjoying her and Lach's little battle of wills. Her jaw ground down and she arched her brow. "Do you mind?"

Kieran snorted, his black eyes sparking with mischief. "No, no, I dinna mind a'tall, sugar. You just keep laying into his worthless hide and I'll stand here minding my own sweet business." He had no intention of telling her that because Lach had been injured by another *Magick*, the wound couldn't be healed with *Magick*, or that he would heal more slowly as a result.

"Kieran, in case you've never noticed, there isn't a single sweet thing about you."

A low, male laugh rumbled deep within his chest, and Té shivered beside him, clearly following his wicked thoughts. "Och, now, Evie," he drawled, rubbing the side of his nose with his finger. "There may be one or two—but none that brute you call a mate would ever let me get near ya."

"Kieran—" Lach warned beneath his breath, and Té couldn't quite catch her very soft, feminine burst of laughter at their crazy bantering.

Evan gave her a look that clearly said *Hey, you're supposed to be helping here, not making it worse*!

"Sorry, Sis," she chuckled around a sly grin, shrugging her shoulders. "They're just too funny. All this male posturing and snarling. I feel like I've landed in the middle of a cockfight."

Kieran cut her a warm look, his deliciously big body crowding her once again, herding her right back into the far corner of the small office. His scent hit her harder this time, warm and male, like a sinful invader stealing into her blood, robbing her of free will. The man was that intoxicating—made her that hungry, that tempted, as if she'd been craving him for years, rather than an insignificant flash of time. There was no logical explanation. How could something like this happen so suddenly? Hell, it'd taken Lexi four weeks of asking her out before she'd finally agreed to go on a date with him, though things had gone lightning speed from that point on. But this man was a stranger, one she'd known no more than a handful of minutes, and yet he smelled like a part of her. Hot and sexy and completely irresistible, the curve of his lips and the wicked gleam of sensual knowledge in his gaze capturing her breath—refusing to give it back.

Those dark, glittering eyes moved over her—her throat, where her pulse beat a pounding tempo, her collarbone, swollen nipples, down to the quivering, melting apex of her thighs—every surface they touched tingling as if he'd boldly stroked her with one of those big, delicious hands. "Tell me," he murmured, his husky voice pitched low, for her ears alone. "Any cock you'd like to fight with in particular, lass?"

"N-no," she whispered. "I just enjoy watching your little show." She hated the telltale quiver in her breathless voice, having never met a man who could put it there before. What was it about this gorgeous ass that had her so turned inside out? It must be stress. God only knew she'd had her share of it lately. But hadn't she learned enough in the past few months to know that sexy studs were *soooo* not her style? Especially the kind that screamed Alpha male and exuded the kind of sexual magnetism that made her just want to shove him up against the nearest wall, rip his monstrous cock out, drop down to her knees, and swallow his burning flesh right down her throat.

Not her style? Hah! Tell that to her unbearably empty, weeping pussy. That traitorous body part was drenching her panties until she began to worry she'd actually get a wet spot on her jeans.

His gaze blazed into hers, the black pupils lost in the ebony brilliance of his stare, the flame of desire leaping outrageously high, and she had a sudden, horrible suspicion.

Oh my God, did he read my mind?

One black brow arched in arrogant humor, but he only said, "When I give you a show, there'll be nothing little about it, love."

Kieran pressed toward her, closer and closer, almost forgetting they didn't have the room to themselves as his hands raised to the wall at her shoulders, caging her in. "And you're welcome to fight with it anytime, beautiful."

She opened her mouth, another sarcastic retort on the tip of her tongue, her pulse beating wildly at the strange fun she was enjoying by baiting the gorgeous stranger, but then Lach's frustrated growl jerked their attention back to the other side of the room for a second time.

Evan was apparently trying to gain her feet, while her husband had ideas of his own. "Damn it, Evie, I'll handle this myself! No fucking doctors!"

"Yeah?" Evan threw back, clearly furious, struggling to rise so she could look her husband squarely in his handsome face as he leaned over her. "And when the time comes, who's going to deliver the *baby*, you ass? *You*?"

"What bloody baby?" he muttered, trying to push her back down onto the small sofa without hurting her as she fought him to get up.

Evan glared up at the giant, pointing one rigid finger at her flat abdomen. "*This* bloody baby!"

There was an absolute moment of stillness, and then Lach jerked straight up to his full height as if he'd been struck by a jarring bolt of electricity. He quickly stumbled back a step…then two, his expression one of pure awe, utterly dumbstruck.

"Sweet Carnissa and Saephus at once," he croaked, staring at his wife's belly. "*Oh, Jesus.*" He swayed, and Kieran lurched forward, catching him by his shoulders before he slumped to the unforgiving hardwood floor.

Supporting Lach beneath his arms, Kieran flashed Evan a boyish grin, while Té rushed forward, smiling, and leaned down to whisper in her sister's ear. Evan giggled while Kieran said, "Congratulations, beautiful." He looked down at Lach's pale face and gave a wicked chuckle, shaking his head of black hair. "Look at the poor wreck. You're no' going to faint on us, are ya, man?"

Lach grunted and jerked in his cousin's grasp, regaining his feet, though he still seemed somewhat unsteady. Staring down at his wife with an expression caught somewhere between bliss and terror, he whispered, "Are ya certain, lass?"

He reached out and cradled her delicate jaw in his large hand, handling her as if she were a priceless, fragile treasure. When he dropped to his knees beside her, Té saw Evan's eyes go glassy with moisture. "Yes, you big oaf," she hiccupped around her tears. "Of course I'm sure. You know, for a *Magick*, your intuition can really suck sometimes."

His fingers trembled as he brushed her hair back from her temples. "Aye, well, I'll admit I canna think very clearly around you, woman. You go straight to my head."

"I only found out this morning," she whispered, turning her face so she could place a gentle kiss in his palm. "Are you happy?"

"Aye," he whispered back, his deep voice cracking with emotion.

His other hand joined the first, and he held her still as he lowered his mouth to hers. Té thought he'd give her a tender kiss to celebrate the moment, but the heat she witnessed as the powerful Warlock slashed his mouth across her sister's, all but consuming her, made Té blush clear to her scalp. Then he spoke against Evan's swollen lips, whispering his words into her mouth.

"Thank you, lass. I'll never understand what I did to deserve you, but I love you so much it bloody hurts. I could no' live without ya, Evie."

Té felt her own eyes go hot at the wrenching beauty of his words, the stunning emotion with which he'd pledged them, and she quickly tore her gaze away, wanting to offer them what privacy she could.

Too bad the first thing she saw was Kieran McKendrick's midnight stare locked right on her—his penetrating gaze seeming to see into her bruised, battered soul.

She waited for the taunt, the baiting remark, but it never came. He just kept those dark onyx eyes fixed on her flushed face, his expression so intense…so focused, she wondered if he'd even notice if the building came crumbling down around their heads in a blast of stone and rubble. Then he gave her a slow, easy smile, and her stomach wasn't the only thing doing somersaults. No, Té could've sworn she felt an answering tremor rip through her chest, settling heavily in the vicinity of her heart.

Well, hell, maybe these McKendricks aren't so bad after all.

Chapter Four

Twenty minutes later, Té was seriously reconsidering her opinion. These McKendrick men were something else all right. Something that strongly resembled a jaw-clenching, teeth-grinding, royal pain-in-the-ass! They may be seriously easy on the eyes, not to mention supernatural, but the killer looks and *Magickal* powers apparently came hand in hand with an exasperating first-class case of bossiness.

And she didn't particularly care for bossy, domineering men, or so her very reasonable mind kept insisting.

Too bad her hormone-ridden body didn't seem to give a damn.

Beside her in Evan's new green Jaguar, Kieran grunted and said, "I just dinna get it."

"Don't get what?" Té sighed, unable to believe her sister had actually suggested Kieran use the car to take her to their home, while she and Lach made a quick stop by the local urgent care clinic in Lach's Land Rover. After Evan's exciting news, the poor guy had been too dumbstruck to argue with her any longer, and she'd quickly won the battle over her ankle.

And now Té was stuck with the Black Knight, as her fanciful imagination had decided to name him. Normally he rode some kind of outrageously expensive motorcycle, or so Evan had teased him, but today he'd been on foot, which had led to her sister's brilliant plan, since she and Lach had been in separate cars.

A motorcycle. Huh, Té could just see that. His big, tall body covered in black jeans and a black leather jacket, that long black hair flying in the wind behind him. Christ, the man was so sexy it should be freaking outlawed.

And her determination to swear off the opposite sex was working worth a damn around him. She hunkered down in h seat, staring out the frosty window, determined to ignore th one man she unfortunately found to be utterly un-ignorable. What rotten freaking luck.

Sneaking a quick peek at him from beneath her lashes, she almost groaned, he was *that* beautiful. His eyes remained on the narrow road, profile ruggedly handsome with his ink black hair tousled from the heavy Edinburgh wind and his golden, suntanned cheeks ruddy from the cold. Té ate him up out of the corner of her eye, loving the smell of the expensive leather interior mixed with his own woodsy, masculine scent. A rich, clean aroma that was sexy-as-hell.

Her body was going liquid and soft, and when he spoke, the rough edge of his voice sent an embarrassing current of heat pooling between her legs, warming her pussy. "How can you just—accept it?" he muttered beside her, clearly perplexed, his deep voice startling her in the quiet of the car, the Jag's powerful engine nothing more than a low, soothing purr beneath the sleek hood. "Most of the *gnach* are no' as willing to believe what they very foolishly consider the unbelievable."

Té gave a noncommittal shrug, wondering how she could feel so desperate for sex while feeling so incredibly irritated. Of course, a lot of that irritation was centered at herself, mainly for being so attracted to a man when she'd firmly promised to lay off the fickle species, if not forever, then at least for a good, long while. She'd been doing so well, too, damn it—until catching an eyeful of Kieran McKendrick. Jesus, the guy was a walking poster boy for hot, wild, uninhibited sex—the ultimate Alpha male personified, completely irresistible. And—she couldn't forget—a Warlock! Hell, talk about a day of revelations. "Yeah, well, like Evan said, you can thank Aunt Ellie."

He cut her a quick glance, expression unreadable. "What was she like?"

"She was my father's younger sister, and a crazier woman you've never known," Té found herself saying, unable to keep

the smile from her voice. "She lived in the apartment above my parents' home office, so we pretty much grew up with her. Then, when we lost Mom and Dad eight years ago, she was the only family we had left. I still can't believe she's gone, too."

"What happened to her?"

"She…well, she had a heart attack, not long before Evan came to Scotland. She was only forty-seven."

"Damn, she was young. I'm sorry," he murmured, feeling the words were completely inadequate, but needing to say them anyway.

"Thanks," she replied around a soft smile, remembering all the good times they'd had with Ellie. "She was the greatest. Beautiful and sexy. The kind of woman that turned every head when she walked into a room." She gave him a sideways grin. "She was in bed when she died." There was a slight pause, and then she added with a wry smile, "In bed with a man."

He shot her a look of quiet surprise. "Damn."

"Yeah. *Two* of them, actually."

Kieran couldn't stop his low chuckle. "Well, hell, if you gotta go, you should at least be having a good time while you're at it."

Té nodded, her deep blue eyes sparkling with warmth. "I think Ellie would've said the same thing."

"It must have been hard to lose her."

She looked out the window, resting her warm forehead against the cool glass, breathing in his rich smell, the completely masculine scent seeming to surround her. "Yeah, I think that's why Evan had to leave. She just couldn't stand to be in the house any longer, with all the memories, and she'd always longed to come to Scotland. And at any rate, Ellie would've wanted her to go and follow her destiny, or whatever she would have called it."

"So you were left back in Chicago, all alone, with no one?"

She shrugged, wondering why she was so easily spilling her guts to this man. "Evan begged me to come with her, but I'd landed this really great job at one of the art galleries in town. The owner had been one of my aunt's closest friends, and I thought it was too important to just leave behind."

"And now you're here, because of some man named Palo?" he all but whispered, his smooth voice strangely soft, long fingers flexing on the leather steering wheel. "Care to explain that?"

She turned to look at him over her shoulder, her dark blue eyes heavy with exhaustion, more mental than physical. "Not really, no."

He could tell from her shuttered tone that there was more of a story there, but Kieran figured he knew well enough when to leave something alone, and when to pick it apart, peeling the surface away layer by layer, until he got down to exactly what he wanted to know.

And that's exactly what he wanted to do to this woman— this mortal—this *gnach*. He wanted to strip her apart, piece by piece, until he uncovered the source of all her secrets, all those shadows in her eyes, and worked his way down to the core of her. He wanted to know what made her tick. What made her laugh. What made her scream with pleasure until she was a frenzied force of passion exploding around his dick as he ground into her hot, wet depths.

Oh yeah, he wanted her. He wanted to fuck her until she couldn't ever take another step without remembering what it felt like to have him buried powerfully between her legs, staking his claim.

And he wanted her taste. All of it. Everywhere. Inside and out.

The taste of his *mate*…if his heart was telling him the truth.

And damn it, he had a horrible sneaking suspicion that it was.

He was two parts savage satisfaction and one part dread — and the satisfaction was making him feel guilty as hell. For years his sexual decadence had been an adequate means of satisfying that feral part of his soul, though he'd known the animal was growing restless.

Restless for a good, hard, grinding fuck.

He had the curse of the wolf upon him, as he'd had from the day of his birth, thanks to his ambitious ancestors, but he hungered not for meat. He never had. No, for him the hunger had always been one of a sexual nature, though he'd carefully managed to resist shifting during sex, never allowing the *beithíoch* that kind of freedom — until Susie.

And one taste hadn't nearly been enough. Especially when it hadn't been the one he truly wanted.

It was a fucked-up situation, to say the least, but he snorted to himself, thinking he could at least appreciate the fact that he'd never gone running bare-assed naked through the night, trying to hunt bloody Bambi for dinner.

Yeah, things could be worse — but he was feeling damn unappreciative at the moment.

He wanted — *needed* — this woman. Needed her in a way that felt as if it were being screamed by every cell in his body, scraped across his sensory receptors like nails down a chalkboard. True, he didn't know her from Eve, but on an emotional, even spiritual level, he felt as if he'd known her forever. Instinctively, he already knew the most important thing, which was that she *belonged* to him. Everything else, all the wonderful details and distinctions that set her apart from all others — well, those were all like precious gifts for him to uncover one by one, at his pleasure.

And the physical need he felt for her was unlike anything he'd ever known.

He craved her. Wanted to sink his teeth into her warm, resilient flesh as his cum blasted like liquid fire from his pumping cock, pulsing in jets of pain-edged pleasure. When the need was riding him hard, he'd always enjoyed his sexual encounters the rougher, the better—had needed the hard, dangerous edge of a relentless, merciless fucking to keep him this side of sanity. But now he found himself wanting nothing less than a complete domination. Absolute control. And suddenly the *only* thing he could think about taking, *dominating*, was the very mortal little Miss Hayes.

And wasn't that just a bloody bitch of a situation? If *Cailleachs*, his own kind, regarded shifters with such superiority and disdain, he was pretty damn sure a human woman would be horrified by the idea.

But there was no help for it. He knew it was wrong, but all he could think about was licking her from head to toe with the greedy scrape of his tongue, claiming possession of every moist, gentle swell and valley. He wanted her marked with his scent— erasing that lingering, disturbing trace of another that still clung to her. Wanted the luscious feel of her skin, the gentle tears from her eyes, and that rich, intoxicating cream he could even now smell slipping tenderly from her slick, moist cunt. Warm and wet and delicious. A unique flavor he'd never be able to get his fill of—not if it tasted half as sweet as the soft scent blurring his mind, making it misty with unsatisfied desire.

And beneath it all, there was that burning need to pierce his canines into her lush flesh, to feel her warm, wet blood spill into his mouth, swallowing it down his throat like the finest of brandies. Or better yet, spread her legs, shove his face into her precious cunt, and pierce the ripe little bud of her clit. Then he'd devour her like a soul possessed, gorging himself on the heady combination of her syrupy cum and the potent, gentle spill of her veins. He wanted to feast on it, to feel his throat working as it pulsed past his lips in a hypnotic rhythm that matched the pounding beat of her heart and the erotic clenching of her womb in the height of orgasm.

Saephus—it'd be so sweet it'd probably kill me.

His body broke out in a light sweat, his big hands gripping the sleek steering wheel so tightly he was amazed it didn't snap in two from the pressure.

And then her voice came back to him in a hollow echo of sound, as if traveling over a great distance of time and space, rather than the other side of the car. "Kieran? Hey, are you okay?"

They slowed at the next red light, the sleek Jag easing to a smooth stop under his direction, and he turned his head to look at her, blinking her back into focus, slowly, realizing with a start that he'd completely zoned out there for a minute. Shit, what was that? Where the hell had he gone?

To the fuckin' la-la-land of screwing, or some crap like that, he thought with a snarl. How friggin' pathetic. He'd only just freaking met her, and already he was playing the lovesick sap and daydreaming about her.

The light changed, but he just kept staring, unable to stop, the silence stretching out between them like an indefinite loss of reality and time. Finally, a horn blared behind them and he looked forward, hitting the gas, the sleek Jaguar hugging the roads like the fine-tuned machine that it was. He worked his jaw, determined to sound calm, and was finally able to say, "You must be fairly knackered after such a long flight."

His voice, so dark and deep, stroked a wave of warmth across the chilled surface of her skin. It was a lover's voice, as seductive as it was hard. Dangerous. Like rough silk, the kind she just wanted to wrap herself up in. She swayed, feeling her body begin to fall toward him, as if an invisible chain were connected between their pumping hearts, pulling tighter and tighter. It was a strange, sudden, powerful force of attraction— and one she could barely resist.

Only by some miraculous force of will, the one that had kept her alive these past months, did she manage to catch herself. She wrenched back, turning her body quickly to break the power of his mesmerizing pull.

He turned his head to look at her, eyes intent, a dark, hard, glittering stare that shone as black as night, fired with what looked like sparks of—*hunger*, as if he were starved for another's touch.

Her touch.

Funny, she thought with a little smile and telling shiver, but she'd always thought of herself as a "blue-eyes" kind of woman. Light and azure and soft, like Lexi's. But there was another new truth pounding in her skull, demanding recognition of its existence.

She liked devil's eyes.

Kieran's eyes.

Actually, to be honest, she thought he had the most beautiful eyes she'd ever seen. They were so dark they were nearly black—and yet they shimmered with light like the black sand beaches she'd read about from Hawaii. Sand born from the fury of a volcano. From the raging of the earth. Powerful. Primal. Explosive. All words to describe how she felt each time she lost herself in this man's—this Warlock's—sensual gaze. Sensual…and decidedly physical, as if he could see beneath her jeans and cashmere sweater, straight down to the tingling flesh buried within.

Her nipples were swollen, aching nubs, pulsing in rhythm to the erratically heavy beating of her heart. It was a pounding, erotic cadence that danced through her system, heating her blood, warming her to a searing intensity, despite the frigid cold, until the blistering need settled possessively between her thighs. It stirred through her womb, swelling her tissues, pooling in a rich, thick wave of need, of want, of writhing bodies and carnal appetites. She was soaked, panties drenched, swimming in her own slick, liquid juices—her pussy a hot, empty, throbbing ache between her trembling legs. A vacant core that hungered to be packed full of Kieran McKendrick—that longed to feel every single mouthwatering inch of his cock sliding in, forcing her open, stretching her apart.

She felt dizzy, disoriented—and then it hit her. Oh crap, he'd asked her a question somewhere along the way, and she'd been sitting here, staring off into space, thinking about sex. About hot, heavy, grinding sex, *with him*. At the nearest, soonest possible moment. In every conceivable position. Violent in its intensity. Yeah, every single raunchy, warped, twisted way imaginable. God, he made her feel like a ravenous sex maniac.

Well, crap. Now on top of everything else, she had to confront the knowledge that she was a shameless slut. Yep, definitely a slut, considering she'd known him for little more than an hour and all she could think about was whipping out his big, beautiful cock and discovering how it tasted and fit against the back of her throat.

He was, for all intents and purposes, a stranger—and yet, all she could seem to focus on was the idea of fucking him till he couldn't see straight. She just wanted to crawl on top of that rock-hard, mouthwatering body wrapped up in jeans and black leather, release the bulging mass of what had to be an absolutely monstrous erection, and impale herself on every brutal inch until they sealed together into one perfect, inseparable unit.

Beside her, Kieran released a low, rumbling growl that he was obviously trying to keep quiet. For one horrifying moment, she wondered again if he'd been able to read her mind—but no, Evie would've told her if that were possible. Of course, that didn't mean that he couldn't sense what she was thinking, considering she had to be broadcasting sex right now like a freaking satellite.

Damn. Okay, it's time to answer him, you hussy, she mumbled to herself.

Yes…an answer.

An answer.

Anssssssswer, please.

Ah, crud. What was the friggin' question?

She hazarded another quick glance at him, trying to be casual, and hoping like hell she didn't appear as aroused as she felt. "Um, I'm sorry, did you ask me something?"

Ooh, brilliant wit there, Té. Negative 5000 points for that line, sweetie. You're so smooth.

He laughed softly, pausing at another light, and reached over to tuck a stray lock of hair behind her ear, his touch hot against her cool skin. She jolted, as surprised by the affectionate gesture as by the licking, curling flames of heat spreading from the stroke of his finger against her skin to the slick, pouting flesh of her pussy.

"Aye, I did. I said you must be knackered — after your flight."

She scrunched her nose as she looked at him. "Knackered?"

He grinned that devilish grin that was fast becoming her favorite. "Tired."

"Oh — I'm — actually, I managed to sleep most of the way. Thought I'd be too excited, but the next thing I knew I'd crashed out."

You're rambling, Té. Get it together, woman. Do not look pathetic.

"That's good, then," he murmured, and damn but his voice sent another wave of chills across her flesh.

The light changed and they made the rest of the short trip in silence, until he pulled to a stop in a wonderfully expensive neighborhood, before a towering townhouse. Té looked out through the window, her jaw nearly dropping at her first look at her sister's new home. Kieran got out of the Jag with an amazing masculine grace, considering his size, and came around to get her door, but she was already scrambling out for a closer look. Shutting the door behind her with a wry smile, he retrieved her backpack and small case from the boot instead.

She watched from her position beside the car as he climbed the short flight of stairs and used the traditional key Lach had given him to open the beautifully hand-carved front door, while she just stood there on the cobblestone sidewalk, staring in awe at the stunning stone front of their home.

"Are you coming?"

Not yet, I'm not. But to Kieran, she simply said, "Yes."

And she couldn't help but laugh a little at herself, realizing she'd been standing there staring like a simpleton, though in truth, she was a little shocked. Being *Magick* was apparently a very lucrative business. "It's…um, very beautiful."

"Aye, it is," he agreed, his black eyes blinking slowly as his gaze remained fixed on *her*, so intent it felt like a caress.

She frowned at the way he was staring at her, the meaning he had put behind his words, simply because she questioned her ability to resist him. Then he winked, that damn grin back in place, and walked through the entrance, climbing the staircase that hugged the right side of the room.

Té followed after him and closed the door behind her with a resounding thud, the fact that she was suddenly alone in a huge house with a gorgeous Warlock whom she very much wanted to get naked with hitting her like a ton of bricks. She stared up after him, liking the way his ass fit inside his jeans far too much for her peace of mind. "Um, what are you doing?"

He looked down at her over his shoulder and his smile flashed, wicked and white. "Showing you up to your room."

"Thanks, but there's, uh, really no need. I'll be fine down here, and Evan can show me everything I need to see when they get home. They said they'd only be an hour or so."

He hesitated, clearly weighing his next words while he set her bags on the wide landing and came back down to her. He was at the bottom step before he finally said, "You're no' afraid to be alone with me, are you?"

She made a scoffing noise beneath her breath. "Hardly," she muttered, her tone somewhat insulted—defiant—but her body language was clearly saying differently as she wiped her palms on her jeans and shifted nervously from foot-to-foot.

His mouth twisted with what looked strangely like regret. "I'm no' going to bite, you know."

Though I'd sure as hell like to…

One slim golden brow lifted, mimicking his earlier expression of mocking humor. "I didn't think you were."

He laughed softly, shaking his head as he walked toward her and reached out, flicking the silver hoop in her brow. "We've got a hell of a problem here, don't we, beautiful?"

Oh…she *so* wasn't touching that one. No way in hell. "A problem?" she repeated, feigning innocence. She spun around, taking in the amazing room, still a little awestruck for the moment at the rugged beauty of Lach and Evan's home. "With what?"

He snorted. "What do you think?"

She stopped to look at him. "Do you always speak in riddles?" She knew she sounded like a twit, but damn it, he'd been pushing her buttons since they first met…and clearly enjoying it.

"Do you always refuse to accept the obvious?"

"The obvious," she said with a smile, determined to hold her ground even as he moved in on her. She wasn't going to flinch, and she sure as hell wasn't going to cower.

I just might pass out though…

"Aye, the obvious. It's so strong I can feel it—*taste* it." His head cocked slightly to the side as he studied her with those magnificent midnight eyes. "Why bother denying something that's so obviously the truth?"

And why dinna you shut your fucking trap, man? What are you trying to do here, anyway? Hell if he knew. Stupid…arrogant…misplaced pride. It got the better of a man, be he Warlock or mortal, every damn time.

He had every intention of turning his ass around, walking away, and leaving her alone…for as long as he could…*forever*, if possible. Though at this point, he was seriously starting to doubt he'd make it five minutes. But before he could even put it to the test, she lifted her chin and said, "I really don't have the slightest clue what you're talking about."

Kieran groaned, recognizing defeat when he saw it. So much for hightailing his ass out of there. Suddenly he was right there, pressing into her, bringing her up hard against the back of the mocha-colored leather sofa.

She blinked up at him, her neck craned back at a sharp angle, their noses touching as he leaned over her from his greater height, her breath warm and sweet against his lips.

"No?" he growled. "Then maybe I ought to demonstrate."

He leaned closer, nuzzling the top of her head, wishing he could just bury his face into the soft, silken mass of her red and gold tresses. His muscles tightened, and he knew he was going to kiss her. There was no other choice. It was taste her or die. Giving over purely to instinct, ignoring the voice of reason screaming in his head, he grasped her hips in his big hands as his mouth found her ear and licked the tender shell, nibbling on the delicate lobe.

Té jolted, lurching against him, and he growled again, the sexy rumble erotically seductive against her sensitive flesh. "I want to be in you—*deep in you*—so damn bad," he rasped, nibbling on her lush skin. His lips trailed up the soft arc of her cheek, pressing a kiss against the corner of one eye while she stood completely still within his grasp, not even breathing. Then his lips grazed the fine skin of her temple and he froze.

Té stiffened within the tight circle of his arms, knowing what was coming, even though she knew it impossible for him to *know*. The bruises had faded weeks ago, leaving only the emotional scars that she'd done her best to ignore.

Acknowledging their existence would have been just what Lexi would've wanted, and she would be damned before she gave him that kind of sick satisfaction. The bastard.

Yeah, she knew it was impossible, and yet Kieran's words were exactly what she'd been expecting. Had known he would say. "You've been hit—*struck*," he snarled, a sudden edge of violence in his deep tone. It sent a shiver of delicious anticipation down her spine, and she wondered just what that said about her. Lord, maybe she really was as twisted as Lexi had claimed.

No! Damn it, Té, stop thinking about him. Don't let the miserable creep poison your mind.

She tried for a smile that she was sure looked as fake as it felt. Crap, at this rate he was never going to believe her, and if she couldn't convince a complete stranger, she knew there was no way in hell she was going to be able to convince Evan. Good Lord, what had she been thinking to come here? Evan had been able to see through her since Té was old enough to know a lie was sometimes easier than the truth. The truth of her life hadn't always been pretty, and she'd learned early on that a clever play on words often kept that sickening look of pity off a person's face, which was just as she wanted it.

But it'd never worked on Evan.

Yep, she was *sooooo* screwed.

But what the hell? Might as well give it a go.

"You mean the knot?" she asked with wide-eyed innocence, at least as much as she could muster. "I got that in the fifth grade when Amy Murray whacked a line drive and I was playing shortstop. Drilled the hell out of me."

Kieran's black eyes drilled into her now, until she began to feel dizzy from following the shimmering glints of light in their reflective surface. "You expect me to believe this was made by a baseball in grade school?"

His warm breath caressed her face as he leaned over her, and she knew she was such a goner. All she wanted to do was keep staring up at him, memorizing the masculine perfection of his body, the strong, corded length of his throat and that perfect spot between neck and solid shoulder where she wanted to nip him with her teeth, hear his empowering growl. His raw, sharp-edged power blasted against her, wrapping around her like invisible claws, imprisoning her within the bonds of his control and savage appeal. Seeking balance, she placed her hands on the hard, warm surface of his leather-covered chest, desperately ignoring the feel of ripped, sculpted muscle beneath her palms.

Good god, this guy was fine. Too damn fine for her peace of mind.

Oh geez, now I'm rhyming, she thought with a low groan. It was time to get her act together before she did something she would assuredly regret and jumped his sexy-as-sin bones right then and there.

"I don't expect you to believe anything but what I tell you," she challenged in a deliberately cool voice, the denial accompanied by an even harder shove against the solid wall of muscle caging her in.

Oomph—he didn't even budge.

"You're lying." The strong, masculine tendons in his neck stood out in anger, a small muscle jerking hard in his dark jaw.

"Yeah?"

"Yeah. I can still feel the energy—the anger. Someone struck you, and it was someone a hell of a lot bigger than you are." And he knew it was somehow connected to that faint trace of watered-down *Magick* that he'd scented on her before, though he could hardly credit such a bizarre suspicion. Until this morning, she hadn't even known that his *kind* existed. It was far from likely that she'd been interacting with other *Magicks* back in America—and even less likely that she could have known any and not realized. A *Magick's* power was so much a part of who they were, the idea of keeping it a secret was damn near inconceivable.

And yet...Kieran knew that elusive trace beneath her light, lush scent was going to drive him out of his bloody mind until he discovered its source.

Té stared up at him, eyes narrowed in frustration, while dread coiled in her belly, a sudden fear taking root at just how well this man could read her. She didn't want him knowing her secrets, damn it, digging into her mind. "He's not your problem."

"He is until he's dead."

That was it. Point blank. Matter-of-fact.

Kieran intended to kill for her.

Té didn't know whether to laugh or smile....or run like crazy and get her stupid little ass as far away from these crazy McKendricks as she could.

Only, she wouldn't ever be completely free of them, because her sister was now one.

Damn.

"Listen, Kieran, because I'm only going to say this once. I'm not your problem. Not now. Not ever. So drop it. I don't need saving."

He smirked in the face of her denial, not backing down an inch. "You, Té Hayes, are most definitely *my* problem."

And she knew there were so many separate, powerfully distinct meanings to that statement.

A strange sort of panic settled into her jittery system, quickening her breath. But she wasn't afraid of him. No, suddenly she was very much afraid of what she realized she could feel for this man...*this Warlock.* "I'm not staying, so whatever you say, whatever you think, doesn't matter. I'm not looking for another meaningless fling—"

"Good," he grunted with a clipped nod of his dark head. "Because I have a feeling I'm looking at forever, whether I want to be or not."

Her chin came up in a surge of anger. "Damn it, I'm not going to let myself feel anything for you."

"Too late, lass," he said with that wicked twist of his lips that made her want to slap him and kiss him all at the same time. "You *already* do."

Her breath huffed out in a hard sound of exasperation. "God, you're irritating."

To her surprise, he threw back his head and laughed, the warm sound pooling through her system like succulent, dripping honey. "Dinna worry, darlin'. I'll grow on you."

She opened her mouth, but before she could say anything, he quickly turned her around and swatted her backside, pushing her toward the stairs while he still could. "I *will* find out what I want to know, but for now be a good girl and go grab a nap. The guest room is the fourth door on the right."

She muttered something under her breath and began climbing the stairs.

Kieran watched the sexy sway of her ass until he knew a second more was going to send him barreling up the stairs after her. Shaking his head at his own remarkable weakness where this little mortal was concerned, and still not having a clue as to what he was going to do about it, he called out, "I'll see you tonight."

She turned to look down at him, those lush lips pulled into a frown. "Tonight?"

"Aye," he drawled on his way to the door, needing to get away from her as soon as possible. It was too damn dangerous being alone with her. One more second of having her pressed against the back of that sofa and she'd have been flat on her back, just like Little Red at the mercy of the Big Bad Wolf. "The family will be champing at the bit to meet you. And there's no' stopping the family, lass." He shot her a sly smirk over his shoulder. "We McKendricks can be pretty persistent when we want something bad enough."

The door closed behind him with a reverberating thump that seemed to echo the sickening drop of her stomach. Nervous energy fluttered across her skin and she licked her dry lips. Shit. She could lie all she liked, but one thing was for damn certain.

She may not want—may not *need* the complication a man could cause in her life, but it sure as hell looked like she had one. What was the point of denying it, when her thundering heart rate and dazed senses spoke for themselves? The sad fact of the matter was that she was already falling hard and fast for the dark, dangerous, *Magickal* Kieran McKendrick.

God help her.

Chapter Five

The nap that afternoon had done her wonders, along with the hot, luxurious shower in her private bathroom and sisterly beauty time spent with Evan. Té felt refreshed and at her best, dressed in a long, light cotton skirt and sleeveless top in a deep, dark blue that matched her eyes and showcased her new tan. Her sister and her new brother-in-law had made her feel completely at home throughout the easy afternoon, but when she walked into the packed family room later that evening, she felt entirely like a fish out of water. The family gathering was in full swing, and there were McKendricks everywhere, along with some of the family's closest friends, not a single space or piece of furniture left unoccupied.

Friendly looking faces smiled at her from every direction, but Evan first introduced her to the High Council, Lach's uncles, which she knew included Kieran's father, Iain McKendrick, thanks to her sister's earlier rundown of the family. Té didn't know what she'd been expecting, based on the brief descriptions Evan had provided her, but certainly not *this*. She supposed she'd imagined anyone who governed over such a powerful people to be distinguishably ancient, but despite their long, silvery white hair and beards, Kieran's father and uncles were a powerful, mesmerizing sight. Their snow white hair adorned rather young looking, handsome faces, the long robes hardly concealing what were obviously still strong, virile physiques. She had no idea of their ages, but they were an intimidating lot, even though they welcomed her with genuine, if not expectant smiles and warm words — Iain even giving her a warm wink that perfectly matched his son's.

And now, thanks to Evan, she was a part of their family.

Jesie Chrisie, as Aunt Ellie would say.

And then there were *the girls*, as the family called them. Five Witches in their early twenties who Seamus had apparently taken under his wing and reared as his own, when their own families were lost during a dark time of hostile feuding among the *Magick*. They'd been welcomed with open arms, Kieran and his cousins apparently adoring them, acting like overprotective brothers if other Warlocks so much as showed even a flicker of interest in the young women. The thought brought a smile to Té's face, though she doubted the Witches found it so amusing. Lord, it probably drove them mad.

Needing to oversee some last minute preparations in the kitchen, Evan ushered her over to the group, introduced her to *the girls* and then left, leaving Té to fend for herself. She plastered on a smile and tried her best not to feel self-conscious surrounded by such stunning beauty. They were breathtaking, even up close, the five most beautiful women she'd ever seen, though each one looked decidedly different from the other four.

"I hope I didn't interrupt anything," she offered apologetically, hating to have intruded on their conversation.

The one named Ivy gave her a warm smile. "Of course not."

"We normally dinna look so fierce, but we were just complaining about how we've been denied the *Ag Ríochan* for too damn long," Willow explained, as if the strange statement made perfect sense.

Té nodded. "At the risk of sounding incredibly stupid, what is that?"

Willow scrunched her nose in obvious distaste. "It's a ritual of sorts, a kind of practice that Witches pass down to the following generations. A spell, actually, in which a young *Cailleach* learns to use her power over the elements to prepare her for the intense physicality of mating with a Warlock."

Té swallowed a shock of surprise, a million and one questions racing through her mind. "And you've all been…*denied* the training? That sounds rather harsh."

The one named Poppy scowled at the group of Council members on the other side of the room, their white heads bent in private discussion. "Aye. Seamus forbade it."

"But, why?" Té asked, the feminist in her clearly appalled.

Chrys, short for Chrysanthemum of all things, snorted at her side. "Because the controlling old bastard thought it would keep us from having sex."

The five Witches shared a smothered laugh, drawing worried looks from Mal and Dugan, who stood near enough to see their devilish expressions. *The girls* winked at the two intimidating brutes, both of whom Té had yet to meet, but had been pointed out by Evan, and she felt a grin tug at the corners of her lips. "Something tells me their little plan hasn't worked."

Ivy shrugged. "Well, it's true that none of the Warlocks will bed us, because our interfering cousins have made sure they all know we've been denied, but that's hardly stopped us from experimenting with some of the *gnach*."

Té's grin fell into a sudden frown. "I'm not sure I like how you guys say that—like it's a dirty word."

Lily clasped her shoulder, giving her a little hug. "Ah, Té, you're no mere *gnach*, love. You and our Evie are special."

"Thanks, I think."

Ivy sent her an apologetic smile. "Lily's right, Té. You and Evie *are* special. And it's not as if we dislike the *gnach*. But it's hard sometimes to be sympathetic toward a race that used to burn us at the stake."

Té shot her a sideways look. "Hmm…good point." She looked over at the Council. "Do you think Seamus knows what you've done?"

Five distinct laughs filled the air. "I should hope not," Chrys replied. "If he did, he'd probably drop a plague on the whole damn city just to keep anyone from touching us."

"But won't he have to let someone share it with you someday?"

Willow nodded her head, sending her white-gold curls bouncing around her smiling face. "Oh, I'm sure he has plans for letting one of the matrons share it with us eventually. Say, like when we're forty."

They all giggled, making Té smile. "And even your cousins won't find the answers for you?"

Poppy snorted across from her. "Are you kidding? Those arrogant heaps of testosterone still treat us like we're five."

"How hypocritical can you get?" muttered Chrys.

"Yeah," Lily sighed, "the philandering fuckheads."

"I hope to hell you're no' talking about me," came a deep rumble from behind the group. The five young Witches turned at the sound, snickering, and Té somehow found herself standing in the center of a perfect semicircle. She glared at *the girls*, each one trying to give her an innocent look that she so wasn't buying, and turned to see Kieran watching her with the intensity of a hawk going in for the kill.

Her mouth went dry at the sight of him.

Lord, he looked even better than she remembered. Gone were the jeans and leather jacket, and in their place were a fine, sage-colored pair of expensive wool pants and a crisp white dress shirt, the fine linen contrasting wonderfully against his dark, olive-toned skin.

"Té," he said, his low voice falling over her like a wave of warm, mellow whiskey. Her belly pulled tight, a strange little fluttering of delicious anticipation racing through her blood.

"Kieran," she whispered, trying not to wince at the breathless, dreamy sound of her own voice.

Chrys gave her a gentle elbow in her side. "Come on, girls, I think we're thirsty. Catch ya later, beautiful."

"Great meeting ya, Té."

Another hug came from the back. "Glad to finally have ya here, Té. You better stick around."

"See ya later, sweetie."

"Ciao, darlin'."

The chorus of feminine voices faded away, and just like that, she was left alone with *him*, albeit in a roomful of people, but she still felt like the final survivor trapped on a sinking ship. Miserable little rotten deserters, she wanted to shout, but knew it would be too rude.

Kieran gave her a slow, perceptive smile, as if he knew just what she was thinking, and she scowled at him, wanting to knock the knowing expression right off his gorgeous face almost as much as she wanted to kiss him.

"Feel better?" he asked in that fine voice, his tone far too intimate for her to handle.

"Just peachy," she gritted through her teeth, wondering why he could so easily rankle her. His crisp, woodsy scent floated through her like an addictive substance, dangerously close to dismantling her resolve, a sensual combination of aftershave and warm, virile male. Her emotions became a chaotic jumble, everything felt in the extreme around this too-sexy-to-be-true Warlock.

His black eyes inspected her from the top of her hair down to her little sandal-clad toes. "You look just peachy, too," he drawled around a wickedly boyish grin, his eyes reversing their path in a slow, sensual caress, lingering in a maddening way over the juncture of her thighs and the slow heaving of her breasts, until finally connecting with her own once again. He opened his mouth, but whatever he was going to say was cut off by the deep voice coming from directly behind him. Té peeked around his side to see another gorgeous giant standing there smiling at her, his hair a bit longer than Kieran's, so black it was nearly blue, with thick-lashed eyes the color of a Caribbean sea.

"And who might this fiery beauty be?" he drawled, the delicious burr in his voice rolling across her senses just like the others.

Kieran's lips pressed into a scowl as he watched Té step to the side and smile, extending her hand with the natural warmth that made him just want to crawl up into her. "Hi. I'm—"

"She's no' someone you'll be touching, Blu McKendrick. Keep your blasted hands to yourself," he muttered, feeling his fist clench involuntarily at his side in an instinctual need to knock the smiling Blu right on his cocky ass.

Té shot an outraged look at Kieran, and Blu let out a low whistle. "Och, now, Cousin, I dinna think the lass is in agreement with ya, man."

Shouldering her way in front of Kieran's huge body, Té grabbed Blu's big hand and gave it a hearty shake. "I'm Bronté Hayes, Evan's little sister, and it's lovely to meet you."

"Ah, so little Té's finally made it home? 'Bout time too, lass," Blu murmured, taking in her changed appearance. "I almost didna recognize you from the photos I've seen."

Her home? What was it with these arrogant Scots? Sheesh, the one at her front seemed to be as bad as the one at her back. And he was almost as gorgeous, with that blue-black hair and those lapis-colored eyes.

Hmm…maybe it wasn't such a great idea coming here after all. If her instincts were to be trusted, she didn't think it was going to be as easy to eventually slip away as she'd initially thought it would be. She shifted nervously, tucking stray strands of her red and gold hair behind her ears like she always did, wondering why she didn't just cut it shorter to save herself the hassle. "Yeah, well, I was, um, ill for a bit," she offered by way of explanation.

Yeah, sick in the head for letting myself be taken in by some sexy stud.

She plastered on her bright "everything's just peachy" smile. "But as you can see, I'm all better now."

Blu placed his hand over his heart. "Lass, if you got any better, I'd be dead."

"Cousin—" Kieran growled the low warning from her back, so close she could feel his mouthwatering heat, and the devil in front of her winked.

"Um, if you two will excuse me, I think I see Evan looking for me."

The two Scots watched her scurry away, their expressions wry, the blatant fact that she was hightailing it away from them rather too obvious to miss. Lach walked over to join them, his look accusing. "What the hell did you two do now?"

Kieran ignored the question. "Keep Mal and Dugan away from her," he snarled, beyond the ability to be reasonable. His eyes cut to a smirking Blu. "And this idiot, too."

Lach gave him an infuriating grin, his expression saying he understood all too well the hell Kieran was going through, struggling to deny the undeniable.

And then a mischievous look settled across Blu's face that had Kieran narrowing his eyes in suspicion—a suspicion which was quickly confirmed when Té's sudden squeal snagged his attention. She'd stopped working her way through the guest-filled room, standing not ten feet away from them, her hands struggling to hold down her billowing skirt as it swirled and thrashed around her shapely legs, lifting into the air.

"Damn it, Blu," Kieran growled, shoving his smiling cousin in the arm while Lach chuckled under his breath. "Cut it out, you ass. Right now!"

Blu's deep blue eyes widened in feigned surprise. "What? Dinna even try to tell me you're no' enjoying the view."

Té's skirt lifted higher, Blu's *Magick* whipping the air around her into a churning frenzy, until she looked like a Marilyn Monroe poster Kieran had often seen. Her hair whipped around her flushed face as she spun in a circle, apparently trying to figure out where the bizarre breeze was coming from. He gritted his teeth as he caught a quick shot of her gorgeous, panty-covered ass, but only a few raised brows and slow grins came from those standing around her—everyone there far too used to witnessing the cousins' crazy antics to rile one another to be shocked by the odd display. A low grumble of soft, heated expletives could be heard slipping from Té's lips, though, and Kieran couldn't help but give a brief, inner smile at her fire.

Standing there with his fists clenched at his sides, he felt torn between enjoying the tempting view of her incredible body, and beating the holy living hell out of Blu. There was a steady pounding in his temples, echoing the pumping of his heart—the need to knock some sense into the man itching through his system.

He couldn't handle this crap right now. Not with the shape he was in. Saephus, couldn't Blu see how close he was to the breaking point?

"Nice view," Mal drawled at his back, and Kieran suddenly began to wonder just how angry Evan would be if he threw a punch in her house. Or better yet—two.

"Damn—best I've seen in years," Dugan added over his other shoulder, his voice a low, aroused rumble, and Kieran felt the sudden possessive need to blind the whole friggin' lot of them.

"Keep your bloody eyes off her," he snarled, turning his back on Té so he could face the three smirking faces sending him knowing expressions that he couldn't wait to wipe away.

As if oblivious to the murder in Kieran's eyes, Mal cocked his head at Blu and said, "Check this out."

Groaning under his breath, Kieran cut a quick look over his shoulder at Té's low gasp. The wind slowed softly around her legs, yet she stood rooted in place, facing them, hands still grasping fistfuls of her skirt, her wide eyes glued to her panting chest. Kieran followed her line of vision, his gut cramping with a staggering punch of lust when he saw that the thin fabric of her shirt was now wet with one tiny drop of water, right at the tip of her left breast. They both stared at the small wet spot where her nipple pressed against the clinging cloth, and Kieran felt his tongue stroke the roof of his mouth, eager for the taste of that sweet little nipple between his lips. He swallowed a painful lump of sexual hunger as her dark blue gaze sliced to his, the vivid color hot with accusation.

He winced as he slowly turned back to her, ignoring the low rumble of his chuckling cousins as he stared…lost to the lust…transfixed by the sight of another plump drop of water materializing in the air just above her right breast this time. It hovered there, catching the shimmering sparkle of the soft lights and flickering candles, then descended with perfect aim to land precisely at the tip of her right nipple.

Kieran growled in the back of his throat, desperate to use his mouth to continue the job and wet the entire damn shirt, sucking and nipping at those luscious tits until she was screaming from the pleasure, her hot little cunt shattering in ecstasy. She'd be wet and silky, glistening on the pretty pink lips of her pussy, down the insides of her thighs—all that sweet cream just waiting for his mouth to eat it, lapping it up stroke by rasping stroke. It was such a hot fantasy, and one he needed to put a stop to right now, or he'd be doing it, going down on her in a roomful of his bloody relatives.

"Cut it the hell out," he grunted at his cousins, his hands fisting tighter, knowing he was getting ready to throw that first punch—Evan's anger be damned.

Blu took a long swallow of his ale and smiled. "Or what?"

Kieran let his own lips curl with warm satisfaction, suddenly realizing, when it came to this particular cousin that he had at least one weapon at his disposal he could use without pissing Evan off. "Or maybe I'll see fit, the next time I see her, to let a certain little pink-haired *Pixie* know you canna keep your bloody eyes off her ass every time she turns around."

Blu nearly choked, sputtering his ale through his nose as Mal gave him a few helpful whacks on his broad back. "The hell you will!"

"Just keep them away," Kieran snarled at a chuckling Lach, watching as Té sent a final glare in his direction and then turned on her heel to storm away.

His mood, which had started out sour as he stood in the corner, waiting for Té to make her entrance, had only gotten worse as the evening progressed. He'd watched with a completely alien feeling of burning jealousy as every eye in the room ate her up while she talked with the Council, and then with *the girls*. The only time his attention had strayed was when he caught sight of Lach seated in a big, comfortable chair beside the fire, his wife cuddled up in his lap, strong arms wrapped around her middle, his big hands settling possessively over her flat belly. It was such an intimate sight that Kieran had been tempted to look away. But then, it had been so beautiful, he could do nothing other than stand in the corner and stare at his cousin's hands soothing over the invisible bundle of his unborn child.

Kieran had felt his own hands tremble, a sharp stab of recognition knotting his gut—a realization that he wanted to have *that* feeling—that same look of bliss that fell over his cousin's fierce features whenever the woman who'd changed his life walked into the room.

And instead, all he had was a temperamental prick and a raging sex drive, with no easy end in sight. Not to mention the complicated puzzle of Té.

He watched her make her way through the crowded room, his eyes taking in every nuance of expression as she turned a tense, but friendly smile to those who came forward to greet her. She wasn't comfortable being surrounded by so many people, especially after his jackass cousins' attempts to push his bloody buttons, and he felt a dangerous need to pull her into his side and offer what comfort he could.

Only, he didn't have any comfort to give her.

Saephus, what in hell's name was he going to do about her?

The added ache of uneasiness that had settled into his bones puzzled him. It went beyond mere protection—though Té Hayes certainly looked as if she could use some—to some foreign sense of raw, primal possessiveness. He wanted to *own* her, in the truest sense of the word—but first he had to find a way to claim her without hurting her.

Because he really didn't think he had a choice in the matter. He *would* claim her. It was a fact. His soul wouldn't let him do otherwise.

The only question was when?

She turned into the back hallway and he was already walking after her when he heard Lach say, "You'll have to mate her soon, Cousin, if you expect to be able to keep the others away."

He stopped, but didn't turn around. He felt raw, exposed, as if every sensation were magnified by the instability of the emotions churning inside of him. "If they touch her, they die."

And with that, he set off to find the woman turning his entire world inside out.

* * * * *

He found her a few seconds later, talking on the phone in Lach's home office, her back to the door as she perched her sweet ass on the corner of the mammoth mahogany desk centered before the back wall. The only light in the warm, wood-scented room came from the flickering blaze of orange and yellow in the grate to his left, the fire crackling comfortably to ward off any chill in the air. He could smell the burning wood, a faint trace of sandalwood incense, and underneath those stronger scents, the subtle, alluring smell of the woman he was slowly closing in on.

He knew the instant she realized she was no longer alone, because her spine straightened, voice going low as she said goodbye to her private caller. Jealousy flamed to life, burning hotter than the blaze at his side, when he heard her say, "I've missed you, too. It'll be great to see you tomorrow night. Bye."

She set the phone down carefully, still not turning around, and he heard himself say, "Who the fuck was that?"

A small laugh reached his ears. "I knew it was going to be you."

"And I asked you a question."

She shot him a sharp look over her mostly bare shoulder, the flames from the hearth doing amazing things to the red and gold of her hair. Shit, she was so intoxicating it made him ache. Made him fucking hurt with the need to take her and claim her as his own.

"Last time I checked, I don't answer to you, McKendrick."

"My name is Kieran, and you sure as hell *will* answer to me."

"You presumptuous ass," she sputtered, slipping off the desk to stand beside it, cutting him with her glare. "Who the hell do you think you are?"

Wide shoulders shrugged casually, the muscles shifting with a predatory grace beneath the fine white linen of his shirt. "The answer to that is easy, Té. I'm the man who's going to be fucking you. The *only* man who's going to be fucking you. So you can just call back and cancel whatever the hell it is you think you're doing tomorrow night."

Her mouth opened and closed twice before she said, "No."

He stopped dead in his tracks. "What do you mean, no?"

"I meant it just like it sounded. You can't dictate to me where I go and with whom. And there's no way in hell I'm canceling tomorrow night. It's important."

"Then I'll be going with you."

She crossed her arms before her still damp chest in a mutinous stance. "You don't even know where I'm going."

"I dinna give a fuck where you're going," he stated implacably, that fascinating muscle jerking in his tight jaw, dark eyes glowing as they reflected the light of the flames. "The only thing that matters is that you're going with me."

She watched him with her large, shimmering eyes, blinking slowly. "I can say no. After that stunt you pulled back there and your seriously aggravating attitude, I *should* say no."

"But you willna do it."

Her eyes narrowed in surprise at his cool, male confidence, her expression completely transfixed. With her lips barely moving, she managed to ask, "And why is that?"

"Because you know damn well that I didna have anything to do with what happened back there, but mostly because you want me just as badly as I want you. Can you honestly tell me that you dinna want me to fuck you? That you've no' thought about what it'll be like between us? What it'll be like to have my cock crammed up tight in your little cunt, and us grinding each other raw?"

She frowned, giving him her best dirty look, but he just laughed softly, the dark sound warm and deep, like slow, thick, melting molasses. It did all kinds of wickedly heated things to her insides, not to mention her quivering pussy. Jesus, at this rate, her panties were going to end up a great sopping mess.

Her attraction to him was undeniable, despite what Evan had revealed to her this evening. She still didn't know what to make of that wild tale. It was unbelievable — and yet, she somehow believed.

And God help her, she still wanted him. If that wasn't a sign she had it bad, she didn't know what was.

What Evan had claimed seemed impossible, but looking at him, Té knew she believed it. It was there in every relentless line of his body, the reined animal just waiting to be set free.

A *wolf*, Evan had claimed. Kieran McKendrick could actually shift into a deadly beast — an animal. It *should* have terrified her, but instead she felt the fascination burning like a hot little ball of fire in her belly, spreading warmth and eagerness through her system. Was it the taste of the forbidden that had her so intrigued, or the simple fact that she was completely knocked out by the gorgeous stud standing before her, looking at her like he wanted to eat her up, piece by piece?

A predator preparing to pounce.

According to Evan, his skin became covered in a gleaming, silky, blue-black fur when he changed, the length depending on how far he let the change progress. His eyes would bleed to a brilliant metallic silver, glowing, and his teeth would lengthen into a lethal set of fangs that could pierce and rip with the ease of any deadly carnivore. A snout would transform his nose and mouth, again depending on how much of the change he allowed, and his already muscle-ripped, mouthwatering physique would gain near a foot in height, muscles expanding with unbelievable, savage power and strength.

Evan had shivered during the telling, a wicked spark of mischief firing her gray eyes. "Actually," she'd said with a smile, "I think it all sounds kinda sexy. I wonder if Lach could—oh, never mind."

Té had laughed and told her she was warped, and then spent the rest of the time getting dressed wondering what it *would* be like to be taken, to be ravished, to be *consumed* by a man as wild and wicked as Kieran McKendrick.

Hell, who was she trying to fool? She wanted him bad, even with a freaking curse or two on his sexy head.

"You want me," he repeated, his words eerily mirroring her thoughts. It was a statement. A fact. Not something he was putting up for argument.

But she wasn't ready to let him win. "No," she whispered, unwilling to admit to him what she'd only recently been able to admit to herself. Something told her that giving in would be the wrong move, because this was a guy who would take the power and run hard and fast with it, never giving it back. "You're wrong."

Kieran couldn't stop the slow smile of anticipation from settling across his face, the animal in him enjoying her challenge. There was something about her that tempted him, called to him, made him—*hungry*. Yeah, that was it. Thinking about her was like thinking about a feast, one prepared specifically for his pleasure, on which he could dine for an eternity and still not get enough.

He took another step toward her, maneuvering her right where he wanted as she back-stepped to keep from touching him. "You're lying, lass. And you're no' verra good at it."

"Like hell," she said with as much conviction as she could assemble, and yet, she knew her look was questioning. How could he read her so well? *God, please don't let him be able to read my mind.* She was going to be such a goner if he caught so much as a glimpse of the things she'd like to be doing to his gorgeous bod. Hell, even she was shocked, and they were *her* fantasies.

One strong hand reached toward her face, cradling her jaw, and she tried not to melt at the exquisite touch of his warm palm, the latent strength she could feel just beneath the hot surface of his skin, the slightly rough scrape of his calluses against the softness of her flesh. He may be a man, a Warlock, of extraordinary power, but he was still a man. A man who worked with his hands. Who had molded his body into a thing of beauty and power. A man who was obviously not afraid of hard work. A man, who as a high-ranking Council soldier, had vowed to protect others with his life.

A man who could make her completely forget why she didn't want a man.

He cradled her face, his expression intense, as if he could see straight into her soul, straight down to the pool of need bubbling to life in her core, gathering like rich cream between her thighs. The corner of his mouth twitched as he took a slow, deep breath, his thumb moving out to stroke the fullness of her lush lower lip.

"You're wasting your breath lying to me, sweetheart. I can smell the way your little pussy is going all warm and wet, melting for me, just waiting for the moment my mouth will eat into it."

Her lips thinned, teeth grinding. "That's not possible."

She watched through lowered lids as his head cocked slightly to the side, smile twisting into a look of carnal speculation that made her womb contract, her pussy swell with the need to feel him right *there*, hard and solid and strong, stretching her so wonderfully wide.

"For a mortal, no. But then I'm no' mortal, love."

Her brow lifted in imitation of his annoying, if not sexy expression. "Have I mentioned that I don't like arrogant men, even if they are Warlocks?"

His lips twitched again, slowly twisting into a grin of unfairly sexy proportions. "Well, your lips say one thing, lass," he said, his seductive voice lowered to a husky whisper as his other hand moved to settle onto her lower belly. "But your little cunt says another."

She jolted at the wicked word on those sinful lips, her face flushing with heat while her body responded with surprising speed, going liquid and soft, liking it…a lot. No one had ever spoken to her this way. Not even Lexi, whose language had been rawer than any of the fledgling men from her youth. She hadn't really understood the attraction of such words, until she could both watch and hear as they slipped from that heavenly mouth that surely belonged to a devil.

And he knew it. The smoldering heat in his eyes told her he knew just what his voice and language did to her.

"Are you reading my mind?" she demanded in a breathless rush, eyes bright with fury.

"Nae." He took a deep breath, his nostrils flaring, eyes dilated with desire. "I can smell it on you—your need."

"No," she whispered, willing it to be untrue.

He leaned closer and drawled in a husky rasp, "You really are wasting your breath, beautiful. I *can* smell the way your little piece grows warm and wet, making those tight little panties slick, every single time you set eyes on me."

His fingers contracted, massaging her stomach as it cramped with need, the edge of his pinky finger nearly grazing her mound. Suddenly there were too many damn clothes between them, and she wondered what he'd do if she just lifted her skirt and shoved his hand between her trembling thighs, proving that every wicked word he'd drawled was true.

He leaned closer, surrounding her with his heat and that smoky, male scent that made her head feel fuzzy with lust. She licked her lips, and tried to concentrate.

"Would you like to hear what it's telling me?"

"Not particularly," she said in a halting rush, a small gasp escaping her parted lips.

"Tough, because I think you *need* to hear it. *You want me.* You want me so damn bad you can hardly stand it."

"No," she sighed, grimacing at the wistful sound of her voice, wondering why she was still bothering to deny something so blatantly obvious.

The corner of his wicked mouth twitched at her tone, the pad of his thumb pressing purposefully into the pouting flesh of her lower lip. "You're lying again, lass. And it isna nice to lie."

Chapter Six

Everything happened in a bewildering, spellbinding blur of movement and sound. One second she'd been telling him to go to hell for calling her a liar, and the next thing she knew, his hot, corded length was plastered against her, his big hands hard on her ass as he ground her up against a mouthwatering erection. With long, purposeful strides, he carried her to one of the immense chairs before the fire, covering her the instant her backside hit the warm burgundy leather beneath her. And then the lean line of his hips was pressing between her legs, forcing her thighs to part while his strong hands held her upper arms in a biting grip and his mouth…

God, his mouth.

His mouth attacked her in ways she'd only read about in books, warm lips moving against her own with torrid intent, slashing from one angle to another, testing and retesting their fit until he found the one allowing him the deepest penetration. He tasted like wine and blazing lust, deliciously addictive, his tongue rubbing past her lips in blatant imitation of the immense, pants-covered ridge stroking the apex of her thighs. It was a voluptuous tangle of hungers and textures, scratchy jaw against baby smooth skin, the soft roughness of his tongue stroking sleek, moist tissues, teeth nipping into the vulnerable fullness of her lower lip.

Her body was on fire, so damn hot she expected to start smoking at any second, combusting into scalding flames beneath the carnal mastery of his seductive mouth and the delicious press of his heavy, very aroused male body.

How in the hell had she gotten to this point?

Where had she gone wrong?

Damn it, she'd been so certain she could resist him, and now look at her.

Tumbling headfirst into the sexual abyss he ripped open at her feet, Té moaned a throaty plea of surging need, tangling her tongue with his. She battled for control and finally won, sucking greedily at the tip the exact way she'd been dying to do to the head of his cock. Slow, deep pulls that had him shouting into her mouth, an answering cry slipping through her sex, leaving her liquid and soft.

Kieran shuddered and tore his hot face away, only to push it instantly into her crotch, knowing he couldn't walk away if his life depended on it. He pressed closer, burrowing into the warm, sweet crease at the top of her thighs, just wanting to eat her alive. Humid warmth met his hungry, passion-dazed senses, spiced with the rich, honeyed scent of her cream, and he began to wonder if a Warlock could actually die from lust. His cock throbbed like an angry beast within the confines of his pants, feeling as if it would simply explode from the mounting pressure, while the remembered taste of her mouth continued to devastate his senses.

And her scent. Saephus, he just wanted to lap at her like a dog. Just shove his muzzle into her delectable pussy and gorge himself on every single delicate inch of her pink flesh. Wanted to rub his face into her warm, slick folds, his tongue stroking her swollen, creamy slit in long, hungry licks. Wanted it spearing into the exquisite clench of her inner muscles, fucking her with deep, greedy strokes until she flooded into him, filling him with her lush, salty-sweet juices.

"Gods," he groaned, the heat from the fire blazing against his back while she seared his front. He nudged the damp fabric of her skirt with his nose, wishing he could have her naked and spread open, his thumbs spreading her lips so wide that her little slit pulled apart and he could look up into her clinging depths. Wanted to search with his eyes what he knew he might never be able to have with his cock, just so he could keep the memory burned into his brain for eternity, engrained on his desperate senses.

This was so ironic, that he'd found a woman who made him finally *feel* more than any other creature he'd ever known—who made him understand how a man could utterly commit himself to one person for the entirety of his life with absolute abandon and joy, giving all that he was because without her he'd be nothing—and he couldn't have her.

He was ruined for any other woman now. But, fuck, what did it matter? He didn't want another woman. What he wanted was Té Hayes. Every little mouthwatering inch of her. There was a fire inside the headstrong American—a brilliant spark of incandescent light—and it called to him like a moth to a flame.

He forced her sweet thighs wider and bit at her cloth-trapped pussy, swearing he could taste her juices in the damp cotton as his big hands grabbed her knees and wrenched them even wider. He could hear her shallow breathing over his low, rumbling groans, her hands grabbing fistfuls of his hair, but she didn't push him away. She simply held on, as if he were her anchor in a world spinning too quickly out of control.

"I just want to fucking eat you alive," he grunted, the wet, slippery feel of her pussy through the thin skirt nearly driving him insane. "Bite by bite. So bloody hot. Sweet. Delicious." The words were short, sharp blasts of sound, so ragged they seemed torn from the depths of hell.

He had to have this. At least *this*, damn it, he thought as he lifted his head and ground his mouth into hers again, demanding she open for him with a ruthless, savage pressure that he knew would leave her pink lips swollen and bee-stung. His hands caught her behind the knees and he lifted her legs, hooking them over the wide arms of the antique chair, while his mouth ate at hers, desperate in its need.

And all the while, his cock throbbed—a painful ache that spread through his groin, poisoning his blood. The blunt head was wet with surging blasts of pre-cum as drops spilled from the narrow slit, so fucking hot and full, he wondered at how it didn't simply pump itself into his pants—but then he remembered.

The curse.

He wouldn't come until he was buried hard and deep inside of warm, wet cunt, and *the one* he wanted was right here, drenched and so ready he couldn't resist.

"Kieran…no! I can't—" she panted when he began to gather the long folds of her skirt in his powerful fist, twisting the light fabric around his clenched hand, the long, sinewy length of his body shuddering, heat blasting against her in overpowering waves of sexual hunger and frustration.

"Please," he groaned against her parted lips. "Please, Té. Just give me this. Let me feel you. I bet you're so fucking hot and sweet, you'll burn me alive."

His eager hand slipped beneath her skirt to find her wet panties and he groaned like a man in an agony of need, cupping her throbbing sex completely within his calloused palm. "Oh hell…you feel so…*fucking amazing*," he gritted through his clenched teeth as he buried his dark head between her quivering, cotton-covered breasts, his words halting and harsh.

Her knees dangled over the wooden arms of the chair, helpless in her pinned position, and he could have howled at the need to lift the loose fabric of her skirt and rip the soft cotton of her panties completely away so he could stare down at her naked flesh, spreading her lush, liquid folds until he could watch the juices flowing from her pink little cunt. But he didn't trust himself with the dangerous visual, so he focused on his other senses, and found them just as deadly to his control.

With deep, panting breaths, he took in the rich, heady perfume of her arousal, nearly drunk on her scent. There was a desperation in his soul to explore the tender folds beneath his fingers with lips and tongue and teeth, until there was no part of her sweet pussy that failed to recognize his ownership—his claim—his possession.

He wanted to feel the shy, nestled slit bloom with pleasure, to feel the grip of her inner muscles as he fucked her with his thrusting tongue and felt her mouthwatering juices flood into his throat. The feral idea of simply eating his way through the crotch of her miniscule underwear, right up into the core of her cunt, was a powerful, painful cramp in his gut—as if he were poisoned and only the tender release of her rich cream bursting over his taste buds could soothe his demons, easing the ache.

He'd had so many different types of women in his life—all that he'd ever wanted or needed—but whatever pleasure he'd taken with a woman before proved a pathetic comparison to the smooth, silky lips spreading beneath his fingers as he deftly slipped his hand down the front of her bikini briefs. She felt so sweet. So delicate. A hot, voluptuous heaven of tight flesh and slick juices, the tips of his fingers moving easily around her puffy vulva to the swollen mouth of her vagina, dipping gently inside, swirling in her syrupy cream.

She felt so perfectly *his*.

"You're already so wet you're dripping," he rasped, the physical ache of not being able to have this woman the way he wanted more intense than any wound he'd ever received in battle. And as his position dictated, he'd battled plenty. Shed his blood and that of others in rivers of pain and broken bones, more times than he could count.

A Warlock's life was truly gifted, but seldom easy, especially for a commanding soldier. There were always those who coveted a higher *Magick's* power, who sought to steal it for their own achievement, the miserable fools. Who thought to secure their power base, and found themselves horribly broken in the process.

But none of it, not anything that he'd ever suffered, compared to this.

Té's swollen tissues tugged gently at his fingertips, as if greedy for his touch, and he couldn't stop his middle finger from slowly pushing within, the exquisitely tight walls of her vagina parting for him as he pressed inside, penetrating the grasping slit while her nails bit crescents into the tops of his shirt-covered shoulders.

Oh Saephus, it felt so good it nearly killed him, her damp channel sucking him so hard he actually had to work to draw the long digit out, then shove it back inside, going deeper than before, rubbing at the silky surface of her inner walls with his rough calluses, killing them both with the pleasure. She was whimpering beneath her breath, eyes closed tight, teeth biting into her lower lip, but she wasn't in any actual pain. No, he understood all too well the agony of physical hunger. The slow, deep throb that felt like death until it was satisfied with a hard, savage fuck.

She needed a man between her silky thighs, riding her with desperate intent, and gods how he wanted to be the one who gave it to her.

Leaning forward, Kieran buried his hot face in the moist, delicate crook of her neck, nuzzling her with his nose, his tongue taking slow rasps of her flesh as he fantasized about dragging it through the wet folds beneath his fingers, nibbling on the lush, bare lips of her cunt protected by no more than a puffy little cloud of curls at the top of her mound. "What color are they?" he groaned, surprised by the guttural sound of his voice. "What color?" he grunted, lowering his head until he could close his mouth over the soft, cotton-covered swell of her right breast, the soft fabric still slightly damp from Mal's earlier raindrops.

Té jerked at the heat and strong suckling sensation, unable to swallow the moans spilling past her parted lips. "What color is what?" she panted in a sensual haze, completely lost to a world that centered only on the commanding press of Kieran's fingers and the searing mastery of his mouth.

"Your curls," he grated around her nipple, nipping it with his teeth while he shoved a second large finger alongside the first, jerking a strangled cry from her throat as they speared into her, thick and hard, her hips surging off the burgundy leather, lifting toward the indescribable pleasure. "Are they blonde or red? Color," he barked. "Now."

"Um…red," she whispered, head tossing from side to side against the back of the chair. "Red, like the red in my hair."

He groaned so deep it sounded like another rumbling growl, and she started with a soft gasp, unaware a human could even make that kind of sound.

But then…he wasn't exactly human…was he?

With a gut-wrenching snarl of pain, Kieran suddenly ripped himself away from her, his lungs heaving like a mighty, storm battered sail and his fingers dripping with her sweet cream. She lay sprawled before him and he screwed his eyes shut against the far too tempting sight, knowing he was only seconds away from scaring the ever-loving hell out of her.

Only seconds away from going dark and furry, in all his beastly glory.

He clenched his fists at his sides, her slick juices pressed greedily into his palm as he struggled to draw it back inside, the sounds of her scrambling away from him like a sharp, hissing slash of pain across his chest.

Hell, he couldn't believe it. Couldn't believe how easily she'd made him lose control. Already he was on the verge of exploding and he hadn't even touched her with his dick yet. No, the bloody thing was still strangled up tight in his pants, ready to fucking kill him.

He opened his eyes with great care, doing everything in slow, calculated movements, lest his beast secret out his vulnerabilities and fight its way through. She stood against the back wall again, staring at him with a passionate glaze of hunger that so perfectly matched his own. His jaw locked, teeth ground together, and he turned to go, not trusting himself to speak, almost afraid of what he'd admit over the crackling sounds of burning wood and their harsh, panting breaths.

She gasped, a soft, urgent burst that was equal parts outrage and unsatisfied physical need. "You're…you're just going to leave me…*like this*?"

With no conscious thought or direction, Kieran found himself right there, pushing her against the wall, fitting his hard body into hers, groaning at the feel of her giving, female softness. "Do you have any idea how much I want you?"

One big hand palmed her crotch again, rubbing her pussy with a delicious, possessive friction. "How much I want *this*? This right here? How much I want to eat my way inside of it? *Fuck it?* Cram it so full of cock that you'll wonder how you dinna bust open around me? Pack it full, with whatever you'll let me put in it. Do you?" he growled, dipping his knees so that he could nip at her fragile neck, his tongue flicking out to scrape her skin for another needy taste while two knuckles trapped her swollen clit and massaged it within their tight vise. "Do you even know what a dangerous game you're playing, tempting me like this, little Té?"

The pressure on her clit was mind-shattering, the orgasm building inside of her almost terrifying in its intensity as it surged back to life. "I'm not doing anything! You started this, you arrogant bastard!"

His free hand gripped the back of her head, forcing her to look up at him. "You're standing here, damn it, and apparently that's enough."

"Is this some kind of sick game?" she panted, eyes glassy with pleasure. "Work up the little American mortal and then cut her cold?"

"Damn it!" he grunted, wrenching back from her, taking deep, shuddering breaths. "I dinna want to scare you," he struggled to explain, knowing he made no sense, barely able to get the words out over the thundering of his heart.

Té slumped lower, palms flat against the cool surface of the wall, seeking leverage. Words ran over themselves in a frantic tumble within her mind, the mesmerizing force of him—of everything he was—nearly destroying her ability to communicate anything but the basest of needs. Primarily that she needed to be fucked—and soon. As soon as freaking possible.

And despite her earlier resolve to stay clear of this man, she found herself ripped open before him, all those dark, inner desires wrenched to the surface. She was starving for the taste and feel of his long, dark length, her senses ravaged by his vibrant, brutal, achingly tempting appeal. The light of the fire burned behind him, setting the outline of his powerful body within a fiery, glowing frame, sparking off the dark, midnight veil of his hair. It was like a curtain of rich, silky mink, falling around the raw beauty of his hard-edged features, giving a sensual balance to the strong line of his jaw, the deep grooves on either side of that incredible mouth and those unreal, otherworldly eyes beneath the dark slash of his brows. That long, magnificent mane set off each individual feature, until the entire effect was a devastating, dizzying blow to her shields.

She wanted to reach out and stroke it, sifting the Stygian strands though her fingers, knowing they'd flow like a smooth stream of warm water over her skin. To be honest, it was almost too beautiful to be a man's—too rich, thick, luxuriant—possessing that natural gloss and sheen of a sleek, primal predator. Something feral and dangerous, but so intoxicatingly attractive that you felt drawn to it against your better judgment. So tempting that you just wanted to get closer…closer…*closer*, until the trap was sprung and you found yourself at the mercy of the beast.

Long and lustrous, the flickering rays of firelight caught at the individual strands, creating a shimmering effect upon its calm, silken surface. Té wanted to bury her hands in all that warm, raw silk and pull him to her—wanted to twist handfuls around her fingers until she could pull him to the hot, melting center between her legs. Wanted to use that gorgeous hair as an anchor when he sent her crashing over the edge.

And damn it, she wanted it now. "Who in the hell says I'm scared? Do I look scared, Kieran? Horny, yeah, but I'm not afraid of you."

He cut her a sharp look from beneath his brows, and she could have sworn his eyes shimmered, the velvet black lost to a liquid, glowing silver. But then he blinked, and the silver vanished as quickly as it'd appeared.

"If you're no' scared," he whispered, "then you bloody well should be."

Her chin lifted, eyes narrowed in defiance—and gods help him, it made him even harder.

"You know what you need, McKendrick?"

The corner of his mouth kicked up in an arrogant smirk, despite the thundering pain in his dick, his hands clenching and unclenching at his sides. "What's that, lass?"

"You need to learn the difference."

"About what?" he demanded.

"The difference between when a woman's afraid…and when she's ready to be fucked."

His jaw worked, but it took a moment for him to get the words out. They were hard, each one bitten through his teeth as if he had to force them out with great concentration. "*Dinna. Push. Me.*"

"Why?" she pressed, her tone sharp with accusation, high cheekbones flagged with twin spots of bright, feverish color. "Isn't that what you're doing to me? Pushing my buttons? You'd be lying if you said no, Kieran. A man with your kind of reputation sure as hell knows what he's doing when he leaves a woman on the edge like this."

He took two steps forward, fingers biting into her upper arms, lifting her clear off the floor as if she weighed no more than a feather, jarring her against the pale plaster at her back. He felt the blood pounding in his temples, knew that at any second his eyes were going to completely bleed to the blinding flash of silver. "Damn it, lass, you dinna think I'd have you face down over that bloody desk right now if I could?" he snarled. "Face down and open, my cock drilling that sweet little piece between your legs. Are you crazy, or just stupid, because it doesna take a genius to see I'm in hell from no' being able to finish what I've started."

"Whatever," she said with forced disinterest, as if she weren't dying inside, refusing to look at him. "It makes no difference. Just forget about it. I won't be staying here long enough for it to bother me."

His lips pulled back over his teeth. "You think you're leaving me?" he nearly shouted, clearly outraged by the idea.

Her eyes cut back to his, the blue so incredibly dark they almost looked as black as his. "Not *think*, McKendrick. I *will* be leaving."

He forced himself to set her down and step away. Holding her — touching her — was just too damn dangerous. "Because of me?" The words were bitter, nearly choking him, a sickly desperation taking root in the quiet recesses of his heart that had remained untouched until this precise moment in time.

She snorted, laughing resentfully beneath her breath. "No, gorgeous, not because of you. How like a man to assume everything revolves around him."

"If it's no' me," he demanded with an angry glint burning bright in his eyes, taking a sudden step toward her, "then what the hell is it? Where in the hell do you have to go from here, Té?"

She smiled sweetly. "I don't particularly think that's any of your business," she laughed, the hard sound cool and brittle.

She tried to wrench past him, but he was too quick, snagging her upper arm in an unbreakable hold, halting her with a slight tightening of his grip. His strength amazed her, and for one heart-stopping moment, she fantasized about how wonderful it would feel to be able to lean into him, to take refuge in that strength and let him help. But she couldn't, could she? She didn't even know him, though she had a case of lust for him unlike any she'd ever experienced.

And this wasn't his fight — if there even was one. Té was no longer certain of anything — anything other than the blatant fact that she was treading into some dangerous territory where this sexy Warlock was concerned.

"Why, damn it?" he demanded, his eyes boring into hers with all the force of his will, stealing into her, secreting out all her hidden places. "You *belong* here."

"Like hell I do. I'm not staying, so whatever you say…whatever you think, doesn't matter."

"The hell it doesn't."

"You don't own me."

"For your sake, Té, I almost hope you're right," he whispered, releasing his hold, leaving her trembling on her own, her face wet with angry tears, lips parted and kiss-ravaged. He had to get out of there, far away from temptation before he ruined everything. Five more seconds and she'd be getting an up close and personal look at just what kind of *monster* he could be.

Five more seconds and she'd understand just what stood between them, in all its beastly horror.

He stormed out of the room, heading straight for the door and the safety of the night, mindless to everything but the protective need to get himself as far from her as possible. She could deny it all she liked. Scream it to the heavens and hell until she was blue in the face. Rage with all the livid force of her will.

But in the end, it would make no difference, because in his soul, Kieran *knew* she was his.

He just didn't have a clue what to do about it.

Chapter Seven

The morning followed a sleepless night, and Kieran found his cousins at Lach's training studio, just as Evan had told him when he'd stopped by the café. She'd looked at him in a way that was somehow questioning...even *expectant*, but she hadn't told him to leave her sister alone. If he were honest with himself, he'd admit that was exactly what he'd expected. Saephus knew he'd have himself strung up by his balls if he were Té's family, but Evan had merely seemed excited, as if she were actually happy her sister had a bloody *beithíoch* sniffing after her.

Kieran shook his dark head, stuffing his hands further into the pockets of his black jeans, the lines of his face set into a fierce scowl. *Mortals.* Gods, would he ever understand them?

He pulled open the heavy wooden door of Lach's private studio and let it crash closed behind him, sealing himself within the main battle chamber. Cool air blasted him from vents imbedded within the ornate tiled mosaics above, and he was instantly surrounded by the metallic clashing sounds of a sword fight, though there were no mortal weapons being used in the intense practice session taking place between Lach and Blu.

The two Warlocks moved upon the gleaming floor in a choreographed dance of violence that would have made most *gnachs* fear for their lives. The large, high-ceilinged room echoed with the crashing, grating sounds of metal against metal, though they fought with no visible weapons. Kieran smiled with pride, and no small amount of anticipation. His eyes, despite their troubled shadows, gleamed with the wicked anticipation of a little boy eyeing a new toy through a lit holiday storefront.

Oh yeah, the *Whispering Blade* was going to be fun.

Lachlan had spent the past month perfecting this new technique in which a Warlock's power over the wind could be compressed into a lethal, invisible blade—the ultimate weapon.

The *Whispering Blade* would serve them well in battle against any rogue Warlocks and Wyzards, or the shifters who so often chose to seek them out in challenge. And those challenges were becoming more and more frequent these days, which kept Lach in busy demand training *Magicks* who wished to know how to defend themselves, though there was seldom a need. It was the Council's soldiers who did the fighting for them, the majority commanded by Blu and Mal and himself, and Lach who did the greater part of their training.

Kieran suspected his lovesick cousin had probably invented the highly effective blades just so he could have more time to spend with his gorgeous little wife. Not that he blamed him. If he had a woman like that of his own, he'd want her by his side every minute of every hour of every damn day, too.

Christ, but was *that* a chilling thought.

And suddenly he realized everything had gone strangely silent around him while his mind wandered a million miles away. He looked up to see Lach and Blu standing in the center of the great room staring at him, their clothes soaked in sweat, chests panting as they struggled for air.

Blu gave him a thorough once-over, taking in his haggard appearance—wild eyes, dark jaw, hair tangled from the fingers he repeatedly ran through it—and smiled. "What the hell happened to you?"

"His woman," Lach laughed. "That's what." He turned a grin on Kieran. "I told you it's hell."

"Hell?" Kieran snorted, pacing from one side of the room to the other, his body burning with all the restless energy of a caged animal. "Oh no, it's no' hell, Cousin. Hell has *got* to be better than this," he hissed. "No...this is—Saephus, I dinna know what the fuck this is."

"You two sound like a couple of wimps," Blu snickered, grabbing a white towel from his bag and slinging it around his strong neck and broad shoulders. "For crying out loud, they're just women. How fucking scary can they be?"

Two sets of eyes, one pale green, the other black as midnight, blazed onto the spot where Blu stood. He lifted his shoulders in an arrogant shrug. "What?"

Lach nodded and gave him a slow, menacing smile. "I think I'm going to enjoy reminding you of that comment when you find the balls to stop running from your own."

Kieran gave a sharp laugh and Blu tensed, fists clenching at the ends of his towel. "Damn, no' you, too. What do I have to do to make you louts understand? That pink-assed little *Pixie* is no' my bloody mate!"

"Methinks he doth protest too much," Kieran drawled.

Blu arched one black brow. "Et tu Brute?"

"Who ever thought the Big Bad Blu would be afraid of a little *Pixie* dust?" Kieran snorted with satisfied laughter.

"It's no' her bloody dust that worries me." As soon as the words left his mouth, Blu's eyes widened with surprise, wide mouth curling down in a set frown. "I mean *nothing* worries me. Life's too bloody short to spend any of it fretting over a lady. There's too many fine ones to choose from."

Lach shot Kieran a knowing smirk. "I say we make this interesting. Why dinna we challenge him a thousand pounds that she has him mated and bonded within three months, kissing her cute little ass like a lovesick pup?"

Kieran smiled. "Sounds good to me." He winked at Blu. "Nothing as satisfying as easy money."

Blu looked ready to combust with frustration, his high cheekbones going dark with color. "You're on, and when I'm still fucking away to my merry pleasure, whoever I damn well please, mind you, I'm gonna make you two little ass-kissers pay up with a big ol' shit-eating grin on my pretty face."

Lach damn near strangled on a bark of laughter. "Hell, only Blu would call himself *pretty*."

Kieran nodded. "Always was the arrogant one."

"Can we get back to the topic here?" Blu drawled. "The important one? I thought we were listening to Kieran whine about how he doesna have the heart to bite his little bitch."

"Blu," Kieran grunted, his laughter instantly forgotten, "dinna fucking push me right now."

"But you know what they say," Lach laughed, using his own towel to dry his hair. "You've never really been ridden until you've been bitten."

Kieran choked and Blu whacked him on the back, chuckling as he groaned, "Oh man, that is so bad. I love it."

Lach grinned from ear to ear, tossing the towel over onto his bag. "I thought someone with your warped sense of humor would appreciate it."

"Aye, I do."

Kieran shook off Blu's pounding hand, finally turning his attention to the purpose of his visit. Looking at Lach, he said, "What do you know?"

Lach flashed him a jackass expression. "Quite a lot, actually."

"I mean about Té," he gritted through his teeth, wondering how he'd managed to keep from killing his smart-ass cousins years ago. Problem was—he loved them as much as they drove him mad, if not more.

The corners of Lach's green eyes creased, gaze piercing. "Yeah, I knew that's what you meant."

Kieran regarded him with keen frustration, grinding his jaw. "But you're no' going to tell me, are you?"

"Well, hell, where would be the fun in that?" Blu snickered at his side.

"Damn it, this isna funny, you ass!"

"No' from where you stand, I know—but it's pretty entertaining from the sidelines."

"Saephus, I canna deal with you two right now."

Blu placed one hand on his shoulder, giving him a hard shove. "Damn it, man, if there's something you want to know, why dinna you just use your power to get it?"

Hell, here it was again, the same damn argument that he was getting bloody tired of defending—and to be honest, no longer even wanted to try. But he wouldn't back down against Blu. Not on this. "I dinna need this shit right now, Blu."

Lach snorted. "Nae, what you need is to get your bloody head out o' your ass, before you do something stupid and lose the lass for good."

"You know, of all people, I expected *you* to understand."

"It's because I *do* understand that I'm tellin' ya to give in gracefully, Cousin," Lach explained in an infinitely sensible tone that made Kieran want to smack him. "There'll be nothin' to gain from fightin' a battle you canna win. And if you were honest with yourself, you'd admit that you dinna really want to."

"It's dangerous enough for *Magicks* to fuck around with *gnach*, but are you forgetting that until recently it was bloody forbidden for a Lupine to take a mortal?" Kieran demanded.

Lach nodded his auburn head, mouth pressed into a thin line. "It was a stupid law, Kieran, which is why the Council abolished it."

"Was it? As a power, there are rules, Cousin, as you well know—though Blu more often than no' chooses to ignore them. But the rules protect the mortals, as well as those of our own kind. If we were allowed to act at our will, who knows what sort of anarchy we could create?"

Blu's mouth compressed with irritation. "Yeah, and some rules are made to be broken."

"Och. Just because you choose to violate every blasted code of honor we have—"

"Oh—so now I'm the black sheep. Is that it?"

"Is that no' what you want?" Kieran snarled, the tips of his fingers beginning to tingle as his irritation began to get the better of him. His claws itched to slip the flesh that bound them, and a cold trickle of fear snaked down his spine at what he might do if provoked far enough.

And wasn't that right there the main foundation for his steadfast belief in upholding their laws?

The sad truth of the matter was that he *needed* them— needed those damn restrictions to help keep the primitive side of his soul in check.

Ignoring the danger he was courting, Blu closed in on him, muscles bulging as his own temper flared with all the power of an irritated Warlock. "What I want is to stop seeing you so bloody afraid of what you are! Why do you think the miserable old bastards cursed your beast in the first place, Cousin? They went right for the jugular with their bare teeth. You think they've no' seen—no' *known*—how this would all play out? Yeah, they may make the bloody rules, but they've no compunction about bending them to suit their own arrogant purposes."

"That's your own father you're talking about, Blu," Kieran muttered, knowing he sounded like Lach.

"Aye—and he's as warped as the rest."

Lach's mouth twisted with grim humor. "And I'm thinking that you're starting to get the itch your own turn is coming."

Blu's smile was suddenly smooth and deadly. "I'd like to see them try."

Kieran looked back to Lach, eyes narrowed, irritated at the distraction. "I need to know what she's running from."

"Aye, but you're no' going to find out standing here and arguing with us, now are you?"

"What the hell else should I be doing?"

Lach sent him a pained look, as if the answer should be obvious. "I'm on my way to join Evan for a meeting with the contractors, so the lass is gonna be at the house all alone for the morning. If you canna come up with an idea of how to keep her busy, I guess I'll have to rely on ol' Blu here."

"Hell, I'm game," Blu announced with a feral smile of pure, carnal intent.

One second Kieran was standing in the middle of the room, and in the next, he had his fist twisted in the sweat-soaked front of Blu's white T-shirt, the owner still inside, his big feet dangling a foot from the floor as Kieran slammed him into the studio wall. "Dinna even think about it," he snarled, knowing his eyes were glowing with the silver fury of his beast.

But Blu only smiled down at him like a loon, snickering beneath his breath. "Och, okay…okay. I was only teasin' ya, man. Damn, but you're sensitive over the lass."

Kieran released his grip, his laughing cousin dropping to the floor with a loud thud. He stared at the smiling ass, wondering if he'd ever be able to laugh like that again. Shit, he just wanted to be free. Wanted to be able to do just what he wanted, which was finding Té Hayes and showing her in raunchy, explicit detail everything he'd wanted to do to her since first setting eyes on her.

Was that really only yesterday? Hell, it felt like a lifetime ago. Felt as if he'd been living the aching nightmare of resisting her for years and years, instead of a measly goddamn day.

Sensitive over her? Fuck, his smiling cousin had no idea.

Without another word he turned and left, leaving Blu snickering behind him, and knowing exactly where he was headed. He could no more fight it than he could control the air that he breathed or the thundering beat of his heart.

He had to see her, to be near her, even if it was a bloody torture.

* * * * *

Kieran told himself it wasn't going to work the entire way to Lach and Evan's. It was an annoying litany that played repeatedly over the nonstop thread of erotic images wreaking havoc on his sanity as the wind howled around his head, the cool morning air doing little to squelch the fire in his veins. Images of him and Té in his bed, their bodies hot and slick as he pistoned his hips between her widespread thighs with a violent desperation, spearing the luscious clench of her cunt with his big, burning cock.

He'd hoped he would be able to touch her the way he had last night, to get his fill that way, by feasting on her pleasure and ignoring his own—but it wasn't going to work. It'd been a desperate, pathetic pipe dream—an anxious grasp at an illusion—one brought on by the gut-clawing need he felt for this woman and his body's need to get his hands on her by whatever means necessary.

He had to *touch* her—that dewy, sensuous skin, like the delicate satin petals of a pansy. That silky, luxurious mane of red and gold. That impossibly seductive *fuck-me* mouth and the little mole positioned just beneath her eye. He wanted to run his tongue over that spot with an intensity of longing that he would have never believed himself capable of. Wanted to stroke it in a blatant act of ownership and then lick his way from her temples down to her delicate little pink toes. Needed to investigate each lush, incredible inch of her soft, intoxicating body. Needed the feel and scent of its heat. The taste of its seductive flavor.

There was every likelihood that he'd go mad if he didn't get it, *all of it*, beneath his hungry hands and mouth and cock at the soonest possible moment. As galling as it was for a man of his reputation to admit, he was *starving* for her—this fiery little American *gnach*—to the point that he bloody ached with it in his bones, the pain far outreaching the tangible limits of his flesh, to settle heavily into his soul like a burdensome weight of *guilt*.

Ah…and wasn't that million-dollar word his very problem? The painful, infuriating crux of the situation? Where it all came back to?

The truth of the matter was that he felt guilty as hell. Not for wanting her, but for the undeniable knowledge of the fact that he knew there was no way in hell he'd ever let her go, whether she wanted him to or not. Not in a thousand bloody lifetimes.

One way or another, he was going to be sinking his teeth into Té Hayes.

He only hoped he didn't scare her to death when he did.

Chapter Eight

Té opened her eyes to the bright flash of the late morning sun glaring through the thin white curtains over the guest room window, and knew she'd slept late. The next thing she knew was that she was definitely not in bed alone. Looking over her shoulder, she gasped at the sight of the beautiful Warlock snuggled up against her back, one heavy, wonderfully tanned arm thrown over her waist, securing her to the bed. "What are you doing here?" she screeched.

The sexy rumble coming from the other pillow sounded suspiciously like, "Enjoying myself."

She swallowed twice before muttering, "Not with me, you're not."

He lifted his head from the pillow and gave her a heavy-lidded, smoldering stare that nearly made her toes curl. The dark stubble covering his strong jaw looked deliciously tempting, and her mouth went dry at the thought of how that stubble would feel scraping gently across the inner faces of her thighs. "Too much temptation?" he taunted with a sexy smirk.

She snorted, trying ineffectually to move out of his hold. "God, you're arrogant."

He laughed and rolled onto his back, allowing her to move, which she immediately did, scrambling to the edge of the immense mattress, eyeing him as if he were a deadly viper that had found its way into her bed. One arm lifted to support his head in the open palm of his hand, the other scratching lazily through the silky, black pelt of hair extending between his small, dark nipples, arrowing down into a fine line that made its way into the low-slung waist of his indecently bulging jeans. Her mouth watered and her eyes went wide, wondering just how many magnificent inches a man would have to have to make that kind of beautiful package.

"It's no' arrogant, love, when you can back it up."

God, did he have that right. Jerking her eyes away from his magnificent crotch, she drank in the impeccable sight of Kieran McKendrick without his shirt on, marveling at his ripped, lean physique, the long, corded muscles and bulging biceps. She even loved the silky tuft of jet black hair beneath his raised arm and the numerous small scars covering his forearms, most likely from battle. She had the strangest longing to soothe them with her lips, healing those past hurts with her kisses.

It took a moment to remember she was irritated with the gorgeous jerk. "What is it with you McKendricks? Do you all run so hot and cold?"

Kieran rolled onto his side, propping himself up on his elbow, his long black hair flowing over his lower shoulder. "Aye," he rumbled, reaching out his hand to play with a lock of hair that had wrapped around the base of her neck, his rough-tipped fingers playing over the rapid pulse of her heart in the hollow of her throat. "Aye, you've got me all stirred up, I'll give you that. Do you have any idea how beautiful you are in the morning, all soft and warm...and *wet*?"

Té shook her head as if to clear it, short strands of her sleep-tousled hair tumbling wildly about her face. She tried to keep her pulse from jumping, but knew he'd felt the revealing leap as soon as that slow, sexy grin once again shaped the corners of his sensual mouth. "Why are you here?"

His thumb lifted to test the texture of her bottom lip in a slow, sexual exploration. "I've got a bad feeling, love."

She wanted to tell him she wasn't his damn love and he had no right calling her such a ridiculous thing, especially after leaving her high and dry last night, but the sharp words wouldn't form, no matter how hard she tried to say them. "About what?"

He watched as the sunlight spilled across her pretty face, dazzling off the tiny silver hoops in her ears and the one pierced through her arched brow. He wanted her so damn bad, it was like a sickness in his soul, something that could only be cured by having her close, having her beneath him, around him. "Whatever it is you're no' telling me. We didna discuss it last night, but I've no' forgotten."

A bitter laugh burst past her lips before she could choke it back. "Really? And what makes you think there's something I should be telling you, McKendrick? Are you psychic?"

"Nae."

"And are you my boyfriend — my husband — my significant other?"

His smile flashed, so wickedly beautiful it made her melt between her legs, his eyes warming to a deep, burning black. "No' yet — but you've got to give these things time, darlin'."

"Why is talking to you always like banging my head against a wall?"

"I'm getting to ya, aren't I?"

She snorted under her breath. "Whatever gave you that idea?"

He couldn't stop smiling, feeling the warmth of having her near flood through his system. It was intoxicating, after so many days...weeks...*months* of nothing but anger and desolation. Loneliness. But now he had Té, and it was like she'd opened a door into a dark, dank, miserable chamber and flooded it with the brilliant, awe-inspiring warmth of the sun.

And no way in hell was he going to be able to let her go. Hell, he wasn't even going to consider it anymore. No, his only concern now was how to do it — how to claim her without wrecking something so vulnerable and new.

Her nipples shone like dusky peaks beneath her thin nightshirt, the soft mounds of her breasts lifting with each breath, and he watched from beneath heavy lids as his long, dark fingers reached out for her. At first he barely stroked one puffy, beautiful peak with the back of his knuckles, loving the breathless gasp that tore from her throat, and the tiny nub hardened into a tight little pearl. He scooted closer, helpless to resist her pull, and nudged the aching ridge of his cock into her hip, wanting nothing more than to rip the clothes from their bodies, pull her over his throbbing dick, and force her gorgeous little cunt down on him until she'd taken every aching inch, her tight little body convulsing with pleasure, sleek inner muscles milking him to a blinding, shouting completion.

"I know I'm getting to you," he rasped in a dark drawl, cupping her breast, rubbing his thumb back and forth across that perfect pink tip, "because you're getting to me, too, beautiful."

"And you're the type of guy who lets lots of women get to him," she stated breathlessly, her eyes nearly rolling back in her head at the feel of his magnificent hands on her body. She looked down to see him cup her breast through the thin fabric of her threadbare tank top, his skin dark, hands decorated with soft, black hairs, faint scars, and heavy veins. He was so ruggedly masculine, so outrageously sexy, it hurt just to look at him. "Am I supposed to be flattered?"

"I don't know," he said on a harsh breath. "But I've been a long time without a woman, Té. It's true I've had my share, but I've no' wanted one—I mean I couldna find one who I—"

She shook her head. "A man like you holds out for no woman. No, you've been without because of your little curse, Kieran. It has nothing to do with me."

His eyes widened with shocked, stunned surprise.

"What?" she asked, her lips twisting with wry humor. "You thought my own sister wouldn't tell me? I even know what happened with that MacIntyre woman."

That guarded look was back in his eyes, and she couldn't help but wonder at what it concealed. He rolled to his back once more, eyeing her with dark suspicion. "Seeing as how it has fuck all to do with her, I didna think she'd be the one doing the telling."

Her head tilted to the side, expression serious as she studied him. "So then, you *were* planning on telling me yourself?"

He blew out a tense breath and his head fell back against her pillow, one arm lifting to cover his eyes, armpit dark with another silky tuft of ebony hair. "Aye, I would've told you, but no' so soon," he admitted with complete candor.

She swallowed, feeling the oddest compulsion to comfort him. It was so bizarrely outrageous. If anyone had told her two days ago that she'd be sitting on her bed with a powerful Warlock who could shape shift into a deadly wolf, she would have laughed her ass off and then promptly informed them they were seriously delusional. And yet, here she was, and the strangest part of all was that she wanted him to stay right here.

And just how badly she wanted it had her going quickly to her feet, no longer trusting herself to stay so close to him and not jump his gorgeous bones. Wrapping her arms around one of the beautifully carved foot posts, she looked down at his striking, masculine length. "That's why you ran from me last night, isn't it?"

His jaw hardened as he nodded. The long, lean, muscled lines of his body were tight with tension, the beautifully round biceps in his powerful arms screaming of strength, making her mouth water. She stepped closer to his side of the bed, voice soft, soothing, like someone dealing with a skittish animal. "You could've just told me, Kieran. I handled the first revelation pretty well. What made you think I couldn't take the second?"

His arm lowered and his eyes shot open, zeroing in on her own with the precision of a laser-sighted weapon, dark and chaotic, so many emotions moving through the liquid black of his piercing gaze that it was hypnotic to watch. "Are you kidding me, woman?" he growled, sounding outraged. "There's a hell of a difference between being *Magick* and telling you I wanna fuck your brains out as a bloody wolf and sink my goddamn teeth into you!"

"Well, you wouldn't have had to say it like that," she snapped, losing her patience. "All I'm saying is that you could've tried trusting me, Kieran, the same way you expect me to trust you."

He snorted. "What world do you fuckin' live in, Té? A fairy tale?"

"No, but I think you do. Look at me, Kieran. I know what you are, but I'm not running from the big, bad wolf, am I? Why can't you just admit you were wrong?"

"Christ, Té, *I* can hardly live with it. What in the fuck makes you think I'd believe you can?"

She looked confused, that small frown dipping between the twin arches of her fine brows. "But I thought you'd always had the curse?"

"Aye," he grunted, clearly not wanting to talk about it.

"And you've never accepted it? Jesus, Kieran, that isn't healthy."

"Thanks for the psychological profile, darlin'," he sneered, his tone heavy with sarcasm. "And to think I never figured that one out on my own."

Té stamped her foot, clearly losing her patience. "Damn it, will you stop being an ass for two seconds and just talk to me?"

There were five seconds of heavy silence, and then, "What do you want to know?"

"How did it happen?"

"It's a long story," he muttered.

She arched her brow, smile slow and sweet as she leaned her back against the foot post. "Yeah, and I've got the time."

"Fuck. Whatever," he grunted, knowing the damage was already done. Hell, if she hadn't gone running at this point, why not open his veins and spill the whole miserable story? "The curse comes from my mother's bloodline. She was the Laird's daughter, of the Lindsay Clan. They're a family of warriors, *Magicks*, who centuries ago had used shifting spells to transform their bodies during battle."

"Why?" she interrupted, clearly more intrigued than frightened.

Kieran stared at her as if she were an intricate puzzle that needed solving, and then proceeded to explain, his tone flat and emotionless. "Because a shifter is all but invincible. In one particular battle over some valuable land, my mother's people defeated the dragon-bred soldiers of a rather nasty Witch named Serena the Sable. In retribution for the defeat of her beloved army, she cursed the Lindsay's bloodline to an eternity of the *beithíoch*—the beast—making it a part of our blood rather than a mere spell to control at our choosing. It soon became known as Serena's Lupine Curse, and it has affected every generation of Lindsay males, and will continue to do so for eternity. The spell was such that it could no' ever be undone."

She licked her lips, staring at him with an open tenderness that twisted his heart. "And you—you've had no choice in your changing?"

He pressed deeper into the bower of pillows. "For the most part I have complete control. Until this fucking mating curse, I've only ever shifted during battle with an enemy, as many of those who would do battle with us use shifters as their first line of attack. There's been times when I've gone weeks, months, nearly a year without shifting, though the longer I resist, the more strongly the beast fights me for control."

"And so that time with that woman—that was the only time you'd shifted during...sex?"

"Aye, but I'll no' lie to ya, lass. The compulsion, the need, has always been there, though I've just been able to control it, partly because the beast had never tasted the pleasures of the flesh, and partly because I was no' bedding my *bith-bhuan gra*. Those others were no' the one he wanted."

"Your soul mate," Té said in a hushed tone, remembering the Celtic phrase Evan had used to explain the nature of the Council's mating curses.

"Aye. And with her, I'll no' be able to control the change. For certain the first time I take her. Hell, maybe never."

She chose to ignore his veiled warning for the moment, and focused instead on getting all the details to his story. "And since that time, the curse has passed to each following generation, moved on from one male to the next?"

He nodded, and neither of them mentioned the fact that the curse could very well carry on to Kieran's own offspring. The answer was too obvious—the subject too tender, considering their tenuous relationship.

"God," she finally whispered. "I would have killed her."

A reluctant grin curled his lips. "You know, for a mortal, you sure are a fiery little thing."

Her head tipped to the side as she stared at him. "You called me that before. A mortal. You're not....I mean you don't...that is, you don't live *forever*, do you?"

His black eyes sparkled. "No' unless we wish to cast a spell for immortality."

Her own eyes widened. "You didn't...haven't...have you?"

"Nae." He rolled off the bed in a smooth, masculine move, one step bringing him to within a mere foot of her body. His voice lowered and he came closer, suddenly crowding her with his tangible heat, his power spilling over her like a tempting, teasing Caribbean breeze. "Though I have to admit, I wouldna mind spending forever with you."

He was so close she could see the small pores of his dark skin, the tiny lines at the corners of his wicked eyes. "Only because you probably think I'm your whatever the hell you called it. You only want me because you think I can help you break this stupid mating curse, Kieran. But you don't even know me. I'm sure there's plenty of other women who would do."

A small smile curved his sensual mouth, tripling her heart rate. He shook his head slowly, his black hair moving like silk around his wide shoulders, dark skin stretched tight across muscle and bone. "That's no' how it works, lass. There's only *one* woman, *one* true mate. Only one *bith-bhuan gra*. I have *your* taste on my tongue, burned into my memory, erasing any other woman I may have known, because they dinna matter. They were no' the one. It's you that I want, lass. No' another."

Not knowing what to say to such an outrageously thrilling confession, she focused on the one part she could safely argue. "My taste? Ya know, I think I'd remember you going down on me, Kieran. And last night sure as hell didn't go that far. I would've come if it had, instead of tossing and turning all damn night."

He gave her an infuriating nod. "Sounds like splitting hairs to me, Té, but if you're no' ready to handle it, then keep on hiding. But I *do* have your taste, smooth and sweet, because I sucked it from my fingers," he whispered, looking down into her upturned face, holding her hot stare. The difference in their two heights was such that he towered over her, though he was able to bring their faces closer, his nose brushing the tip of her own, by leaning over her as she stared up at him. "The taste of your cunt, Té. And, ah lass, it was so hot, so sweet, I nearly died. If no' for this curse, I'd have come in my bloody pants then and there."

He leaned down, dipping his knees, and nuzzled the side of her throat, grinning as he felt the shiver quake through her sleep-soft body. "Or better yet, I'd have shoved you over that desk and crammed my cock up your hot little cunt," he rasped in a low voice heavy with dark promises of sin and seduction. His hand slipped between her legs, one finger circling the rim of her panty-covered vulva. "Right here, where you're so tender and wet, and I'd have fucked you until the only bloody thing you knew in this world was me. *Me*. My taste. My scent. The feel of my cock breaking you open, stretching and filling you so full and wide, pulling you so far apart, until you couldn't decide whether it was pain or the best fucking thing you'd ever felt. Hot and hard and deep, Té, holding nothing back."

The tip of his finger slid through her slick, cotton-covered slit, finding the swollen crest of her clit and applying just the right amount of pressure to make her moan. He circled it in a dizzyingly slow pattern, changing tactics every few seconds and skimming the calloused tip across the sensitive nub, teasing her to the point where she thought she'd go mad. "Have you ever been fucked like that? Has this sweet little pussy ever been hammered into one orgasm after another, until you're so hot and wet it's dripping down these smooth little thighs, drenching you in cum?"

She trembled beneath his touch, undone by his wicked words, barely able to recall the fact that she was still irritated with him. Damn it, she was—wasn't she? "Do you...do you normally make it a habit of coming on to women you barely know, in their bedrooms, *uninvited*?"

His finger drew back, immediately replaced by the intense pressure of his palm completely covering her sex, pressing hard, as if holding her possessively within his strong hand. "Do you normally make a habit of letting men you've only just met shove their fingers up your cunt?"

Her eyes narrowed, flashing with irritation. "What can I say? You got lucky."

He couldn't help but smile, despite the throbbing pain in his dick—the primitive need to push her over, shove her legs apart, and then fuck her the way he'd wanted to since first setting eyes on her. "Lucky? I'm no' so sure that's how I'd put it, seeing as how I woke up with your sweet taste on my breath. Do you know what that does to a man, lass? I'm so hard I could knock the bloody wall down. As stiff as a fucking spike."

"Your fault," she huffed. "*You* ran."

His free hand, the one not shoved between her trembling thighs, stroked lazily up and down her spine, fingers spreading goose bumps in their wake. "And you can be relieved that I did, or you'd no doubt be more than a little sore this morning, Té."

Her face went hot at the decadent thought of being ridden that powerfully by a man—by *this* man. "That sure of yourself, are you?"

"Aye, I am."

The simple, honest conviction of that statement made her breath catch, her blood race to the frantic cadence of her thundering heart.

His fingers flexed against her moist pussy, the drenched fabric of her panties teasing her sensitive tissues with its delicate rasp. "I want you, Té. More than anything I've ever wanted before. *Anything.* I want to feel your cum on my skin, want my cock soaked in it, drowning in it. Want it filling my mouth and slipping down my throat. *That's* the only thing that could ever come close to fucking you. Just shoving my face in your pussy and eating you out for hours on end, my teeth nipping at your swollen lips and aching clit, my tongue shoved up your tight little hole, parting those hot, tight walls, filling you, making you come till it hurts. It'll be so good, angel, I willna ever be able to let you go."

She trembled, and he nipped at the sensitive connection between her neck and shoulder, tasting her need on the warm flush of her skin. His gut cramped, balls aching, and he licked a long line up the edge of her throat, his teeth nipping at her earlobe, making her squeal. "*But*...for now I'll settle for the pleasure of going with you tonight."

What?

Té pushed away from him in shock, unable to go far within the sudden circle of his immovable, steel-roped arms. The change in topic was jolting, and she struggled to form her words. "You don't even know where I'm going."

"I know you're going to meet a man," he announced in a hard voice. "And that's all I need to know."

She pushed against his chest, harder this time, and he loosened his arms, allowing her to pull back and step away. "I won't be alone, Kieran. Evan's going to go with me."

He sat back on the edge of the high bed, watching her with hot eyes, and shook his head. "No' anymore."

Té narrowed her gaze on him, not liking the thick satisfaction in his words. "What do you mean? What did you do?"

"Nothing. But I saw her this morning at the café and she was all but busting at the seams about her first meeting with Meggie tonight."

"Remind me to thank her for abandoning me to the wolves," Té drawled with a cool look, knowing this little change in plans reeked of Evan's relentless matchmaking.

"Dinna be thanking her yet," he replied with an arched brow. "You've no' seen just how wolfie I can get."

"Yeah, yeah," she threw over her shoulder, looking for wherever she'd left her makeup case the night before. She couldn't take it anymore. He looked like a dark god sitting there atop her white sheets, and here she felt like something the cat had dragged in. Damned jetlag was such a bitch. "And who the heck is this Meggie?"

"The McKendrick midwife."

"Ooh, you guys have one of everything, don't ya?"

"We like to be self-sufficient, aye," he agreed, shrugging his wide shoulders.

Her lips twisted into a reluctant smile as she turned back to him. "Did I miss another fireworks display?"

"You mean when Lach informed her she'd no' be having the baby at a hospital?"

"Yeah."

His lips answered with a boyish grin. "Nah, I'm sure she took it in stride, as soon as she realized it was Meggie they were going to see. Meggie's an angel."

Té tried to look uninterested while she ran her wooden-handled brush through her hair, giving up on finding her makeup for the moment. "An angel, eh?"

"An eighty-year-old angel, darlin'. You dinna need to be shooting daggers at me with those stormy blue eyes of yours."

She gave an elegant snort of humor. "Keep dreaming, McKendrick."

"Aye, well, considering I spent all night dreaming about you, it'd be my pleasure," he rasped, enjoying the simple luxury of watching her brush all that thick, gorgeous hair. It was strange, but he couldn't remember the last time he'd stayed with a woman, once the fucking was done, long enough to witness her daily rituals, all those fascinating things women did to themselves in preparation for the world. He'd never realized how personal it was—how intimate.

"I just bet it would."

"So it looks like you're stuck with me. Your sister seemed to think I'd make the perfect escort."

Té's look clearly said otherwise. "Yeah, I'll just bet she did."

"She'd be hurt by that tone," he tsked, giving her an infuriating wink. "You really need to learn how to control that temper, sweetheart."

She snorted again, telling him exactly what she thought about that little remark. "I just wish you'd trust me that this is *not* a good idea, Kieran. It's an exhibition at an art gallery and if Evan can't go with me, then I'd really rather just go on my own. The last guy I was dating didn't particularly care for it, and I'd rather not have to go through a repeat performance."

His eyes narrowed as he worked through the many possibilities of that statement. "But I'm no' the last guy, now am I, lass?"

Her lips curved, blue gaze devouring him from his big, bare, hair-sprinkled feet to the shoulder-length black silk of his hair. "No," she agreed, swallowing hard. "You're *definitely* not the last guy."

His eyes smoldered, dark and intense. "And now you're going to tell me about him."

Kieran tried to keep his voice calm, but the undeniable thread of anger was clearly audible. He wanted—*needed*—to know if this was the prick who had dared to raise his fists to her.

"Am I?" she tossed back, seeing right through him.

"Aye. I've been patient, and I'm no' feeling patient anymore."

"Hmm…that sounds bad for you, then."

"Damn it, Té, we need to talk about this." His big hands fisted in the bedding at his sides, sensual mouth hard, lips pressed thin with determination.

"Why?"

"Because it's important to me." His hands flexed against the white cotton, clenching, knuckles going white. "*You're* important to me."

The way he said that, the rough words spoken with such intense meaning and emotion, melted right through her. Sheesh, she was amazed she didn't just fall over him, begging him to take her then and there. Without conscious effort, she heard herself saying, "Look, it's no great mystery, okay? I got mixed up with the wrong guy, is all. No biggie. It sucked, but I learned my lesson, so you don't need to worry. There's really no story here, Kieran."

"Why dinna you let me be the judge of that?" he replied in a silky rasp.

"Because it's not your problem. I'm handling it—I mean, I *handled* it just fine."

"Damn it, you have a family now, Té. You have a sister who loves you and anyone by the name o' McKendrick who would give their blood to save you were you in danger. When are ya going to bloody well realize that you dinna have to do everything alone?"

Avoiding the touchy subject, she said instead, "I wouldn't think some stuffy art gallery would be your cup of tea, Kieran."

"You'd be surprised at what I like," he answered with deliberate challenge.

Té lifted her chin. "And you think you'll be able to keep your hands off of me if I let you take me to this thing?"

"No' really," he said with a shrug, "but I'm sure as hell going to try. Until you're ready. And then you had better be prepared, because I want you so fucking bad, there's no way in hell it'll be easy."

Setting her brush down on the antique dresser, Té walked back to the bed and wrapped her arms around the sturdy foot post. She stared straight at him, feeling as if she'd fallen into a strange, intoxicating dream. "That big, eh?"

"Yeah, I am," he said with so much confidence she actually believed him. It was on the tip of her tongue to ask just *how* big, when he stood before her, his voice a low, rumbling growl of intent. "I want to make you come so hard that you cry. Scream. Claw. *Beg*. Till you can barely breathe. You've been waiting for someone to release that insatiable, wild, cock-hungry little animal inside o' you—but you dinna have to wait anymore. So you better be ready, beautiful, because from what I hear, it can be hard when a cunt as tight as yours is crammed full o' dick for hours on end."

She nearly fell on her backside as she tried to stumble away from him, saved only by the quick hands pulling her hard against his chest, his dark eyes smoldering, blazing down into her shocked gaze. "So dinna—for even one bloody second— think of running on me, because once I get it in you, Té, that's where I stay."

"Is that a threat?" she demanded as he just as quickly let her go. She watched through wide eyes as he pulled on his T-shirt and gathered up his leather jacket and boots.

At the door he stopped, turning to look back at her, one of the first genuine smiles she'd yet to see transforming the harsh lines of his sexy-as-hell face. "That? No, lass—*that* you can consider a promise."

Chapter Nine

The tension in the car was so thick, Kieran felt as if he could feel it moving through his lungs as he breathed. It was an added element to the air, full and heavy. He felt strung out on lust, and to make matters worse, Té sat beside him wearing nothing more than a scrap of transparent, strapless black silk. The dress was so see-through, it was actually nothing more than an elegant cover-up for the matching strapless bra and panties set he could glimpse beneath—evocative shadows of lace and skin nearly driving him mad.

She'd walked out of Evan and Lach's guest room not twenty minutes ago, wearing the pitiful excuse for a dress, and he'd damn near come in his friggin' pants. Hell, he was still hard, shifting uncomfortably in the too small seat of Evan's Jag and the too tight crotch of his boxers.

He'd taken one look at her and told her to turn her ass around and go finish getting dressed. Of course, being Té, she'd given him a very sexy, very female smile and informed him she was wearing the Betsey Johnson, or whatever the hell she'd called it, with or without him. Then she'd turned to walk out the front door, treating him to an exceptional view of her perfect little heart-shaped backside, and he'd found himself wanting to blister those lush cheeks and fuck her senseless all at the same time.

Instead, he'd stalked to the car, opened her door, and kept his bloody mouth shut, allowing his temper to simmer on a low, roiling boil. The only words she'd spoken were to give him the address of the gallery where they were headed, and then she'd settled into an equally heavy silence of her own.

And they'd been like that ever since, the tension slowly grinding away at their resolve, wrenching the taut lines of their composures to a snapping point.

Té shifted her legs, crossing them, and his eyes moved to the smooth length of her calves as if he needed the mere sight of her to exist. From the edge of his vision, he saw her small smirk, and realized she knew *exactly* what the damn dress was doing to him. Feeling ornery and confined, and generally pissed, he decided to push her a little as well.

Looking straight ahead, he kept his voice calmly mellow, one hand curled casually around the Jag's steering wheel. "You know, Té, I canna help but wonder if you wore this little get-up tonight understanding full well that all I'd be able to think about was what I'd be doing to you—after I rip it off."

Her shoulders stiffened, but her eyes remained glued to the straight line of the road ahead. "You won't be ripping anything, McKendrick. And for your information, my aunt gave me this *get-up* as a gift."

"No shit?" he laughed. "Aunt Ellie had a penchant for the risqué, huh?"

She shot him a hot glance. "What she *had* was an understanding of the value of a woman's sensuality, and she wasn't afraid to let people know it. She bought me this for my birthday the week before she died."

He shifted uncomfortably in his seat, suddenly feeling like a complete jerk. "Why do you always say just the right thing to make me feel like an ass?"

Her smile was soft and smooth. "I think you take care of that all on your own, Kieran—or maybe you just make it so easy."

"Touché, sweetheart, and before you rip my heart out, I've no' told you how beautiful you look in it."

"Rip your heart out?" One slim golden brow arched. "And here I was, unaware you even had one."

"A little hard, but aye—it's there," he muttered, slanting a shuttered glance in her direction.

"Actually, I thought you wanted me to take it off," she countered, smile going sugary sweet.

His own smile returned, boyishly hopeful. "Are you offering?"

The soft snorting noise sounded ridiculously cute coming from her. "You wish."

He grinned again, that damn dimple in his cheek casting him in an easy, teasing light that made her heart do this funny little stutter. "Only because I dinna want every other prick tonight getting the same view as me. But I *will* enjoy taking it off you later, have no doubt of that."

"Hmm...remember what I said about running hot and cold?"

His hand flexed on the leather wheel, though his manner remained easy. "Aye."

"You should give it some thought."

A sin-packed chuckle filled the warm interior. "Maybe, but then I'd rather think about fucking you."

Té nodded slowly. "See? That's what I mean. I think you're trying to drive me crazy."

"Yeah? Well, it's good to know I'm no' the only one going crazy here."

She looked across the dark interior of the car, the downtown lights flashing through the window, painting the masculine perfection of his face with vivid, iridescent splashes of color. The beauty of him took her breath away every single time she looked at him, but that was far from the source of her attraction—and she was honest enough with herself to admit that when it came to this man, she was seriously attracted.

Dangerously tempted.

There was something in him that simply called to her. That brooding darkness, tempered by his wry sense of humor. The desperate struggle he waged to resist her, while snatching each opportunity to seduce her with an almost single-minded purpose. The loneliness in those beautiful black eyes, that need to connect with a woman and be completely accepted for what he was. His incredible sense of honor and duty, and the sexy-as-hell spark of intellect always burning bright in that midnight gaze. It was an irresistible package—and damn it, she didn't want to resist.

It suddenly came to her again, as it had when he'd left her today, the knowledge that she would resent this for the rest of her life—resent leaving without getting her fill of this magnificent man, or Warlock, or whatever the hell he was.

She wiggled in her seat, feeling the dress shimmer across her thighs, and for once in her life, she was happy with who she was. Growing up, she'd always longed for Evan's height, the simple grace of her figure, her unshakeable confidence. It was Ellie who had tried so hard to convince her that although she was so different from her older sister, she was in no way less special.

Palo had tried to further his close friend's cause by helping Té to find her own confidence, to recognize her unique beauty, as different from Evan's as it might be. But even Palo hadn't completely succeeded, though he did manage to show her that she could be short and curvy and still look sexy. Not a knockout like Evan, maybe, but a woman who could command attention if she wanted. Lexi had tried to kill that in her, but she was going to be damned before she let him win.

And maybe this sexy-as-sin Scot at her side was just what she needed to get the job done.

Warlock or not, she wanted him—arrogance, curses, and all. And God only knew she'd probably regret it later, but she was going to take him. She didn't have any other choice.

Yeah, she needed to get her fix of him and fast, because soon she was going to have to bail. The sooner the better actually, now that she knew Evan was pregnant. She'd never be able to forgive herself if the evil stalking her somehow followed her here and threatened her family. It seemed incredibly paranoid, but she just couldn't shake the strange "feeling" that this was all going to turn out badly in the end.

But before she left, she needed...*had* to get the sexy stud sitting beside her the hell out of her system. If she didn't, there was every possibility she'd go out of her freaking head from the unsatisfied hunger twisting her stomach into painful knots of desire. It seemed a simple enough request, except for the fact that he kept running from her.

And damn it, she was tired of letting him get away.

Turning on her hip, Té looked at him across the dark interior of the Jag, loving the way the bright lights continued to illuminate his face and hair through the car window. Her head cocked to the side as she studied him, drinking in all the delicious details that made him so appealing, feeling drunk on his rugged beauty. Nibbling on the corner of her bottom lip, she finally said, "I understand you have rules."

"Rules about what, darlin'?" he asked, slanting her a sideways glance.

She touched her tongue to the bow of her top lip and he groaned beneath his breath. "About things that can and can't happen between *Magicks* and mortals."

He swallowed, his strong throat working, tendons bunching, begging for the press of her lips. "Aye."

She sent him a wickedly provocative smile that shot straight down his spine, only to curl around his balls and shoot up through the core of his cock in a jaw-clenching explosion of need. He ached. His head. His sac. His blasted prick. She was turning him into one throbbing, tortured mass of pain and physical need...*and unnatural hunger*.

"Don't you know that some rules are made to be broken?" she asked in a conversational tone, while the cradle of her arms pushed her lush breasts together in a way that made him want to drool. The sound of her voice licked across his skin, and he ground his teeth together to keep from releasing a telling moan.

Saephus only knew what the wicked lass would do if she knew what hell he was in. Damn, she was ruthless enough as it was.

"These rules," he finally muttered through his teeth, fighting the urge to rip that insubstantial scrap of silk off her blasted body right then and there, just so he could feast on those luscious tits in all their bountiful glory, "serve a purpose that canna be thrown away so carelessly, lass. Can you imagine what my kind could do if we dinna have honor restrictions placed upon us? Any Warlock could have you stripped and spread, his cock rammed between your legs with no more than a thought, and there'd be naught you could do about it. And when he was finished with you, he could take the memory from you with equal ease, and leave you wondering why you ache and have no recollection of a man. This isna child's play, Té."

Her eyes narrowed, the blue so dark they looked near as black as his. "Is there a rule against sleeping with non-*Magicks*?"

He gave a sharp, agitated twist of his neck. "*Gnach.*"

"Excuse me?"

"Non-*Magicks*, they're called *gnach.*"

"How lovely," she drawled, voice oozing with sarcasm, thinking it sounded less than flattering.

His head turned and his eyes drilled into her with a piercing intensity, spearing straight through to her soul, stroking her desire until she could have sworn she heard it purr. And she could only thank God that the gorgeous ass returned his eyes to the road before she made such an embarrassing sound, knowing the last thing his ego needed was more fuel for the fire.

"Until recently, there were some restrictions, but they've since been lifted. So, to answer your question, no, there are no rules against it. The *Magicks* are not a racist people. We find ourselves no better than others, and would never think to dictate who a Witch or Warlock can love. The laws that existed were thought to be for the protection of the *gnach*. Though, there are some *natural* laws of nature that make certain things…difficult."

If not damn near impossible.

"Difficult? Sounds like an easy out to me. What relationship isn't difficult, whether it's between *Magicks* or *gnach* or friggin' pussycats? That's the nature of the beast, Kieran. If something's worth having, you can sure as hell bet it isn't going to be easy to get—or keep."

He shifted in his seat, his hand reaching between his hard, long-muscled thighs to rearrange his thick, angry dick, and she felt her mouth go swiftly dry at the gripping sight of his hand on his crotch. "I was no' exaggerating when I said I willna be easy for you to take, lass. So be mindful of just what you're tempting me with, beautiful."

Té shook her head, trying to regain her focus. "For such a clever guy, you can say the most ridiculous things."

His mouth twisted with humor. "Are ya questioning my size, then?" he drawled around a smoky chuckle. The fingers of his left hand flexed, stroking the mouthwatering bulge of his cock beneath the fine cloth of his pants.

"No," she said around a small laugh. "Not just yet. But the 'beautiful' part is starting to get a little rich, don't you think?"

The look he shot her as he pulled into a narrow side street beside the gallery was one of genuine shock. "You dinna believe you're beautiful?"

She groaned beneath her breath, fidgeting with the hoop in her brow. "It's uh, nice of you to say so, but there's really no need," she said with perfect honesty while he just shook his dark head in disbelief. "Really, Kieran, I'm quite aware of what I am."

An interesting subject, Palo always said. His candor while they worked together had made it so much easier to model for him when he'd asked. There'd been no pressure to be something she wasn't, to live up to the expectations she'd always set for herself but could never achieve. Evan was always going to be prettier, taller, skinnier...but Té felt she'd finally grown up enough to say *what the hell*. Palo had helped her to see—through the talent of his lens—that even though she may have scored the average height, fleshy curves, and quiet shyness from the family gene pool, there was something in her worth celebrating.

And as he parked the sleek Jag, coming around for her door, she couldn't help but wonder if Kieran honestly felt the same.

* * * * *

They stood in the main viewing room, a small raised area at the back of the gallery where a show's spotlight items were most often displayed. To Té's surprise, that was where they found her photographs, the ones for which she'd modeled. What was even more surprising was her sexy Warlock's reaction.

His eyes blazed as he moved from photo to photo, the tasteful black and white nudes never showing anything more provocative than the gentle swell of a breast or the rounded curve of her hip, but blatantly erotic in their use of shadow and form. "Bloody hell," he growled beneath his breath. "I should blister your little backside for this, Té."

She couldn't help but feel a warm, soothing flood of relief at his outraged expression. Outraged, but in no way frightening—such a vast difference from Lexi's strange, imbalanced fury when she'd taken him to the first showing in Chicago. With a wry smile, she said, "I tried to warn you that you shouldn't have come."

One black brow cocked up, dark eyes thoughtful as he studied her smiling face. "We'll see how funny you think this is when I spend tonight walking around here with a fucking pole in my pants."

Her eyes dropped to his heavy crotch, and she licked her lips, feeling unbearably tempted. "You. Can't. Do. That. *Here.*"

Kieran made a masculine sound of disbelief. "You drag me to a bloody roomful of naked pictures of your beautiful ass, and you didna think I'd be hard the entire time?"

He watched as she shrugged her bare shoulders, shaking her head, the soft lighting playing over the silky sheen of her hair in a sensuous caress, glinting off the little ring of silver in her brow. "First of all, I didn't drag you here, remember? And, to be perfectly honest, considering your reputation, I didn't expect you to be so…um…*affected* by a couple of photographs." She shot him a considering look. "I mean—think about it, Kieran. I'm hardly bombshell material. Palo's the one who makes them so incredible. I seriously think the man could make a sheep look good."

He would have thought she was shitting him, if it weren't for the open honesty in her expression. He didn't get it. How could someone so outrageously sexy be this clueless about her appeal? Saephus, she was so intoxicating he could hardly think straight around her—could barely pump sufficient blood to his brain because it was always rushing to his damn dick.

"Aye, the man is talented," he agreed. "But it's the *subject* that makes these so fucking good." He did a slow turn, dark eyes taking in all twenty-four photographs. Looking back at her, he said, "That must've been one hell of a photo shoot."

"Is that jealousy I hear in your voice, Kieran?" she gasped with mock alarm, fully expecting him to deny such a "human" fault.

But he surprised her with a low, heartfelt, "Aye."

Té watched him from beneath her lashes, feeling one more wall crumble, knowing she was soon going to be utterly defenseless where this man was concerned. Shaking her head, she answered with as much honesty as he'd given. "It was actually quite comfortable, but then women aren't exactly Palo's thing, if you know what I mean. I think that helped me to be able to relax as much as I did, plus the fact that he was such a good friend of Ellie's."

He didn't like hearing *any* man referred to with such warmth by *his* woman, but was able to choke back the "caveman" routine in favor of staying on her good side. Not that he was there yet, but he figured a little optimism couldn't hurt. "I canna stop looking at them," he rasped, voice gone guttural as the need he constantly carried for this woman began to churn with dark, sharp-edged focus.

His eyes found hers, midnight gaze blazing with desire. "In fact, I'd be willin' to bet they'll be playin' front and center in my mind—till I replace them with the real thing."

Her breath sucked in on a sharp stab of arousal, a carnal groan sticking in her throat at the primitive, smoldering look in his eyes. Kieran took a step closer, and she felt her muscles quiver with anticipation.

"Your body is beautiful in these pictures, Té Hayes. Soft and womanly and so sexy it makes me want to come just looking at them—but you know what really gets to me?"

She swallowed, shaking her head, not trusting herself to speak. "It's those damn pictures of your face, sweetheart—those expressions that make me so bloody hard that I ache, because in every single one of them, you look exactly…*exactly* how I imagine you will when I'm inside of you."

"I won't apologize for them." Her voice was soft, challenging, as if she honestly expected him to object. "They were my choice and I'm proud of them. I'm proud to have been a part of something so beautiful. Palo is truly an artist. An artist and a wonderful friend."

His smile was slow and sweet, fingers warm as he tenderly brushed a dark red lock of hair off her forehead. "I didna ask you to, beautiful."

Té shook her head in a small burst of frustration, honestly not knowing what to make of him—her thoughts a rioting jumble, emotions no better. Needing to find Palo to let him know she'd arrived, not to mention a few moments away from the sexy stud to get her head together, she took a deep breath and said, "How about you take a look around while I go get you a drink and let Palo know we're here?"

He didn't like the idea of her going off without him, but figured he had to give her at least a little space, whether he wanted to or not. Shoving his hands deep into his pockets, he nodded, the corner of his mouth kicking up in a teasing grin. "Just make sure it's a bloody stiff one."

She looked back at him with a warm gleam in her luminous eyes. "And here I thought you were already *stiff* enough."

He laughed softly beneath his breath, eyeing her the entire way across the room, wanting to kill every single man who stopped to stare. She drew their attention like a flame draws the helpless moth, entrancing them with her stunning, unique appeal.

And he was as snared as the rest of them — if not more so.

Hell, who was he kidding? All she had to do was snap her little fingers and he'd be hers to do with however she damn well pleased — body, heart, and soul.

Beside him, a small group of Americans climbed the carpeted step up into the room, walking from photo to photo, heads bent close in private discussion. Kieran watched them with narrowed eyes, wanting very much to go and throw his body across the black and white photographs like an overly dramatic, lovesick pup. He snorted to himself, not knowing he had such a possessive streak. Of course, it could all be attributed to the headstrong little American turning his entire world on its ass.

Damn, what a startling little bundle of surprises Té Hayes was turning out to be — each one making him fall for her all the harder.

"I know what you're thinking," the cultured voice murmured beside him.

"Is that right?" Kieran drawled. Hell, he wouldn't be surprised. Seemed *everyone* knew what he was thinking these days.

He turned to face the short, stocky man holding out a well-manicured hand. "I'm Palo Daumier. And you must be the man Bronté told me she would be bringing when she phoned this afternoon."

"Aye," he replied, reaching out to shake the artist's cool hand. "Kieran McKendrick."

Palo gave him a small smile. "Well, I do know what you're thinking, young man. Aside from dreaming about how you'd like to physically dismantle me piece by piece, you're wondering how someone as inherently modest as our Bronté can manage to look so sinfully erotic, so painfully enticing—the consummate seductress."

"Is that right?" he repeated. His voice this time was tighter, the words darker than before, but Palo remained undaunted.

"Oh definitely. It what's we *all* think, dear boy."

A bitter flavor that tasted remarkably like that jealousy she'd accused him of soured his mouth, and he shook his dark head in fascination. Who would have ever thought that after thirty-three years he would finally fall victim to that little green monster? Here he was, a lethal combination of wolf and Warlock, and he was fuckin' jealous of some *gnach* photographer. "From the way I heard it, sexy females aren't quite your thing, Daumier."

The older man had the grace to blush slightly, looking somewhat guilty in his severe dress black. "Yes, well, you don't think Ellie and I could have really persuaded that beautiful girl to model for me if she suspected I enjoy a little variety from time to time, do you?"

Kieran's black eyes glittered from beneath lowered lids, pinning the stylish older man in place. "So you lied to her," he stated softly.

Despite the rise in his blood pressure, Daumier managed another small smile, though the line of his lips now appeared strained, looking white around the edges. "Through my teeth, if you must know. But for these," and he swung his arm wide, indicating the array of photos displayed on the wall before them, "I would do it again and again. I can assure you the experience was nothing short of torturous hell, but we artists must often suffer for art's sake."

Kieran wasn't sure whether Daumier was referring to the fact that he'd had to lie to Té about his sexual preference, or the fact that he'd had to keep his attraction to her well hidden that had been such hell. Either way, he found himself reluctantly liking the old guy for his ballsy admission. So long as he stayed the hell away from Té, Kieran figured he could hold off on kicking the guy's designer ass all the way back to Chicago.

With a dark laugh, he jerked his head toward the wall, indicating the photographs. "I really should beat you senseless, but it's hard to hold a grudge when I find myself so admiring of the end result."

The gleam of success burned like a flame in Daumier's golden eyes. "So am I, Mr. McKendrick. So am I."

Chapter Ten

Kieran hadn't planned on kissing her, but it happened before either of them could stop it. The group of Americans, including Palo, had left by the time she returned with his Scotch, leaving them in the relative privacy of the viewing room. They stood close, devouring one another with eyes troubled by mounting lust and the inherent understanding that the other held a vital part of their soul, as strange as it seemed. Then, before he knew it, he'd taken one long sip, set the glass down on one of the low tables arranged with exhibit brochures, and his arms were pulling her to him, her own going eagerly around his broad shoulders, soft body falling into him.

No, he hadn't planned on kissing her. What he'd planned on doing, every damn time he laid eyes on her, was fucking her so hard and so deep that she'd never again have any doubt just who her sweet little ass belonged to. It'd been that way from the first—a lightning bolt of hunger and recognition the second she walked into that blasted coffee shop.

No, he hadn't planned on kissing her now, surrounded by an unwelcome crowd of strangers, where he could hardly do all the things his starved body was so adamantly demanding.

And the hell of it was that she was kissing him back. Not just accepting the dominating sweep and thrust of his tongue as he forced his way between those lush, wine-red lips and ate his way inside. No, she was kissing him like she had last night, sucking on his tongue as if she drew nectar from the tip, making his head damn near explode from the sudden steam-capped pressure building inside of him.

No longer caring that they were in a roomful of friggin' *gnach*, Kieran's big hands found the soft curves of her ass and squeezed hard, claiming possession. With a feral sound of impatience, he pulled her into him, molding her soft body to his until she was groaning at the huge mass of his cock ramming into her belly from behind the strained fly of his dress pants.

It was monstrous—as unbelievably huge as it'd felt the last time it'd been pressed against her. Every feminine cell in her body went hot, liquid and soft, at the thought of having that massive erection thrusting inside of her—of that magnificent cock pounding her apart. Everything about this giant Scot was fierce and dangerous, intoxicatingly so, and Té knew he'd be no different at sex. No, he'd probably stake her out and drive himself into her until she no longer recognized the stars and the moon, or the earth beneath her—but only the pounding of his body into hers. Total and complete possession, while the rest of the world simply fell away.

Without warning, a sharp cry burst from her throat, but he swallowed the raw sound of need, giving a gruff growl in return. She felt that growl against her nipples, the way it rumbled in his chest like a beast—like an animal—and suddenly her vivid imagination was conjuring up all kinds of hot, mind-shattering visions of being taken on her knees, with Kieran behind her, driving his point home with every hard, pounding thrust of his cock into her open, juice-soaked sex.

In her vision, her mouth was open, face flushed as she silently sobbed and screamed and begged for more. Begged him to pull the cheeks of her ass apart—to spread the swollen, ravaged lips of her pussy and fuck her into a heart-stopping orgasm that nearly killed her. The kind that stripped her skin and sanity—leaving nothing but a pulsing, writhing mass of ecstasy in its wake, and all without harming a single hair on her head.

The kind that settled into her blood, burning her alive from the inside out.

The kind that destroyed her.

And all she could moan was one whispered refrain, soft and pleading—

Fuck me…fuck me…fuck me…

"Stop it, baby," he breathed against her neck, just beneath her ear, his lungs working hard for air. "Saephus, you're killin' me, lass."

Oh, God, it hit her like a punch to her trembling belly. She was whispering that wicked refrain *out loud*—not loud enough to be heard by the curious eyes watching their embrace, slanting them fascinated glances while trying to conceal their attention— but loud enough for Kieran to hear.

She'd been telling him to fuck her.

Begging for it—in the middle of Palo's freaking exhibit!

She moved to pull away, to put some distance between them, her mind dizzy, thick with desire, but his arms held tight, his hold unbreakable.

"*Dinna do that.*"

Té stared up at him, not even pretending to misunderstand. She was the one who'd gotten herself into this, and she was going to be damned before she chickened out like a coward. "I'm sorry."

"Dinna—dinna *ever* tell me you're sorry for this."

His incessant contradictions were driving her crazy. "Then what do you want me to say, Kieran? That I can't help myself when I'm around you? Well, I can't, damn it—and I don't like it. I hate it! Especially when you seem to have no interest in ever taking it any further."

"No interest?" he snarled. "No interest?" With his back to the roomful of mortals, he grabbed her cool fingers and pressed them against the pulsing ridge of his cock beneath the fine cloth of his pants. "What the fuck do you call this, Té? If this isna *interest* then I dinna know what the hell is."

"Yeah, well, you have a funny way of showing it," she grumbled, still struggling in his grasp, trying to pull her hand away. "And that's fine, Kieran. Really. I have enough to deal with in my life right now without butting heads with you every five minutes."

"I'm trying to protect you." The words were harsh, tortured, forced out between his clenched teeth.

She heard the tiny noise like a deafening blast of sound. The small, significant click inside her head that suddenly sent everything tumbling free. "Damn it, will you stop trying to protect me from what you are? In case you haven't noticed, I'm not running. I'm right here, ready and aching, going outta my freaking mind because I want you. But no—no, you've got to *protect* me, because I'm just some puny little human *gnach*, huh? Well, fuck you, Kieran. I may be human, I may not have freaking lightning bolts shooting out my friggin' fingertips, but I have my pride and I'm tired of you stepping all over it."

She jerked out of his grasp, gaining two steps of freedom before his grip on her arm brought her back around. His nostrils flared with his harsh breathing, hot color burning along his strong cheekbones. "Where the hell do you think you're going?"

"I'm hot and horny and if you're not going to do anything about it, then by God I'll go find someone who will," she vowed, rapid breaths setting the soft mounds of her breasts above the strapless neckline trembling. "Someone who isn't afraid I'll break at the slightest touch."

The moment the words were out of her mouth, she knew they were the wrong ones, but there was no way to pull them back. No means of recapturing the threat, the challenge, she'd just thrown at his feet like a gauntlet. And one look at his hard-edged face told her that this time she'd pushed him too far.

God help her, she was finally going to get what she'd been asking for.

One moment they were trapped in a roomful of people, and in the next, she was being pulled along behind his tall form until she found herself utterly alone with him in what must have been the gallery owner's private office.

Kieran spun her around with more force than he'd ever used with her before, slamming her up against the hardwood of the door the second it clicked shut, the lock clicking into place without the help of his fingers, and she knew he'd used his *Magick*.

"Is that what you think?" he blasted into her flushed face as she stared up at him, eyes glassy with desire. "You think I'm afraid of fucking you too hard? Saephus, you dinna know the half of it, Té. Yeah, I'm scared shitless of hurting you. In case you've failed to notice, you're so goddamn bloody tiny and I'm built like an effing animal." *More so than you can even imagine.* "So yeah, I'm worried about losing control—giving you too much when I finally get inside o' you."

"You don't even care that I want it, do you?" she demanded, knowing she was pushing him, yet unable to halt the breathless stream of words.

"Shut up," he ordered with desperate appeal, long fingers biting into her bare arms. "Just shut up and let me get this said, damn it."

Her lips pressed together, deep blue eyes suddenly shooting daggers.

"I want you too bad to be gentle or even safe," he grunted, the words a harsh blast of sound, like the crackling of autumn leaves in the eerie stillness of the night. "I want to take you hard and rough and fuck the memory of every other man you've ever known right outta this sweet little head o' yours. I want to pound it right out with the head of my dick. Shove it past those beautiful lips and shoot my cum down your throat, watching you suck it—fill you so full of it you canna even breathe around my cock stuffing this sexy little mouth. I even want your sweet little ass, Té. Want to pack you full every way there is.

"I want *all* of it—want to show you again and again, for the rest o' my life, how much you mean to me. But first...*the bloody curse—*"

Té wanted to scream with frustration. "God, Kieran, I thought we had this settled. I already know about your curse. So you can turn into a *wolf*. Enough already, damn it. I get it. It's crazy, I know, but I *get* it. I'm not trying to shoot you with a freaking silver bullet, so can't we just drop it?"

His dark face lowered, black eyes sparking with fire. "And do you know what I'll do the first time I fuck you? Do you know that I'll take you like a *beithíoch*? That I'll cover you like an animal and sink my fangs into you—*fucking bite you*—just so I can leave my mark on you?"

Her eyes widened, but she didn't pull away. God bless her, she looked fascinated and curiously...*arousingly* intrigued. "So?" she whispered, licking her lips, blinking slowly up at him, blue gaze burning with desire. "And is this the part that's supposed to send me running, Kieran? I hate to be the one to break it to you, but I kinda like the sound of you nibbling on me."

He pressed his forehead to hers—the agony of wanting her practically killing him. "You dinna really understand what I am, Té. You're coloring this all in some kind o' soft, romantic light, when it couldna be farther from the truth. It's no' a nibble I want, damn it."

"Then what, Kieran? How the hell am I supposed to understand if you won't just spell it out for me?"

"*I want your blood.*" There it was. Out in the open. A harsh, guttural declaration of intent. Crystal fucking clear.

Hell, he couldn't have been more blunt if he'd tried.

He raised his head, and with a sudden catch in her breath, she saw that his eyes had bled to the icy silver of a wolf, mesmerizing in their beauty. There was a tiny crease across the bridge of his nose, like when a dog growled, and a low, rumbling vibration in the back of his throat.

It was the warning before the strike. The signal to run, so that the beast could enjoy the exhilarating satisfaction of the chase.

Only Té didn't want to run. Not anymore. She was so friggin' sick of it.

No, she wanted something else entirely.

And what she wanted was to be caught.

Trapped.

Taken.

Goddamn it, she wanted to be *fucked*.

And it looked like she was *finally* going to get it.

Kieran stared down at her as if he wanted to eat her alive. There was no other name for it. Nor any way to deny what it did to her body, the sharp stab of pleasure beginning to pulse between her thighs, secure in the belief that he would never actually harm her.

He may be *more* than a man—but he wasn't the monster he believed.

He wasn't looking to hurt her.

No, what he wanted was to consume her sexually, and she was more than ready to give him whatever he needed, *even if it was a few drops of blood.*

"Do you know why it's so dangerous for a mortal to fuck someone under a Lupine spell?" he rasped, a deeper roughness to his voice that stroked her skin like a tactile touch, teasing her senses.

"N-no," she whispered, her breath hitching with excitement, the scent of her creaming cunt filling the air, assaulting the predator within him just waiting to be unleashed. It was lusciously rich, like honey and cream, and his beast wanted to shove its muzzle between those silky, pussy-pink lips, burying its tongue up the tight, constricted channel of muscle, until those earthy juices flowed freely down his throat, sating his hunger. Sated it, at least for a time, until he craved her all over again.

He *might* have been able to fight it—if only the man in him didn't want the same damn thing.

"Have you ever seen two wolves mate?" he asked, lifting his right hand to tuck a silky red lock of her hair behind the fragile shell of her ear. "It isna soft, and it sure as hell isna sweet, lass."

He moved one arm to wrap around her waist, using the other to lift the front of her dress, twisting the soft fabric around his big fist. The black material lifted higher as he twisted, revealing first the silky golden skin of her thighs, then the black scrap of her bikini panties, the fragile lace doing little to hide the seductive secrets nestled there between her trembling legs.

"It's dangerous," he growled, leaning down to run his rasping tongue along the sensitive column of her throat, shuddering at her taste, an erotic mix of lust and innocence, "because you never know when the beast will finally break free, ready for his own turn to fuck. Have you ever seen an animal mate, Té? It's raw, primal, hard. As hard as the cock I have shoved against your sweet little belly. Brutal. Rough. *Violent*.

"The beast doesna wait to make sure you want it. He takes your cunt, packs it to its limit…and beyond…until you dinna know whether it's pain or vicious pleasure, and then he pounds the hell out of it. He fucks it, and if it bleeds, if it hurts, he doesna apologize. He just licks it clean, savoring the sweet taste of your blood, and then he fucks it all over again."

Her chin lifted, expression mutinous. "You can threaten all you like, fuck me as hard as you dare, but you'll *never* make me believe that you could actually harm me." Holding his stare, she lifted her hands to cradle his ruggedly beautiful face, his skin fevered and scratchy against her sensitive palms. "I *know* you, Kieran. You may kill me with pleasure, but there's too much good in you for you to ever actually hurt me. I'd be willing to bet my life on it."

His eyes blazed, like a gleaming flash of mercury caught in the blinding rays of the sun. The color began at the outer rims of his irises, slowly swirling its way inward, dizzying in its effect. "I hope you're right, lass—for both our sakes."

A fine tremble danced through her limbs as she moved her hands to his shoulders, whether from fear or arousal, he wasn't certain and was too damn far gone to care. He jerked her hips against him, pulling her up hard against his front, grinding the heavy weight of his cock into her stomach, watching her big eyes go round with shock at his now outrageous, inhuman dimensions. A cock so big, he had no idea how her tight little piece would ever take it. And yet, to take her—to do all that he ached for—was no longer something he could deny either of them...for long.

When their time came, he'd fuck her so completely, she'd never again doubt the hold he had on her, or the undeniable fact that their lives were now so intricately woven together, they couldn't ever be torn apart. And it was for damn sure she wouldn't ever talk about leaving him again.

But, Saephus, how he wished that time were now. The effing wait was killing him.

"When an animal fucks, it bites. *I bite.* Just like I tried to warn you last night. But you didna listen, lass. Hell, you're still no' listening, and sooner or later I'm goin' to give in. Do you know what that means, Té? Do you understand what it is I'll do to you? Do you?"

"Mmm, yes, I understand." She reached between them and wrapped her fingers around him through the fabric of his pants, moaning when she realized they were far from long enough to enclose his wonderfully thick width. "God, you're *huge*," she whispered, the embarrassingly naïve words seeming to fit thickly in her throat. *Massive. Monstrous. Nothing sounded quite right to describe the incredible beauty of Kieran McKendrick's cock.*

"Is that a problem?" he gritted through his teeth, the feel of her little hands on him making him want to throw back his head and howl. "Did your other men no' fill you up? Did they no' make your little pussy ache when they fucked you?"

The anger he was searching for wouldn't come, though Té knew he was being a jerk on purpose, still trying to push her away, at least for now. But she was too far gone in want and need, drunk on the lust and irrefutable emotions this magnificent creature made her feel. "Problem?" she whispered stupidly, her thought processes, including the ability to make intelligent, or even coherent conversation, shot to hell. "No one's ever made me ache before, but no...there's no problem here."

Kieran felt the slow smile spread across his face, her obvious fascination hitting him with the crushing force of a tidal wave crashing down over his head. "I guess no', then. Maybe those mighty Americans are no' so mighty after all, eh?"

"How can you be thinking of other men when I've finally got my hands on you?" she huffed, gripping him hard enough to make him jerk in her grasp.

With a sharp sound of frustration, he ripped open the fly of his pants, shoving her eager little hand inside, needing to feel her touching his naked dick before he went out of his bloody head.

Her breath came out in a low hiss that echoed his own, her cool hand exploring him with greedy fingers, and he almost lost it then and there. Probably would have, were it not for the effing curse that held him back.

Hell, he loved it. Couldn't get enough. Loved the feel of her soft palms on his burning skin. Loved the awe he could hear in her husky voice as she moaned beneath her breath. Male pride pumped like thunder—a mighty battle cry—through his veins, roaring through his cock, the satisfaction of knowing she was "impressed" with him burning ridiculously hot through his lust-filled body.

Saephus, how the hell did she do this to him? He was a *Magick*, damn it, not some green boy needing reassurance about his manly dimensions. He was used to women, *Cailleachs*, oohing and ahhing over his imposing size. Hell, it'd grown so old, he knew what they'd moan down to the syllable. But there was a fresh, wonderful, bursting force of excitement at the sound of awe in Té's voice, and maybe even that tiny edge of her fear….her uncertainty.

The sound of it bloomed in his blood like a wickedly dangerous concoction, spreading with a wave of heat from his heart, centering in the throbbing head of his cock, the cum gathering hot and swift in his heavy balls. Shit, he *knew* it made him a monster, but there was no denying that feral part of his soul that loved, reveled, *howled* at the fact that she was just that little bit frightened of what he could to do her. It liked the fear. Liked the knowledge that he could dominate her and force her to submit with no more strain than it'd take him to snap a twig. Not that he'd ever hurt her. Hell, he'd sooner gnaw off one of his limbs than cause her even the simplest moment of discomfort, but that fine line of what *could be* and what *would be*, of action and intent, remained one that his beast trod with fine, hungering steps.

If he wasn't careful, he could rip her apart, and the animal inside of him loved that knowledge.

The animal craved the taste of her fear.

The man hated him for it.

And the Warlock felt trapped between the two.

She trembled in his arms, and he pulled her closer, trapping her hand between their bodies, his pulsing cock still clutched firmly in her small, possessive grip. And from the tightness of her hold, she didn't seem to be thinking of releasing him anytime soon.

Fighting the reins of his control, he leaned down and pressed his lips to her temple, his breath growing ragged, rough cheek rubbing against the silken heaven of her hair. "When the time comes, you'll take me. *All o' me.* You'll be so hot and hungry, your sweet little hole so fucking empty…*tight*…you'll be begging for it—for every goddamn inch."

And even as he said the words, he knew he was trying to convince himself, as much as her.

She moaned, lost in his dark promise, fingers tightening, palm shifting so that she moved the hot, silky covering over the granite, blood-filled root buried within. "You really think you can make me beg?" her inner wild woman tossed back in challenge.

"Aye," he groaned, mouth open, lips moving desperately across her warm cheek, the feel and taste of her flushed, moist flesh making his head feel as thick as his cock, dizzy as the blood rushed out of his brain, gathering with a mounting force, ready to blast her with his seed.

He'd never, in all his life, had it that way. No rubber. No latex. No barriers. Just her sopping little cunt clutching at him, pulling him into her humid warmth, soaking him in earthy juices and clinging flesh. "You'll *beg*, angel. Beg me to go fast, to pound you open, but I'm going to make you pay for teasing me. I'm going to give it to you so damn slow when I go in, one aching inch at a time, so you can feel *all* of it. I want you to know who's breaking you open, shoving that tight little cunt of yours so wide, forcing those sweet walls apart as I hold you down and make you take it. And when I'm in, I willna damage you, Té, but I willna hold back either. I want you too damn bad for anything but a hard, hammering, merciless ride."

She panted against his throat, taking a tentative lick of his skin above the collar of his shirt. "I'm not sure you'll fit," she sighed, measuring him with her hand, and he wondered almost wildly if she was pushing him again, daring him to prove his point here and now.

"Oh, I'll fit. When it's time, I'm going to pack you full of this big, hot cock, sweetheart. Slow and sweet, so you're there with me for every second of it, and then it's going to get rough. I'm going to look into your beautiful eyes, and then I'm going to fuck you so goddamn hard—stuff you so bloody full—it breaks the blasted bed."

"That sure of yourself, huh?" She nipped the cord between his neck and shoulder, and a low growl erupted from his chest as a hot drop of pre-cum sizzled in the wet slit on his blunt cockhead. She found it with the thumb of her other hand, rubbing it in with excruciating, intoxicatingly delicious circles. Then she damn near killed him when she lifted her thumb to her mouth and sucked it between those bee-stung lips, making his breath hiss out between his teeth.

Before he knew it, his big hand was bracketing her jaw, shocking her eyes wide, his tongue storming into her mouth, eager to taste the evidence of himself where he knew he'd find it.

The hot pad of his tongue swept her own, forcing submission, which she gave—for the moment. Hot and salty, right *there*, and he wanted to die at the eroticism of it. Couldn't wait to be holding her pretty face in his hands, her on her knees, while he pounded his dick between her lips and fucked the little hole of her mouth until he was spewing down her throat, filling her full with blasting spurts of cum.

Filling her full of his seed.

Sure of himself? "You bet your sweet little ass I am. I'm sure of the fact that fucking you is going to be the best damn thing to ever happen to me, and that I'm going to spend the rest of my life proving it to you."

"And when you go furry on me, Kieran? Will you run and hide—will you leave me wanting?" she taunted, throwing his reason for still not touching her here—*now*—in his sinful, sexy face.

For a moment his look became so guarded she thought he'd push her away, as if she'd wounded him, but he shook it off as quickly as it came. "No, I'll no' be running," he said with a quiet, unsettling calm. Her hand was pulled from his cock as he lifted her by her upper arms and carried her across the room, pushing her against the smooth opposite wall, pressing into her. He felt his teeth slip his gums with a sharp, piercing pain, mouth slightly transforming, her words nudging his tenuous control that fraction past the point of his hold, and he let them go with a wet hiss of sound.

The long fangs gleamed as they reflected the bright, iridescent lights from the street through the open window, and he knew they looked deadly. Lethal. Terrifying. The challenging, possessive look in his eyes daring her to fight him.

"You may have to go through life getting fucked by an animal," he snarled, his deep voice more savage than she'd ever heard it before, as he breathed through the mouth of a monster. "But I'm going to make you fucking *love* it."

She jerked at the wicked promise in his words, and it was a shocking realization to feel her body respond with need rather than the horror he kept expecting.

Hah! She wanted to rub the knowledge in his arrogant face, only she was too stunned with lust. But she'd known she was made of stronger stuff than he was giving her credit for.

"I'm going to fuck you so good, you *will* be begging. Even if it kills me."

"Then bring it on, Kieran," she panted, voice husky with the need to have him right then, at that very moment. Christ, this man really did it for her, no two ways about it.

Feeling the need to rock him as hard as he was rocking her—her life...her core...her foundation—Té leaned forward and curled her tongue around one elongated canine, then slipped it across the front of his teeth. She smiled as the powerful hands holding her upper arms shook with an uncontrollable tremor. Satisfaction pooled like thick syrup in her womb, warm and sweet, trickling to smooth its way down her cunt until she felt it slipping from her warm slit, drenching the black scrap of her panties. She pulled back, smiling at the stunned look of base, primitive need in his glittering gaze. Even with the mouth of something that was no longer quite human, he was decidedly deadly to her senses.

The most wickedly beautiful thing she'd ever seen.

And the sudden spasm of vulnerability she glimpsed in the swirling silver depths of his eyes made her ache to comfort him, to hold him to her chest and show him the acceptance that he longed for with every facet of his being. She couldn't touch all of him with her arms pinned the way they were, but she could show him with her lips...*her kiss*. Pressing her open mouth to the corner of his, she licked a slow path across his stubbled cheek, nipping at the lobe of his ear. A heady sigh of desire escaped her lips, and she whispered, "I'm ready and aching, Kieran, wondering just what in the hell you're waiting for."

The need in her blood was like an insatiable beast of her own, something that would slither past her control at any moment and transform her with a rabid, taking hunger. "I dare ya to sink these sexy teeth into me," she taunted, dipping her tongue into the shell of his ear, loving the feel of his heavy cock grinding against the vulnerable flesh of her belly. "I wanna feel them break into me just as that big, beautiful cock is filling me up—and I'm ready to feel it *now*."

He growled a dark sound that could have been torn from hell, scraping and harsh, and she felt the blast of power blow through him, singeing her with its fury. The power in his hands altered, became a living thing she could feel just beneath the hot surface of his skin, and the expression on his face turned to a sudden look of horror mixed with indescribable emotion…lust…and carnal craving.

Burning, uncontrollable appetite.

She did everything she could to focus on the thread of emotion. That shining spark of want she'd never seen before—for her.

All for her.

This was her man, damn it. Warlock, wolf…whatever the fuck he was…*he was hers*.

"I'm craving it, Kieran. Craving it—hungry for it—just like you. Don't you think it's time you did something about it?"

"Christ, just tell me to stop," he growled, the grating sound strangely pleading, his voice no longer human, but something roughly guttural, trapped between man and beast. "Now is no' the time. No' here. No' like this, damn it!"

Her head shook from side to side. "No…now. And don't ever ask me for that, because I'll never tell you to stop."

"I'm trying to protect you!" he all but roared, clearly losing his composure.

"I'm not a child, Kieran. I don't *need* your protection," she argued, small hands tugging eagerly at his hips, desperate to pull him into her. "What I need is to have you *inside* of me. It's time to make good on all the talk, gorgeous."

"Damn it, Té. You're asking for something you willna be able to handle, no' when I'm this on edge."

She glared up at him. "What in the hell do you know about what I can handle?"

"I know your little cunt's so bloody tight I nearly lose it just putting my fingers in you."

"How poetic," she snapped.

"You want poetry, beautiful, then you're shit out o' luck. When I look at you, I can barely remember my effing name, much less talk to you like a lover."

His forehead lowered to the vulnerable side of her neck and he breathed in huge lungfuls of air, his magnificent body held tight with tension. His muscles bulged, hardened, overwhelming in their weight and strength, but she didn't panic. Instead, she felt safe...secure...protected — while at the same time experiencing the most terrifying rush of physical need. It was consuming, this desire for him — this hunger to have everything he could give her both as a lover and a man.

Only...he wasn't really a man at all, and she honestly didn't give a crap. Whatever the hell he was, she wanted him.

"Té," he rumbled, his intoxicating voice spilling into her senses like the warm, decadent taste of sex, rough enough to warn her that this was going to be anything but easy. "Please...tell me to get the hell away from you. Tell me to fuck off...to get lost. Shit, tell me to leave you alone, Té, before I hurt you."

She turned her face to the side, eyes squeezed closed, and his lips trailed across her cheek, sipping from her flesh, his tongue flicking out to take tiny licks, as if he couldn't help but taste as much of her as he could while he had the chance. "Goddamn it, Té, dinna let me hurt you. *Please*. I couldna take it if I ever hurt you."

Everything she knew about this man, this Warlock, rioted through her brain in a dizzying flash of images and emotions. What was happening between them? If all he wanted was a fuck, then why wasn't he taking it? Why was he so tortured by the thought of hurting her? Why did he care? What did he really want...and why did he fight so damn hard against it?

Just how far did his feelings for her go?

Just how much of herself was she prepared to surrender?

And did she really have a choice? Could she honestly protect her heart, when she knew, if she were honest with herself, that she would admit it already belonged to this magnificent man?

His lips trailed down her chest with hungry urgency, his fevered mouth closing carefully over one silk-covered breast, and even through the layers of bra and dress, she could feel the deliciously wet heat enveloping her. Feel the strong pull of ecstasy as he wrapped an agile tongue around her nipple, suckling with a strong, steady pressure that made her eyes roll back in her head.

He worked his way over to her other breast with a rough growl of hunger, but just as his lips touched her nipple, his head lifted, eyes narrowed in concentration, his entire body held utterly still.

A whispery sibilance of noise from the gallery had caught his attention, his senses going on full alert, while Té continued to writhe against him, destroying his concentration. He started to lean back down to her perfect, heavy breast, wanting it naked and vulnerable, but then he heard it again.

"What the fuck was that?" he snarled beneath his breath, pulling back from her. Big hands moved quickly to refasten his fly, his muscles flexed with tension as he turned toward the door, putting himself between his mate and anything that might come through.

"Oh God, don't you dare!" she gasped behind him, feeling ridiculously close to the edge of a breakdown from having him pull away from her *again*. The urge to scream crept up the back of her throat, almost impossible to stop.

Kieran took a quiet step forward, his weight light, poised on the balls of his feet for quick movement, and she wanted to kill him. "Oh no, don't you dare leave me, Kieran. I swear to God you're going to force me to rape you if you do this again. And I am *not* a violent person. I'm a member of Greenpeace, you miserable bastard!"

"Damn it…quiet," he commanded over his shoulder, his voice a steely whisper, face slipping back to its original shape, though the man, the Warlock, looked no less dangerous than the *beithíoch*.

"Is this just another excuse?"

And then she heard it. Or rather, she heard nothing. No sound at all coming from the outer gallery. The eerie silence felt heavy and strange in place of the light music and conversation that had been filling the air only moments before.

"Kieran?" she whispered, scowling at the sudden, quivering sound of fear she heard in her voice.

His muscles bunched, tightened, and she knew something bad was coming.

In the next instant, the door to the office crashed inward, splintering wood flying in all directions, and what stood in the doorway was enough to let the scream she'd been fighting down break free in all its shattering terror.

She looked into the face of Richard Pinella, Lexi's brawny personal assistant, a man who'd always made her uneasy. She'd never liked him, but she'd never seen him look quite so frightening as he did in that moment, his normally brown eyes burning red in the dim light of the hallway, thin mouth twisted into a gloating smile as he glowed with a sickly light. And from between his pale lips flicked a long, ribbon-thin tongue with a forked tip, like that of a serpent.

Kieran pressed back against her, pinning her to the wall with his broad back, blocking her view of the horror at the door.

All she heard was one snarled, hissing statement before she felt herself floating in a strange, black, whirling vacuum of space, Kieran's arms holding her tight, keeping her safe.

But that one statement of intent meant that she was in more danger here than she could've ever imagined.

She heard Richard's sickening words, over and over, like a repeating record skipping in her mind, spreading a cold chill over her skin that seemed to reach into her soul with its icy claws.

Maldari.

Wants.

His.

Woman.

Chapter Eleven

Pulled in opposite directions, Kieran was torn between the savage need to tear the serpent shifter to shreds and the burning necessity of getting Té to immediate safety. The two desires battled against one another — but in the end, there was really no question as to what he would do. Because of what she meant to him, the need to see her protected quickly won out over the thirst for battle and vengeance.

And just as both Blu and Té had proclaimed, it turned out that some rules really *were* made to be broken. Knowing her life was in danger — that it was Té Lexi Maldari wanted — he'd broken one of the most ancient laws of his people and transported them to his father's home with a spell now only allowed to the Council members themselves.

And if they didn't like it, Kieran figured they could bloody well go bugger themselves.

Té sat on the low, hunter green sofa before the hearth in his father's library, a chenille throw wrapped around her slim shoulders as the dizzying effects of being transported by *Magick* slowly wore off. He'd already informed his father of their presence, along with a brief explanation, and phoned Blu on his cell, sending him to secure the gallery and bring Evan's car to the house. His last phone call had been to the gallery itself, and he'd taken the news that no one had come to any harm with a great, heaving sigh of relief.

Knowing that would be Té's first concern, he'd told her as soon as he walked back into the room. "I just talked with Daumier. Everyone at the gallery is fine. A little shaken up by all the commotion, but no one was injured by Lexi's thugs."

She'd nodded, her sigh of relief nearly as loud as his own had been.

And now he knelt before the log-filled grate, holding out his palms, and within seconds a roaring flame sprang to life, sending a curling wave of warmth spiraling through the chilled room.

Té looked back and forth between him and the blazing fire, blinking slowly, and then laughed softly beneath her breath, the sound somewhat odd considering her teeth were still chattering.

He wished he could return the smile, but there were too many unanswered questions running rampant through his mind, and he had only a short time to get them answered before Blu arrived. With his hands planted firmly on his hips, he took two slow, deep breaths, and then said, "Do you mean to tell me that the bastard you've been refusing to tell me about is Lexi Maldari?"

She nodded her head again, pulling the throw around her more tightly.

Shit, that sure as hell explains the scent, he thought with a low curse, knowing now where the watered-down smell of *Magick* he'd kept getting had come from. "He's goddamn mafia, Té. Not to mention a fucking *Gan Bhrí.*"

Her mouth went thin, lips pressed hard in irritation at his explosive tone. "What's a Gan Bree?"

Kieran went on as if he hadn't heard her, pacing before the now roaring blaze. "I canna believe you didna tell me it's fucking Maldari!"

Té shrugged. "It didn't seem important. I mean—I didn't even know you *knew* him. And anyway, it's not like you couldn't have just picked it out of my head if you'd really wanted to," she snapped with accusation, nerves too frayed to deal with his anger at that particular moment.

His black gaze cut to her. Sharp and focused. "I told you I canna do that."

"Right," she said, clucking her tongue, clearly not believing him.

"Goddamn it, Té, this isna a joke. And I canna read your bloody mind."

Blue eyes narrowed with intent. "Then how do you always know what I'm thinking?"

He stepped closer. "Your scent," he growled. "It's rich, sweet...delicious. And it tells me you're in this just as deep as I am."

"Then maybe you need your nose fixed," she muttered, fighting the childish urge to stick her tongue out at him. Damn but she was in a bad mood, not to mention seriously frustrated. *Sexually frustrated*, thanks to the overprotective beast pacing before her. Lord, how could she worry about anything when he clearly worried enough for the both of them?

"And maybe you need to stop changing the bloody subject. We're talking about the mafia here, Té."

Before she could question him on that bit of astounding information, considering she'd thought Lexi's "family business" was vineyards, he blasted ahead, another sudden revelation occurring to him. "Saephus, no wonder you accepted it so easily," he snarled with a sudden, strange force of accusation. She felt a warm wave of air surge around her, lifting her hair from her face, and knew she was feeling his magnificent power firsthand.

Hmm...interesting. She'd never argued with a Warlock before, and for some remarkable reason, she was finding it incredibly arousing. Then again, she was still damned horny from before. Tilting her head to the side, she regarded him with narrowed eyes. "Just what are you getting at, Kieran?"

"Maldari," he gritted out between his clenched teeth, dark eyes alive with fury. "He's a fucking *Magick*, Té. You must have known that."

She couldn't help it—she laughed. "Uh no, he's not."

He shot her a look that seemed to be asking if she was really so stupid as to disagree with him. "Aye, he bloody well is."

"Are you sure we're talking about the same guy?" she asked, scrunching her nose in disbelief.

"He's a criminal, Té. A bloody *Gan Bhrí*."

"Well, I take it from your tone that you don't much care for them, whatever they are."

"Care for them?" he snarled. "His kind were responsible for the attack that killed my mother."

"What?" She could feel the color draining from her face—a hollow, queasy ache bubbling in her stomach.

"They're fucking murderers, Té. The entire lot o' them."

"Evan," she whispered, panic taking hold of her lungs, making it difficult to breathe. "I've got to warn Evan," she stammered, lips feeling numb.

Kieran shook his head, grabbing hold of her arm as she tried to rush past him to the phone. "Lach will take care of your sister, Té. No harm is going to come to her, or the baby."

She sank back down onto the sofa, holding her head as if her pressing palms could somehow keep her scrambled thoughts together. "I had no idea." She snorted, trying not to giggle, it was so fantastically unbelievable. "The *Magick* Mafia. Jesus, I feel like I've fallen into a deranged episode of *The Sopranos* meets *Bewitched*."

Kieran gave her a worried look. "Are you okay?"

"Just so long as I don't get a dead horse head in my bed courtesy of Aunt Esmeralda, I'll be just peachy," she mumbled, pushing her hair back from her face as she tried to absorb everything he was telling her. "So then, I take it these Gan Bree or whatever you called them are the bad guys, huh?"

"You could say that. They're a bloody pest. A menace. Just ask the Council. It was a rogue faction of these assholes who murdered their lovers. *Our mothers*, Té. Every damn one o' them, not to mention my Uncle Robert and my Uncle Kyle, Lach's father."

She shook her head, wishing it were anything but true. The thought of all the things she'd done with Lexi, how she'd found herself so hopelessly attracted to him, until the night she surprised him with the gallery showing and his true colors finally revealed themselves, made her ill. "I didn't know. I swear."

He made an exasperated sound. "How could you? Apparently, you didna even know he was *Magick*, though how he kept that from you I dinna have a fucking clue."

"But how could they? I mean — you're all so *powerful*."

"My Da and his brothers made many mistakes when they were younger, lass. Mistakes which could have easily been avoided had they no' been so bloody arrogant. They...*refused* to bond with our mothers, and in doing so, they left the family with an unforgivable weakness."

"And these men, these Gan Bree, exploited that weakness?" she asked softly, not sure that she really wanted to know.

"Aye. A *Gan Bhrí*," he sneered, "is one who has been stripped of his own powers for unspeakable crimes. He has nothing left but his spells, and those he must be granted use of by a higher power, one willing to share his or her own *Magick*. There was a traitor within the ranks of our people when they last attacked, who gave the *Gan Bhrí* the information they needed. And once they possessed the ancient knowledge of forbidden spell-making, they were nearly impossible to defeat — their vendetta against the leaders who'd stripped their *Magick* utterly merciless."

She was so pale from what he'd told her that her sudden flush shone like twin bright spots of color on her high cheekbones. "You mentioned spell-making. What kinds of spells?"

"Any kind you can think of, from shifting spells, like the one whose curse I live under, to death and lust and everything in between. Though many of the *Gan Bhrí* are no' capable of performing more than one or two. It depends on the will of the *Magick* they are feeding from."

"What do you mean?"

"For a Warlock or a Witch, the *Magick* is their own to control and do with as they desire. For a *Gan Bhrí*, the *Magick* is no longer his to call, only his to manipulate as best he can when granted the right by a higher power. If the *Magick* doesna feel like obeying, it doesna have to."

"And so these…these *lust* spells? If a *Gan Bhrí* wanted to cast a…spell on a mortal, and the *Magick* allowed him to do so, then what would happen?"

His voice was a soft tear across the heavy blanket of silence surrounding them within those ancient walls. "Why do you ask, lass?"

"Because—" She broke off, swallowed, and then tried again. "Because I think Lexi Maldari put one of these *lust spells* on me while we were dating."

Deathly silence followed her words, and then he asked…again, "Why?"

She rocked back and forth in a soothing motion, feeling almost ill at the thought of what Lexi must have done. "Because I couldn't control myself around him." She paused to lick her lips, throat feeling dry. "I didn't even like him, but then one day when he asked me out for about the umpteenth time at Palo's gallery, where I worked, I just couldn't say no. It was like I had no choice in the matter."

"I'm going to fucking kill him," Kieran snarled, his evident fury visible in the tight, tension-held lines of his body. "He's a dead man. A walking, fucking dead man."

And then suddenly the import of her discovery hit her. A smile bloomed across her face with all the refreshing splendor of a fast summer rain—a warm, blinding rush of joy suddenly unfolding inside of her. She'd spent so many stupid months questioning herself, her sanity, for getting involved with a man like Lexi, and now it was over. As disconcerting as the thought of being under his "lust spell" was—it couldn't compare to the relief of knowing *he* hadn't been her *choice*.

She looked up at the man standing before her now, and the thought of how delicious he was sang through her senses, surging through her blood, without the aid of any spell. It cleansed her—making the nightmare with Lexi something so insignificant she could crunch it beneath her toe and chalk it up to him being a total bastard.

And a soon to be dead one at that.

"There's still one thing I canna figure out, though," Kieran murmured, a small frown between his black brows.

"Yeah?"

"Why did you run to Mexico?"

Té shrugged, sobering a bit, but still deliciously relieved. It felt as if she'd rediscovered a part of herself that she'd never thought to find again. "I have this friend, Jamie, who teaches at this school down there, and I figured it was as good a place as any to lay low for awhile, just until he forgot about me and moved on. It seemed perfect, really. I mean—he'd never go there because he hates warm climates."

Kieran blinked down at her slowly, his expression blank. "He hates warm climates," he repeated, simply stunned at her reasoning.

Té scowled, knowing it sounded stupid. "Honestly, he does. He'd have never gone down there. The bugs and humidity would've driven him crazy. So I stayed until his letters stopped being forwarded from Chicago, figuring he'd finally found someone new to obsess over. And that's when I came here."

He shook his head. "Amazing."

Amazing she hadn't managed to get herself killed!

For the second time that night, Té resisted the childish urge to stick her tongue out at him. "You needn't look at me like I'm an imbecile, Kieran. It worked, didn't it?"

"Only because you got bloody lucky," he snorted. "I'd be willing to bet he probably had his eye on you the entire damn time you were down there, making sure no one so much as sniffed after you."

The thought was uncomfortably sobering. "So then he was just waiting to make sure no one touched what he psychotically considers his?"

"Aye."

She shivered, hating that he was probably right, which meant that she *had* been incredibly stupid, not to mention naïve. She'd seriously underestimated what Lexi was willing to do to keep her.

Suddenly, she was very happy that she was there, instead of going it alone in the wilds of Central America.

But most importantly, she was happy to be with Kieran.

As if he'd read her mind, his expression slowly shifted, nostrils flaring, and then a small smile kicked up at the corner of his wicked lips—the same lips that had been so delicious against her own. She shivered, and the smile widened.

"Aye, I think you're delicious, too, lass," he drawled with a sexy wink.

Her eyes widened—stunned, and she blinked slowly. "How the hell do you keep doing that?"

"I canna read your mind, no' really, but then some things are too easy no' to pick up. Sorry, lass."

"Oh yeah? Then why don't you look sorry?"

There it was—that damn grin again. "Maybe because I'm no' really sorry a'tall?" he said with an audacious smirk.

She crossed her arms before her, trying for a hard look. "If you think I'm so damn delicious, then why do you keep leaving me high and dry?"

He took a step closer, each one bringing all the sinful, sexy, mouthwatering details that were Kieran McKendrick into sharper focus. "We're no' mortals, Té. Our strength, even when we try to temper it, can be deadly to the *gnach*. It's even harder to control during sex—much less when you're screwing with a curse on your back. This is gonna take some concentration, lass, no' a blind dash to the finish."

That spark of arousal he'd ignited at the gallery sprang to life, a hot, piercing flash of fire, building as quickly as the flames in the hearth had bloomed beneath his *Magickal* palms. "Kieran, I'm warning you, don't you dare leave me on the edge like this again," she said with a breathless urgency she hadn't known she could feel. "I'll go crazy."

He shook his head, knowing he had no choice. Nailing her on his father's sofa with Blu on his heels was *not* the way to do it, no matter *how* bloody tempted he was. "I canna touch you and no' fuck you—and I'll no' be taking you in a rush the first time I get completely into you, Té. It'll take hours...*days*...to take the edge off this first time."

A mutinous expression crossed her face, her chin lifting at that cute, defiant angle he so loved. "Fine. Whatever. I can just take it off without you, then. God knows it wouldn't be the first time I've ever done it."

With preternatural speed, he was on top of her, his palm cupping her crotch in a tight, possessive hold as he pressed her into the giving cushions at her back. "Dinna—dinna dare touch this cunt without me? Do you understand me? If I have to go hunting for some bloodthirsty dick from your past, dinna even think about coming without me here to eat it."

"You self-righteous ass," she hissed, pushing against his chest. "Nobody asked *you* to do this. I can handle Lexi. Damn you and your overbearing attitude, McKendrick. And get the hell off of me!"

"Like hell. And I'm no' blaming you."

She snorted at that. "Don't do me any favors, Kieran."

"Shit...*I'm sorry*," he breathed against her temple, trying to pull himself back together. "I'm so fucking furious right now I canna think straight, Té. Cut me some bloody slack. All my damn blood is still throbbing in my poor dick, none of it going to my brain."

She'd have laughed if she weren't suddenly so angry at his stubborn-headed attitude. "I don't need you to fight my battles for me, damn it. I'm not so useless I have to be tucked away and guarded."

"I may no' have to, aye, but it's my bloody right and one that I'm damn well claiming. No one touches *my woman*. No one. Ever. And that bastard is going to realize it. The second I get my hands on him, he's going to understand with crystal fucking clarity."

A hard knock sounded on the closed door, and he pulled away from her, leaving her glaring up at him as he stood before the sofa. "I'll be back by morning," he murmured, "so try to catch some sleep." Glittering black eyes moved swiftly over her from head to toe, smoldering with primitive hunger. "Trust me, lass, you're going to need it."

And with that warning, he left her fuming on the sofa, pulling the heavy door closed behind him as he joined his father in the hall.

"Blu is waiting out front," Iain said, his mouth pulled into a worried frown.

Kieran nodded, his long legs taking him quickly down the hall, his father right on his heels. "I'll be back by morning. No telling where the bastard is hiding or how long it'll take for us to sniff him out."

"Aye, and dinna worry over the lass. I'll keep her safe, you've my word."

Kieran stopped at the door, looking back to pin his father with a hard glare. "And dinna even think of bloody touching her," he warned.

Iain blinked slowly, a crimson flush ruddying his cheeks beneath the silver-threaded white of his beard. "Och, I'm a little too old for her, so dinna be so bloody insulting."

Kieran snorted. "Aye, but just because *I* know it, doesna mean *you* do."

His father narrowed his midnight eyes, the perfect mirror of his son's. "I resent the implications in that statement, Kieran McKendrick."

"Resent them all you like, just keep your damn playboy paws off my woman."

"Playboy paws," Iain sputtered. "You insolent little—wait! What? Did you just say *your* woman?"

Kieran gave him a hard nod. "Aye."

"So then you *will* claim her?" Iain asked with obvious relief.

"After I kill the bastard who dared to lay his hands on her."

Iain nodded with understanding. It was only a matter of time. Maldari was already dead. A walking shell waiting for Kieran to deliver him to death.

The *Gan Bhrí* just didn't know it yet.

Chapter Twelve

The sky was exploding in a breathtaking spectacle of color and light as Kieran pulled up in front of his father's house, his eyes gritty from lack of sleep and his dick heavy, still aching with unquenched desire. He looked up at the darkened windows and felt his lungs fight for air, his heart contract on a violent wave of emotion. She was in there, safe, protected…waiting for him.

Waiting for the devil to lay claim to her soul.

He leaned forward, resting his forehead on the cool leather of the steering wheel, not knowing how he could do it—not knowing how he could *not* do it. Té was everything he'd never thought he'd have, and goddamn it, he wasn't going to let her go.

Curse or not, their time had come. And the gods only knew he was more than ready for it, his body buzzing with a raw, sharp-edged anticipation.

He'd wasted the entire damn night searching through the dark alleys and streets, prowling the hells of Edinburgh, hunting Maldari, but he and Blu had been unable to find him. Today, Evan would stay with Seamus while Lach and Mal and Dugan continued the search, and if he still wasn't uncovered, then tonight he and Blu would search again.

It was a cycle they'd repeat as many times as they had to, because there was no other choice. Hell, even Blu understood what was at stake.

And they all wondered if perhaps this was the start—the beginning of whatever the Council had feared was coming. Had another *Magick* opened their power to the *Gan Bhrí*? And if so—who?

None of them had a clue, but they each understood the importance of what must be done.

Sounding far more serious than he ever had before, so unlike the carefree Blu that Kieran had always known—the wild boy of the bunch—his cousin had clasped him on the shoulder and said, "If she's the one, Kieran—if you love her, use your power. Against someone like Maldari, you're going to need it. He hides behind his evil and connections, and he'll no' be easy to find. And that's what you have to do if you want her safe. You have to ensure he'll no' be a threat to her ever again. You'll have to end him."

Kieran looked back up at the house and knew his cousin was right. It mattered not what he had to do to get him. All that mattered was seeing that bastard pay for what he'd done to Té.

A handful of minutes later, he was staring down at her sleeping form curled into a tight ball on the sofa, right where he'd left her. The door to the library was locked behind him, ensuring their privacy—his hunger sharp and demanding.

Settling himself onto the dark oak table before the sofa, he simply sat and stared at her with tired eyes, her precious face cushioned by her folded hands, so beautiful it hurt for him just to look at her.

Somehow, that quickly, she'd become his entire world.

She moaned softly, shifting in her sleep, the throw long forgotten with the fire he'd left burning to warm the room. The hem of her dress rode dangerously high on her sweet thighs, and he felt a sudden, searing compulsion take hold of his will.

He'd touched her cunt with his fingers, sucked the sweet, honeyed juices of her from his skin, but he'd yet to have the pleasure of feasting upon it with his eyes—of spreading it open and investigating every perfect little succulent inch.

Careful not to make any noise, he shifted the table closer, and then, using exquisite care, he slowly shifted her legs toward him, pulling her forward until her tight little ass lay perched upon the edge of the sofa, thighs sprawled across the top of his own. With shaking fingers, he carried the hem of her dress up to her navel, revealing the tiny black scrap of her lace panties, the crotch still visibly damp with her juices, and his breath rushed raggedly through his lungs.

His chest ached.

His dick ached.

Grasping the straps at her hips, he pressed the thin fabric between his thumb and forefinger, calling on his power of fire, and then with a soft, sibilant hiss, the fabric sizzled into nothing, his fingers unburned. With a rough sigh, he pulled the front panel away, letting what was left of her panties fall silently to the floor, and felt the air surge from his lungs in a violent whoosh of sound.

Ah gods, there she was.

More perfect than he could have ever imagined.

His gaze flamed, black eyes bright with lust and dark, deeper emotions, as he stared down at her open, quivering sex. She was pink and, ah, so damn delicate. Above, the silky puff of her mound was as red as she'd claimed, like a flaming little cloud, and below, her perfect, demure lips deliciously bare, already slick with pearly cream, the heated scent intoxicating to his reeling senses. She smelled like sex and woman and hard, unforgiving fucking. The kind where you lost yourself in the pure, blinding pleasure of the moment. Where your entire world constricted, narrowed, focusing down to the exact, perfect point of penetration. Where you knew nothing beyond the feel of your cock cramming into a woman's cunt, the slick fluids of her body coating your skin, the rhythmic clenches of her muscles as they pumped your thundering flesh to completion.

He'd never had it—not like that. Oh, he'd had good fucks, better ones than most men ever deserved, but he'd never had that *one* perfect woman. The one who fit him in every way. Who brought everything she had to the moment and offered it freely, trusting her heart as well as her body into his hands. Even her soul.

And he wanted it with this one.

She sighed, her head rolling across her shoulders, and he knew he should cover her back up and take her home—to *his* home—where they could do this properly. Knew it as surely as he knew that it was far from what he'd do.

With a shaking hand, he trailed one fingertip through the thick seam of her folds, gently opening her so he could look his fill of the even pinker flesh within. Ah, Saephus, she was so beautiful. It stole his breath, thickened his cock to the point where he knew the buttons of his fly were in danger of busting.

Come to think of it, his cock was pretty damn close to busting, too.

"Gods, I want to fuck this—*eat it*," he rasped beneath his breath for his ears alone, his tongue restless within his mouth, waiting for its chance to explore the glistening flesh beneath his fingers. "I could eat you out for the rest o' my life, lass, and never get enough."

Bringing his other hand into play, Kieran used his thumbs to spread her lips wider, stretching them, and looked his fill of the prettiest little cunt he'd ever seen. Her clit swelled, rising at the top of her sex, begging for the gentle bite of his teeth. She took a deep breath in her sleep, and her cunt breathed along with her, the nestled slit so small he wanted to howl. The animal call burned at the back of his throat, his mind filled with image upon image of his cock right there, the heavy, blunt head forcing her open, stretching that fragile skin so wide...stretching it to take his thick, brutal width.

He'd work it in with forceful, intent precision, wetting himself with her warm cream, and then he'd hold her wide-eyed stare as he braced her hips, fingers digging into her silky flesh, and cram his throbbing cock right through the fist-tight clench of tissue. He'd part her inch by delicious inch, not stopping until he was buried up to his balls and her cunt was packed wonderfully full of hard, pounding cock.

He wanted as deep into her as he could get—wanted to measure her pulse with the tip of his dick. Wanted the grip of each breath squeezing him, working him like a strong, wet fist.

With one callous-tipped finger, he tested the tender rim of her pussy-pink vulva. It was soft and sweet, the slit within slipping cream as it pulsed—slick, slippery fluids streaming from the shy hole. He wanted to shove his face right *there*, pierce that narrow mouth with the thick thrust of his tongue, dig into her as deep as he could, and suck the juices right down his throat. He wanted her taste in his mouth, on his lips, sliding down as he swallowed it, filling his gut. And after he'd eaten his fill, after he'd brought her so many times he was full on her cum, he'd break that tiny hole apart with his aching cock and give her the fucking she'd been asking for since the moment they met.

How strange that was only a few days ago. Gods, it felt like he'd been waiting for her forever. Days and months and years—instead of a measly number of hours.

His finger slipped deeper, up to his first knuckle, and her muscles sucked at him so damn perfectly it made his breath hiss between his teeth. He knew there was no way he'd ever get his dick in there without hurting her, and yet, he knew enough to believe that if she was *the one*—if this was meant to be—then she *would* take him, as impossible as it sounded. And Saephus, it would be so damn sweet. To part those hot little cunt muscles and feel her suck him deep inside. To tease her with a steady ride until she clawed and begged and he couldn't control any of it—until he finally let loose, plowing and driving and pounding her so hard it felt like heaven and hell.

He prayed she liked her sex a little rough, because there was no telling how long it'd be before he could give it to her sweet and easy. Damn, the way she made him feel was so forceful, violent in its intensity, he didn't know if he'd ever be able to give it to her that way.

But he'd try. If that's the way she wanted it, he'd do everything in his power to love her the way she needed.

He closed his eyes and took a deep breath, wondering where the hell his mind was going as he pulled his hands away, fisting them on the baby soft skin of her thighs. She was so fragile, and here he was plotting the fuck of the century. Damn woman didn't understand what she was playing with here. She probably had visions of tender moments and gentle caresses, and all he wanted was to fuck her raw, catch his breath, and then give it to her even harder, showing her the force of pleasure a true Warlock could give his mate—a vicious pounding of cock into cunt over and over and over again.

Cracking his lids, as if he didn't trust himself with a wide-eyed view, he reached down and spread her silky lips wide once again, opening her like a ripe, juice-filled peach, exposing every hidden bit of drenched flesh, blushing pink and so exquisitely pretty. She was shiny and wet, soaked in her fluids, her sweet scent making the beast in him want to drool.

And out of nowhere, the heinous, jealous thought of what Maldari must have thought of this perfect cunt slammed through his gut with the crushing force of a sledgehammer, painful and wrenching.

"Té?" he rasped, suddenly needing her to be right there with him. "Té, wake up, baby."

"Mmm…" she sighed, her thighs shimmying atop his, slumberous eyes blinking slowly open as she tried to bring him into focus. "Did you find him?" she asked sleepily.

He shook his head, expression hard, and she tensed, question-filled eyes taking stock of her exposed position. "What's wrong?"

His jaw locked, that tiny muscle jerking in his cheek as he moved his hands away from her sex, resting them lightly on the tops of her thighs again. "Did Maldari like going down on you?" he rasped, knowing he had no right to ask—knowing it was an asshole's question—and yet, unable to keep the ugly, intrusive…entirely unfair question inside.

She stiffened against him. "That's none of your damn business," she said carefully, voice husky from sleep, shocked that he'd mention Lexi at a time like this.

"Aye—I know I have no right to ask," he grunted, rough palms smoothing up and down the outer surfaces of her thighs, wondering why he didn't just shut the hell up before ruining everything. "But I'm doing it anyway."

Té tried to temper her happiness at seeing him safely returned with the irritation she felt at his infuriating attitude. "What are you doing, Kieran?"

His long fingers tightened on her flesh, then instantly released, as if afraid of his strength. "Just answer the question, lass—and you'd best do it now, while I can still listen."

Her bare, left foot planted itself against his shoulder, trying to push him away while her hands fumbled through the gauzy fabric of her skirt, her intent to pull it back down, but he didn't budge. She gritted her teeth, the churning frustration spiraling through her system nearly enough to make her choke. "Is this how you get your little kicks?" she demanded, voice rough with chaotic emotion.

His large hands caught fistfuls of her skirt, holding it in place, and she slapped at his fists, her body suddenly flailing as she tried to struggle against him in her slipping position against the cushions.

"Stop it," he ordered, giving up on her skirt and catching her fragile wrists instead. "Damn it, stop fighting before you hurt yourself. Is it so damn hard to just give me a bloody answer?"

She glared up at him. "Jesus, Kieran, why would you even want to know?"

His jaw ground down so hard she winced for his poor teeth. His breathing was heavy—more from arousal than their skirmish—black eyes flecked with supernatural silver as he stared down at her.

He swallowed once. Twice. "I just—damn it, I canna explain it, Té. *I just have to know.*"

She blew out an edgy breath, trying to gain enough leverage with her elbows to where she could push herself up. Her eyes met his in a flash of anger, then shot to the side. "Yeah, he did." Another breath, this one tight, and her deep blue eyes cut back to his. "Does that make a difference, Kieran? Lexi used to shove his face between my legs every chance he got. He was the first guy I ever let go down on me—and he said it was the sweetest cunt he'd ever eaten. Is that what you want to hear? You want all the dirty little details?"

"Aye," he gritted through his clenched teeth, even though it killed him to hear it. Angry emotions twisted his gut, but none of it was centered at Té. Hell, she was the only innocent in all of this. No—it was all self-directed, because he placed all the hateful blame on himself. Blamed his own jackass hide for not being there for her—for not protecting her from Maldari's viciousness. For not going after her when he'd first suspected something was wrong. For wallowing in his own misery, instead of following his instincts and tracking her down.

For not being the one to find her first.

Damn it, she was *his*—and he'd been fucking his way through Scotland while she was left back in Chicago, unprotected, at the mercy of a vicious *Gan Bhrí*.

"And what do I get, Kieran?" she sneered, the sound of her fury ripping him back to the moment. "An account of all the women you've eaten out?" Her heel pulled back quickly, and then struck out against his shoulder with all her strength, knocking him off balance for the flash of time it took her to scramble to her feet. She swayed and reached out to steady herself against the nearest wall, holding his dark stare, her expression daring him to take one step toward her as he rose to his feet. "I'm afraid I'll have to say thanks, but no thanks."

No more than five feet separated them, and it wasn't enough. She could feel the force of his need—his will—and knew there wasn't enough ground in this entire freaking world to get her far enough away from this man. His hold over her was that strong—that complete. Where in God's name was she going to run to when this was over?

And why did the idea of leaving—*of leaving him*—put a sick feeling in the pit of her stomach? "You're being a total ass," she hissed. "And a crazy one at that."

"Aye," he agreed with a sharp nod. "Maybe. I've felt a little *mad* ever since I set eyes on you. And I go a little more out o' my bloody mind every time I think about Maldari fucking you. I've been searching for the bastard from one side of Edinburgh to the other, all damn night long, and all I could think about was him covering you...sinking inside of you. Damn it, Té, that alone is enough for me to want him dead."

"You can't kill a man for fucking," she snapped, though to be honest, she understood exactly why Lexi deserved to die.

Kieran took two slow, stealthy steps toward her, his movements smooth with the kind of lethal grace that could only be attributed to a deadly predator. "I can if he fucks *you*. And Maldari does die, Té. Understand that now. I'll no' let him live for what he's done to you. He'll no' harm you ever again."

She said nothing, simply stared back at him with those brilliant blue eyes that made him feel completely stripped of his shields, as if his demons were displayed on a rack for her to see in all their brutish glory. He lost count of how many minutes they spent frozen like that, gazes locked together, until he finally cleared his throat, searching for a civil tone he wasn't altogether certain he could find. "It's time to go home."

She arched one golden brow. "And where would that be?"

He worked his jaw, eyes dark with intent. "With me."

A spark of challenge fired her gaze. "This should prove interesting," she drawled, obviously still pissed at him, though he couldn't blame her, considering he was being a complete dick. "*If* I decide to go."

"That's one way of putting it, sweetheart," he warned, the knowledge that she would soon be his pounding through his veins with the raging fury of a tempest, powerful and unstoppable, even if he had to get on his knees and grovel to get her there. "Let's just hope it's no' more than we can handle."

* * * * *

As Té made use of the downstairs bathroom to change into the clothes he'd collected for her from Evan's, Kieran went in search of his father to tell him they were leaving—though Té was still arguing his high-handed tactics. He found the scholarly elder sitting before the fire in his private study, studying an ancient text that looked nearly as old as the gleaming amulet hanging from beneath his snowy white beard. Kieran stood in the doorway, his voice worn-through as he said, "I'll have her back tonight, Da."

Iain nodded, setting the book aside, then stood and closed the short distance between them, his hand heavy on his son's shoulder, keeping Kieran from turning away. "You need to give in, boy. Stop fighting the inevitable. No good will ever come from it."

Kieran felt his breath heave within his chest, his eyes glued to the floor as his father's words ran over and over through his weary head. "I want to, Da." His voice was quiet, the words halting and soft. "I want to—but I'm afraid of what I'll do to her."

"Och—I dinna think there's any need for that," Iain replied with a soft chuckle, patting his son's powerful shoulder. "That lass fair eats you alive with those dark blue eyes every time she looks at you."

Kieran stiffened. "This is no' something to laugh about, damn it. I'm in hell here thanks to your fucking meddling with my life."

Iain waited until Kieran's black gaze met his own, then nodded with understanding. "Aye, you and Lach have always been the fighters. And Blu's no better." His mouth lifted with a proud smile. "We expected the three of you to give us a good struggle."

Kieran looked equal parts anger and stunned surprise. "You old fools actually think Mal and Dugan will take these bloody curses any easier?"

"Well, Mal will just take what he wants, with no concern for the consequences, and Dugan—Saephus, we'll all be in hell when his turn comes."

"And your point?"

"We've only helped you to see what your heart would have already known, but your eyes may have been too blind to see. It's time, son. *She's the one.*"

"I know that, damn it. Why do you think I'm so fucking terrified?" he admitted in a low rumble, walking away. He stopped at the end of the hallway, turning back to look at his father over his broad shoulders. "And dinna even think of pulling that crap you did on Lach. I should think getting ridden by a bloody wolf will be more than enough for her to handle, without the lot o' you five dropping in."

"Aye, you're probably right," Iain agreed with a heavy sigh of disappointment.

Kieran shook his head, a small smile twisting his lips. "You're a dirty old man, Iain McKendrick."

His father's black eyes twinkled with wicked mischief. "Aye, all the best ones are."

Chapter Thirteen

As soon as Kieran had the Jag cruising smoothly down Wallace Avenue, Té could feel the force of his attention shift fully back to her. Huh, she thought to herself. So much for her wild woman streak. Instead of launching herself across the center console and jumping his sexy bones—as she'd promised herself she'd do the entire damn night, driving herself crazy with worry till exhaustion had finally claimed her—here she was fuming in her seat, ready to strangle the gorgeous ass. "Damn you, Kieran, you *cannot* just whisk me off because you feel like it. Not after that little stunt you pulled back there."

"The hell I can't, woman. *You're mine*—that gives me the right to claim you. The right to do whatever I damn well please."

"I'm not a prize. I'm not something you just *get*. I don't stay when I'm told."

"Nae, you're definitely no prize, lass. No' with that vicious little temper, but you *are* my mate."

"Yeah? Did I miss something? Because if you've fucked me, it must've slipped my mind." Her hand motioned between them. "We—you and me—we've never *mated*, you overgrown ape. What we've done, *that* isn't mating, Kieran. That's not even sex." She turned on him, magnificent in her fury, glorious, stealing his breath. "You know what it's been, Kieran? A sadistic little game. Pure freaking torture, and I don't have to take it."

"Wolf."

She shook her head at him. "What?"

He scrubbed his hand down his face in frustration. "Overgrown *wolf*. If you're going to call me names, make sure you get them right, sweetheart. And just because I've no' *claimed* you doesna mean you're no' my mate."

"Well, I hate like hell to break it to you, but that's *exactly* what it means in my book. And you don't look very *wolfie* to me. That thing you did with your eyes and your teeth could just be some kind of spell, for all I know. In fact, I'm beginning to think this is just some lame-brained excuse you've got going for never following through on what you start."

He slanted a glittering look in her direction, before giving his attention back to the road. "Damn it, Té—what the fuck do you want from me?"

"Just that—a fuck," she muttered, turning back in her seat to face forward. "Something to get you out of my system so that I can get on with my life."

He stopped at the next red light and grabbed a fistful of her shirt, pulling her closer, until she all but sprawled across the center console. His eyes drilled into her, piercing her skin, the muscles in his arm bulging. "It willna *ever* be just once," he gritted through his teeth, his warm, sweet breath fanning her face. "Once my cock is packed up tight between your sweet little legs, it's going to be staying there day and night. So you better be sure that's what you want—because there willna be any going back. No other women—no other men. Just you and me and the rest of our lives together. Every damn day and year…*forever*. An eternity, Té. So you think about *that*."

She met his challenge—and raised him. "I don't tolerate 'other' women."

He let go of her shirt and his beautiful mouth curved in that wicked way he had of grinning. God, she was such a sucker for that expression. Who was she kidding? Any expression on his sinful face and she was ready to strip down and do whatever he asked.

But he wasn't asking right now—he was telling.

"Did you no' just hear me, darlin'? I dinna want another woman. No' today—no' ever. I've no' wanted one since I set eyes on you." With the tip of his finger, he traced the outline of her mouth, the calloused skin rasping against her sensitive flesh. "Since you opened these little fuckable lips of yours and told me you dinna play with men." The corner of his mouth kicked up and he admitted, "I never have been one to resist a challenge, lass."

Té slumped back into her seat and made a groaning noise that to Kieran sounded sweetly erotic, but then he was in such a bad way, he figured anything she did would turn him on. Her head fell back to thump against the headrest once, twice, three times.

And when she turned her head to glare at him, he found himself getting lost in those soft eyes of hers all over again. Thank the gods they were still stopped at the red light or he'd have probably driven them right off the bloody road.

"You expect me to believe you wouldn't have had more than your share of women in the last few days if it weren't for that curse? If that's so, then I have some killer real estate in Florida to sell ya, babe."

He watched her with a small frown, realizing she didn't believe him. Amazing. Just fucking amazing. "It doesna matter what women came before. All that matters is what comes *after*."

"I keep telling you, you arrogant ape, that there is *no* after!"

Not unless he gave her what she needed, and Té still wasn't sure he'd be able to do it. Wasn't even exactly sure what *it* was that she wanted, the feelings unfolding in her heart still too new…too fragile in their budding development. And she was smart enough to know—no matter how hard she'd fallen for him—that nothing could be built upon a foundation lacking unconditional trust.

"Well, I'm knowing differently," he drawled. "And…if this *asinine* turn in the conversation is your ass backwards way of asking if I can be faithful, you should know that a mated Warlock is *always* faithful. Our bonds are permanent and everlasting—never to be broken, lass. And when I fuck you, it *will* be a mating, dinna be doubting that."

Her teeth snapped together with a distinct clink as the light changed and they moved forward. "I'm still finding that very hard to believe."

"Whatever," he replied, skillfully maneuvering the sleek Jag through the crowded Edinburgh side streets. "At this point, it doesna really matter what you think, because it's true. I just didna want it to be."

"Oh gee, thanks." Her voice dripped with sarcasm. "Really, I'm just so flattered."

"Dinna give me that crap. You know what I mean. You've seen our power, and that was only a mild showing o' what we're capable of. I wouldna have wished this on you, Té—no' with what I am. You deserve more, no' someone more beast than man, but you're going to have to bloody well settle for me, because I *willna* let you go."

"And what's to say your rules should apply to me?"

Ooh…he didn't like that. Uh-uh. Not a bit. Té could already see the quiet heat in his eyes preparing to leap into a full blown, raging inferno—the slight, imperceptible tightening of his jaw as he slanted her a dangerous look.

She didn't take another breath until his eyes returned to the road, the Jag purring smoothly beneath them. "The mating rules *will* apply to you, but you're right in that your past is your past," he finally grunted, the words somewhat choked as they blasted from between his tight lips. "Though I may have to track them all down and kill them, just to save my bloody sanity. Exactly how many were there?"

"Oh, you want a number?" she asked with wide-eyes, fighting to hold back the mischievous smile blooming deep within. She knew she was being evil, but the gorgeous guy was just too much fun to bait. All she had to do was cast out her line and she got him every time—hook, line, and sinker.

His eyes became mere slits, nostrils flaring. "Aye, a number. Have there been so many you canna give me one off the top o' your head, lass?"

Té cocked her head to the side, careful to keep her tone and expression neutral. "Would it matter if there had?"

A small tic developed above his left eye, just at the tip of his eyebrow, but to give the Scot credit, he didn't scowl. Though Té could tell that was exactly what he wanted to do.

But before she could tease him again, they'd pulled to a smooth stop at the curb in front of a beautiful three-story Victorian that quite simply took her breath away. Kieran turned the key, cutting the engine, and looked at her, his eyes moving over every detail of her face, as if seeing it for the first time. Seconds ticked by that felt like forever, like an eternity, and then he finally said, "Nothing matters but what happens *now*."

Té climbed the steps to his front door, her delicate hand trailing along the wrought iron railing, silver bands glinting on her narrow fingers, and Kieran thought he was going to lose it. It was taking a goddamn eternity and he couldn't wait to touch her. Couldn't wait to get his hands under all those layers of civilized clothes until he was touching cool, soft skin that he knew was going to taste as good as it smelled.

He kept his eyes glued to the naturally sexy sway of her ass beneath her jeans, fighting the temptation to bend her over and shove his face into her cunt right there on the front steps for everyone to see. He'd never been so hungry for a woman in his life. Never wanted one so badly that he literally shook with the need to get inside of her. His dick was rock-hard, pumped so full of blood he should've been feeling lightheaded. It was all he could do not to push his hand between her legs, feeling her through the worn denim—but he knew it wouldn't be enough. He wanted to cup her naked pussy and thrust his fingers deep inside, finger-fucking her until she screamed in ecstasy.

And damn it, he'd waited long enough already.

With a harsh, rumbling sound, Kieran lifted her in his arms, holding her against his chest as she squealed in surprise, his long legs making short work of the few remaining steps.

The world spun before Té's eyes, all restless motion and heart-pounding adrenaline at the feel of being in his arms, pressed close against the heavy thudding of his heart. Before she could get her bearings, they'd made it through the front door, which was promptly kicked shut behind them, and he'd dumped her on the nearest available surface.

She took a quick, wide-eyed look around what was obviously his dining room, and realized she was perched on the edge of a massive, gleaming rosewood table, while Kieran set to work on the systematic destruction of her clothes.

He cursed low as he worked his way down the endless row of small buttons on her plain, white shirt—his nostrils flaring as her chest rose and fell beneath his fingers, her beautiful breasts heaving. He'd made it halfway down, only to see her nipples had hardened into two distinct little points beneath the soft cloth and knew he'd reached his limit.

Taking the delicate fabric in each hand, he ripped, scattering buttons across the hardwood floor with a soft, wrenching cry of sound. But before he got lost in the sight of those magnificent tits under the pale pink satin of her bra, he did the same to the fly of her jeans, wrenching them over her hips and down her legs to be tossed aside with the tattered remnants of her shirt.

And then his mouth was on hers, and he couldn't think about anything but how delicious she tasted, her mouth a liquid-soft heaven of sensual pleasure. He held her jaw with trembling fingers, moving her head from one side to the other, changing the angle of deepening penetration into the moist, honey-flavored cavern.

And Té was right there with him, gasping as his tongue tangled with her own, learning every surface and texture.

She could feel the power riding him—that of his *Magick* and of the wolf. It was in his blood, prowling beneath the hot stretch of his skin, aching for release within the tensed length of his powerful muscles. It wanted to breathe and howl and be free—and it wanted to fuck.

Wanted to fuck *her*…so wonderfully hard.

Wanted to claim her in the most elemental way two animals could mate…bond…possess one another.

Breaking his mouth from hers with a soft snarl, Kieran lifted and turned her, forcing her facedown over the edge of the table. Beautifully crafted rosewood chairs were quickly kicked out of his way, his hands hot on her skin as he ran them down the delicate slope of her spine, unhooking her bra, over her quivering cheeks, to where they pushed her thighs wide. Her lungs burned with excitement as she held her breath, gasping when she felt him rip her pink satin panties out of his way and shove her thighs even farther apart, obviously wanting her wide open, completely exposed to the cool air of the early morning and his blistering gaze.

And then his tongue was there, unfurling instantly inside of her, somehow too long to be human—and God help her, she didn't freaking care. She wanted it. All of it. Wanted it eating inside of her with such greedy, carnal abandon. Wanted the delicious press of sensation as he speared deep inside of her gasping slit, searching out the sensitive hot spot and probing it with his rough tip in a spellbinding rhythm—over and over until she thought she'd die from the pleasure.

She clenched her teeth, wanting to make it last…draw it out…but she couldn't help it. Damn it, she was going to come.

Hard.

Now.

It broke out of her like a thing of terrifying beauty, erupting with the savagery of a roaring force of nature, gripping her body so tightly she thought her muscles would shatter from the pressure. And then the tension broke, her flashpoint igniting, and everything released in a great rippling wave of ecstasy and heart-stopping, passionate emotion. She sobbed out his name while his tongue pierced the shuddering depths of her flesh, eating at her pulsing cunt like something starved and desperate, digging farther and farther inside of her, her juices flowing so freely she felt soaked in her cum.

Kieran grunted in pleasure as his mouth worked, tongue and lips and teeth choreographed in a dizzying, primal assault of need, eating into her as far as he could get, his heartbeat roaring in his head like a violent reverberation of sound. Té spilled into his mouth, flooding him with her heady flavor, and it was too much.

Growling in the back of his throat, he shoved her up onto her knees atop the antique rosewood. Her ass lifted into the air before him, legs spread so that her cunt was an open, weeping sin simply waiting to be committed, and with his hands holding her still, he shoved his face back into her. The soft, honeyed fluids flowed over his sensitive tongue, warm and intoxicating, so much bloody better than anything he'd ever had. The coiled pressure of hunger burning in his belly, knotting his dick, exploded—and he felt the beast roar to life, his fangs slipping painfully free, burning his gums.

Panicked, he tried to jerk out of her, but her tight flesh suctioned to keep him deep inside, his rough tongue scraping her delicate tissues, and another shivering wave of hot, sweet cum flooded into his mouth, dripping down his throat as her hoarse cries filled the air.

Fuck—he couldn't hold it…couldn't bloody handle it.

Grasping her by her hips, he quickly pulled her back to the edge of the table, pressing her down with one hand on the base of her spine, then reached down and ripped open his bulging fly, freeing the hot, aching mass of his cock.

His lungs bellowed like great, wind-filled sails as he stared down at her, all the perfect details presenting a banquet of opportunity to his starved senses and appetites. She was all soft lines and smooth skin, moist and fragrant, not with perfume, but her own, uniquely fresh scent. Fisting his hand in her hair, he pulled the short, golden-red mass out of his way, desperate not to harm her with the lethal, sharp-edged claws beginning to slice through his fingertips, nearly mindless with the lust and painful ache of emotion storming through his system. She lay panting beneath him, eyes screwed tight, her face pale against the dark wood, the color in her cheeks a full bloom of arousal that made him want to howl.

Leaning down, he licked the vulnerable column of her neck, the heady, musky clean scent of her fluids filling the air. He growled so low in his throat, the rough sound vibrated through his body, centering in the core of his cock as he pushed it into the wet valley between the round cheeks of her ass, the heavy shaft moving easily through the slippery essence of her warm cum. His eager lips skimmed across the slope of her shoulder, slipping slowly down the lithe line of her spine, until he came back to that sweet backside, the rosy skin glistening with her cream.

Unable to resist, Kieran spread her cheeks wide with his fingers and his eager tongue lapped across the tight pucker of her bud while he forced his claws to retract, his thumbs pressing into her juice-soaked pussy. He lapped at her ass as if she were a mouthwatering delicacy, fucking her with slow thrusts of his thumbs, forcing the pleasure on her until a series of short, sharp screams were being pulled from her throat, her palms pounding against the table as wave after wave of clenching release rippled through her pleasure-ravaged cunt.

Té was mindless to anything but the endless, raging orgasm spiraling through her body, its edge becoming acutely sensitive, and instinctively struggled against it.

Her legs sawed at empty air, kicking back against his shins as she writhed atop the table, struggling to lift up on her elbows in a futile attempt to crawl away. Kieran snarled against the shivering flesh of her bottom, catching her around the waist with one powerful arm, and pinned her back down with ridiculous ease, holding her in place.

Té cried out, not really wanting to escape, but unable to work her way through the crushing pleasure he kept pushing through her passion-wrecked system. She pressed her hot cheek to the cool surface of the table, tears streaming from her eyes as she felt him force her thighs wider, and she wanted to scream for him to take her now.

Now, damn it. Now, before she went out of her ever-loving mind.

"Please…please…*please*," she pleaded, not even certain of what she was begging for, just knowing that she couldn't keep coming without him inside of her, without her pussy being filled and stretched and packed full of his hot, hard, beautiful cock. She needed him to anchor her to this world. Needed the root of his powerful shaft to ground her—to keep her from falling, tumbling helplessly over the edge.

His head lifted, and she looked back at him over her shoulder, the harsh lines of his face etched with unforgiving need. His eyes no longer burned black, but a shimmering silver that seemed to slice into her, seeing everything they wanted, peeling away the layers of civilization until he was looking at the wild, primal thing living deep inside of her. She felt stripped, raw, exposed—and utterly vulnerable.

"Dinna run…dinna *fight* me," he grated through his teeth, his voice so low and rough it hardly sounded human.

She swallowed twice before locating her ability for speech. "I'm not afraid of you."

He ripped at his clothes as if they burned against his fevered skin—that eager to shed them—and then quickly flipped her over with such ease it was unsettling, as if she were but a doll. And when he had her where he wanted her, he stared down at her shivering body with a delicious intensity, his long black lashes casting shadows beneath his bright eyes, mouth and chin glistening and wet with her fluids. Holding her stare, he lowered his face back between her legs, his hot breaths bathing her sensitive clit. "*Then. Dinna. Fucking. Fight. It.*"

Then his face pushed into her again, his tongue untamed in its need to taste all of her, and she knew it was that of the wolf. It was warm and wet, yes, but far too long and rough, and God help her, it felt incredible. Everything in her lower body tightened with unbearable bliss, her cunt feeling hot and swollen, like a balloon being slowly inflated with a carnal overload of physical rapture, while her inner muscles contracted so wonderfully hard, making her incredibly tight. She could feel her channel pulling at his tongue as he pushed it in, the tip stroking repeatedly over that special little knot of sensation buried deep inside of her in a way that made her feel as if she'd explode.

And then suddenly it was happening again, her world falling apart in a shattering wave of pumping, grinding release as he took two thick, wet fingers and shoved them up the painfully tight mouth of her ass. At first it hurt like hell and she screamed, shocked, twisting beneath him—but then the pain was almost immediately followed by a strange, foreign pleasure that she couldn't have described if her life depended on it. It was dark and forbidden, deliciously savage in its intensity, and Té found herself pressing down, eager for more, taking his fingers just that little bit deeper, until he laughed into her pulsing cunt.

"Have you ever been fucked here before?" he grunted, his voice a vicious, grating slash of sound, rending the breath-filled silence.

Tears of passion overflowed her hot eyes, wetting her face, mixing with her sweat until her hair became damp, sticking to her temples, one red strand slashing across her pink cheek. She was crimson and flushed, her head tossing from side to side, mouth open and panting, arms flung helplessly wide at her sides. "No...no...no," she chanted, her heart hammering so fiercely she wondered if she would die.

His fingers pressed deeper, twisting slightly inside of her, burning the rim of her ass with a delicious stretch. "Dinna even think of fucking lying to me," he warned.

"I'm not," she sobbed, nearly lost to reason, ready to beg for him to come inside of her, needing it more than she needed the lemon-scented air to breathe. "I'm not lying."

She felt rather than saw him smile against her open pussy, his lips pressed softly to her shivering, demure hole. "Such a sweet little virgin ass," he rasped, "and it's all mine."

His tongue snaked out to rim her swollen vulva, dipping just inside with a teasing thrust, taking great pleasure in lapping up the honeyed cum that continued to slip the tiny, ravaged slit. He laughed again, a dark, delicious, fallen-angel kind of sound. "It willna be virgin for long, darlin'. But first I want this gorgeous, perfect little cunt, and I canna wait any longer."

"Thank God," Té cried, boneless and weary with need as he pulled away and deftly flipped her back to her stomach, bra twisting beneath her, pressing her down against the now warm sheen of the table, the citrus scent of the polish filling her head.

"I wouldna go thanking him just yet," Kieran warned.

She made a groaning sound of frustration, bucking against his body as he folded himself over her, covering her fragile form even as he felt the complete change overtaking him, his bones cracking as they lengthened, reshaping within his skin.

"Do you really expect me to turn away from you?" she demanded, supporting her head within the cradle of her folded arms.

Gods, why didna she understand?

"I'm a monster, Té. I could kill you with no more than a flick of my wrist…a snap of my jaws."

She took a deep breath beneath him, aware that he was now even larger—more solid and heavy against her back, his skin outrageously hot as it pressed along her length. "I'm more than aware of what you are, Kieran McKendrick—and if you don't hurry up and fuck me, you're going to be damn sorry."

"Close your eyes," he ordered, feeling the fur overtake his burning flesh, fingers and teeth and claws fully extending, speech coming with greater and greater difficulty as his mouth reformed. The soft, rending sounds of transformation filled the heavy air between them—expectant whispers of what was to come.

Her head shook from side to side. "No."

Careful to stay behind her, out of her line of vision, he hissed a frustrated sound of disbelief. "Damn it, woman, close your bloody eyes."

"No," she shouted, adamant in her denial.

"Té…"

"Make me."

"*Woman!*"

"Stuff it, Kieran."

His mouth pressed right to the tender shell of her ear, his breath sweet and warm. "Oh, I'll stuff you, you beautiful little bitch," he snarled. "I'll stuff you so deep you canna breathe—pack you so full you canna swallow without tastin' me at the back o' your throat."

"Then do it already," she sobbed, giving in, screwing her eyes tightly shut. Her arms spread out wide in an act of surrender, her flushed cheek pressed to the gleaming rosewood. Anything, damn it. Anything just to get him where she finally wanted him.

Everything came to her in blinding, perfect detail, like the wrath of the sea at the moment when it breaks itself upon the jagged rocks of the shore in a violent fury of nature. The air was heavy with hopes and desires—her body even heavier, as he pressed fully against her, a solid, impossibly hard wall of muscle and bone, the raw energy of his power and his male, animal self slamming against her like those waves, her body turning like the thrashing foam.

Colors danced against her closed lids, and she pictured him as he'd looked only moments before, determined to memorize this moment forever, to hold it in a perfect crystal within her mind, suspended there for her to revisit again and again. The texture of his lips as they brushed against her nape, so warm and enticing. The rough feel of his masculine hands on her body, lifting her into position. He didn't seduce her, didn't ask for permission, but simply took what he wanted, his tongue licking across her shoulder while the hot, blunt head of his cock probed between her legs with the confidence of a man who knew he had her right where he wanted her. And he did. She was utterly taken, completely in his thrall, every spellbinding detail making her drunk with lust and what she terrifyingly feared was an emotion far more dangerous. The heady warmth of his breath — the intoxicating scent of his skin — all of it tempting her far beyond control.

Kieran reached between their bodies with one hand, opening the kiss-ravaged lips of her pussy, and then he was *finally* there, pressing within, his cock like a hot brand as it forced its way through, the heavy head shoving past the tight rim of her strained vulva with a powerful thrust he could barely contain. She cried out, trying to find her way through the burning pull, but he just kept going, his hips working with driven purpose until he'd pushed at least half of his long length into her. A hoarse, scraping sound of pleasure ripped from her throat, her pussy clamping down hard on inches and inches of pure male perfection, and she could have sworn she'd already found her limit.

But then he pulled back, held, and shoved through her with a hammering drive that buried him all the way inside, the swollen ridge around the head of his cock ramming through tissues that had never before been penetrated. Two consecutive short, grinding thrusts followed, and she felt that final inch rip into her, his balls slammed up tight against her sensitive clit, teasing it with his heat.

Té took in great shuddering breaths through her open mouth, raw cries spilling helplessly from her throat as she tried to assimilate the sensory data overload rioting through her fully penetrated, trembling body — but it was as impossible as trying to lasso the moon. She was too full for thought. And yet, she craved more. Needed to feel him *move*—taking her with all the fury of his need.

As if he read her mind, Kieran growled near her ear, his breath warm and sweet with the scent of her juices, and began to thrust. His cock became a thick, plowing force of possession, claiming everything she had, forcing her to accept even more. She lay on her stomach, gasping and screaming, throaty cries of ecstasy being pounded past her lips with that massive organ, the blunt, heavy head reaching so far into her that she could have sworn it invaded her mind. He took her with thick, plunging strokes, cramming his raging length in again and again, separating the tight, sodden walls of her pussy with ruthless intent.

She could feel the delicious stretch, the dizzying burn as her body clamored to make room for him. His cock was so wonderfully large, so long and thick and powerful, knotted with a heavy network of veins—and though she was no virgin, the tight-fisted clasp of her cunt had *never* known anything like him. Nothing that even came close to the mind-shattering reality of being fucked by Kieran McKendrick.

And then she felt it, that first tentative stroke of his tongue against her vulnerable shoulder, and fiery anticipation blazed through her system, the thought of what he'd do somehow unbearably arousing. She flooded with juices as he breathed heavily against her skin, his body slamming into her with more and more power, a great driving force of possession—and then it happened. A blinding flash of icy, white hot pain as his fangs sank through the fragile skin, sinking deep, her blood rushing free in a warm, steady flow. He lurched against her, his mouth clamped down hard and tight, hips pistoning with maddened frenzy between her thighs, her soft flesh trapped within the vise of his powerful jaws, and she felt the impossible pull of another orgasm gathering within her womb.

Her mouth opened on a soundless scream that shattered her senses, destroying whatever images she'd ever held of herself, replacing them with one that was breathtaking in its power. She felt reborn…transformed…*created* into a magnificent thing of beauty and strength that knew no equal. In crystal clarity, she understood all that he'd tried so desperately to make her see — the meshing of their souls into one intricate, powerful entity — each giving a part of themselves to make one ideal pair. And in that union, their power was equal, a perfect balance that could never be destroyed.

His lips pulled back, sharp growls blasting against her flesh as his teeth remained locked into her burning shoulder, and then he pulsed into her cunt with one hammering thrust, holding himself hard and deep and high. There was a wonderful, painful thickening, and then his magnificent cock exploded, erupting into her clenching depths, triggering her own, his cum spurting in a violent stream, filling her up.

She came until she passed out, lying limp beneath him, replete with soul-altering satisfaction, completely unaware of when he drew his fangs from her body, collapsing helplessly against her.

Kieran took great, sobbing gulps of air, her blood warm and rich in his mouth as he felt the satisfied beast pulling back inside like a well-fed animal, finally content. He pressed a wet kiss to her nape, marveling at the wonder of her — a pure, untainted joy spreading through his veins, springing from the knowledge that they had broken the Council's mating curse together — that he'd found the woman he'd worship for all eternity with every facet of his being and marked her as his own.

And to make it even more extraordinary was the undeniable fact that she was so much more than anything he deserved or had ever thought to find. She was the foundation of his soul, the beat of his heart, the blood pounding powerfully through his veins, giving him life.

In the midst of hell, she'd brought him heaven, and now they were *one*.

His fingertips stroked possessively across the raw wound at her shoulder, a burning happiness filling him so full it was a wonder he didn't shine, shafts of light erupting from his fingers and toes, gleaming from his eyes.

Struggling to his feet, he lifted her into his arms with extreme care, pulling her close against his chest, and carried her through the heavy silence of the house, up to the bedroom that he now accepted as theirs.

He just had to figure out a way to make the headstrong little *gnach* snoring softly into his shoulder accept it, too.

sensual with intent, as he reached out to curve the long, dark fingers of one hand around her left breast, testing the heavy weight. "I'll enjoy it, too."

She gave him a skeptical look that clearly said she wasn't buying it.

"I'm serious," he insisted, his tone going hard with resolve. "No' that I dinna enjoy you like this, but I'd like to see those soft curves again, like the ones you showed off for ol' Daumier."

Té snickered. "Sure you would."

His head cocked to the side, eyes thoughtful as he studied her. "Aye, I would," he replied, voice gone husky with desire, imagining the sweet perfection of sinking into Té's soft, womanly body. He thought she was gorgeous no matter what size she was, but he couldn't deny the eroticism of riding her with those gentle curves back in full force. "You've probably been starving yourself these past months, worrying yourself sick, but there isna anymore need. I want you to be comfortable enough—*happy* enough to simply be yourself."

"Yeah, well, I should, um, call Evan and let her know I'm okay," she mumbled, wanting very much to turn the conversation to something besides her blasted weight. Sheesh, she'd always made herself sick over the fact she wasn't bone skinny, and now that she'd finally toned down, he wanted to fatten her up again. She'd have laughed at the irony of it, if she didn't find it so damn sweet.

Lying on her side, she watched him in the quiet darkness, heavy brocaded curtains keeping out the afternoon sun, the only light a shimmering glow of gold coming from the two thick, pear-scented candles on the mantelpiece. The molten gleam painted his long body like a god, illuminating the sensual line of muscle and bone, the long, heavy weight of his cock as it rested against his hip, still half-hard and purple at the head, the thick width sculpted with bulky veins that corded his length. And what a mind-boggling length it was. But she loved the thickness even better, the way it stretched her so wide, until she could feel her vulva strained to her absolute limit, and then pushed past that point to a searing, pleasure-edged pain as he crammed himself in to the broad root. Shoved himself deep until their bodies sealed together, grinding against one another in sobbing ecstasy.

She'd never known sex could be like that—something that ripped the world out from under your feet, hurtling you to a plane where nothing existed but mind-shattering passion and the undeniable knowledge that you'd shared everything you are with another person. Allowed them to penetrate not only your body, but your heart and soul, as if you could feel them flowing into you, the warmth of their being becoming an essential part of your own.

It was breathtaking in its beauty—stunning in its absoluteness.

She sighed, falling into a decadent, sensual reverie, when his next words struck a jarring chord of irritation.

"There's no need to call Evan," he explained, collecting the tray and glasses, setting everything on his bedside table. "I talked to Lach last night and told him you'd be staying here with me from now on."

Forever.

Té blinked up at him slowly. "And did he ask if I was agreeable to this decision, or do you McKendricks just think you control us little mortals like pets?"

"He didna ask, and considering you now belong to me, he doesna have a right to."

"I'm not a dog, Kieran," she muttered, sitting up beside him, the sheet clutched tightly against her naked chest once again, the beauty and warmth of her thoughts only moments before dimmed by a sudden chill of annoyance. "I don't just *belong* to you. I'm not wearing your damn tags around my neck, am I? Lach should have asked if I wanted to stay here, instead of you two just deciding my future. Who's to say where I'll stay? I can go anywhere I damn well please."

He watched her like one might watch a wild animal, trying to anticipate her next attack. "You wanna know why he didna ask? Maybe because we trust one another."

"Right," she snorted. "You don't trust anyone, McKendrick."

"What the hell is that supposed to mean?" *Shit*, he cursed beneath his breath. *First Lach…and now Té.*

"Are you serious?"

"Aye."

"You fuck me, you *come* in me without any protection, but you won't let me look at you. And then you expect me to believe that you *feel* something for me — something that will last forever? Huh! Nothing lasts without trust, Kieran. Nothing."

"I didna just fuck you, Té. I changed on you…*in you*. I fucking bit you." *Christ, why wasn't she getting it? Why wasn't she running, screaming, hightailing her sweet little ass to the other side of the world?*

"Yeah, I know," she said with a cool, hard voice, shifting her shoulder, the angry puncture wounds swollen and bruised. "I'm not likely to ever forget it. And you know what really sucks, Kieran?"

His shoulders fell. "What?"

One delicate, silver-banded finger poked him hard in the chest. "I liked it, you big idiot!" she seethed, feeling the need to shout and rage well up from within the untamed core of her body. She had years worth of frustration coming to the surface, all of it set free because of the stubborn ass lying beside her, refusing to recognize the truth even though it was staring him right in the face.

"Pretty fucked-up way you have of showing it, Té," he muttered. "*You keep refusing me!*"

"Marriage, if that's what you're even talking about, is difficult enough, without building it upon a careless foundation. Without unconditional trust, everything else just falls apart."

"It's more than bloody marriage I want from you, woman. Once it's done, there's no going back."

She gave him an infuriating nod. "Then all the more reason for me to refuse."

"*You. Willna. Bloody. Refuse. Me,*" he gritted through his teeth, dark eyes glittering like shards of black ice. "I've claimed you, and now no other man will *ever* touch you, Té. I'd kill him first. Fucking beat him into a miserable little puddle on the ground. Do you understand that?"

"You can threaten all you like, Kieran, but the truth is that you don't feel enough for me. If you did, you'd have given me all of you. You'd believe enough in me to know that I could take it, instead of hiding."

"That's bullshit," he growled, hating that she was partly right—only it was himself he didn't trust, not her.

She leaned closer, blue eyes alight with passionate anger. "Is it? You fucked me. You bit me. Your curse is broken. But guess what, gorgeous? You're still going to want to get furry and fuck. You can deny it all you want, but it's what you are, Kieran. Are we supposed to go through the rest of our lives with you turning away from me, hiding, because you don't think I can take it?"

The muscled length of his golden body shuddered with tension. "This isna fair, Té."

"And what you're asking isn't fair, either. Why don't you think about that?"

"Why dinna you fucking think about *this,*" he hissed, catching her—pulling her into him.

His mouth slashed over hers, a violent force of need that demanded submission, and her lips felt bruised from the delicious assault as she eagerly tangled her tongue with his, determined to give as good as she got.

Her aggression jolted him for the mere span of a second, and then he kissed her even harder, his head moving from one angle to another as he struggled to get deeper into her, his chest heaving, the air filled with his masculine groans.

She lost herself in the wicked demands of his kiss until she felt him wedge one large, incredibly warm hand beneath her bottom, lifting her into him, one long finger playing at the puckered entrance of her ass. She started, but recognized the hiss of acceptance pouring from between her lips. "*Yesssss.* God, Kieran, yes."

Her slippery juices slid into the crease between the round globes of her cheeks, and it was a carnal thrill to feel the way he wet his fingers in her cream, rubbing the slick fluids into the tiny entrance. He played with her, teasing her ass with the tips of his fingers, while the desire threatened to erupt between them, building and building to a fevered pitch that felt like death and life all at once—both a wondrous beginning and a mind-shattering end.

It was so fucking hot—as frightening as it was intoxicating, the knowledge that each moment between them led them deeper into the other, binding them together until they felt like two halves of one complete entity—an utter loss of self while at the same time thrilling with the discovery of new life.

Blistering heat seared between their sweat-slick skin, burning, running in rivulets across the blazing surface of their writhing limbs as they each tried to crawl into the other. With mouths open, their breaths coming in sharp, rushed bursts of hunger, they reveled in the damp slide of hot flesh and the erotic scent of sex. Kieran's muscles bulged, hard as iron, mastering her feminine, quivering form with expert care, and she willfully surrendered.

She was so full on lust she felt drunk. So full of Kieran that she thought she'd burst from the pressure as he fitted the blunt head of his massive cock against her creamy entrance and crammed himself in with one hard, powerful, hammering stroke. They cried out as the snug channel of muscle gave way to his force with a stunning, delicious friction that gripped him like a fist, her wet cunt contracting to hold him tight within her.

His mouth was hot, open against her own, but he didn't kiss her. No, he simply breathed into her, filling her lungs with his own breath, and it was nearly as erotic as the blissful feel of that magnificent cock pulling the muscles of her pussy so wide they felt stretched beyond bearing. And yet, she held him so greedily, demanding more again and again, unable to get enough of this magnificent creature to whom she longed to give everything she was, for all eternity.

"Saephus, you're the hottest little cunt I've ever had, Té. The way you squeeze me so tight. The way you're so tender and wet." His cock stroked her narrow sheath in a heavy rhythm, pounding her with the full force of his strength and weight, the entire mass of his granite-hard, blood-filled shaft ramming her with an almost vicious intensity, as if each deep shove could make her understand what he wanted...*needed* to tell her, but couldn't say. And all the while, his fingers played provocatively between her cheeks, teasing the puckered entrance of her backside, her thigh thrown over his strong, hammering hip.

"And this sweet little virgin ass," he growled, pounding the heavy mass of his shaft in and out of her, forcing her pussy to accept those long, wide, intimidating inches of hot, thick cock again and again. Her vision blurred and she knew she'd reached the limit of her senses, her body flushed and writhing with an overload of sensation as another insanely intense orgasm seemed to build up from the very depths of her soul.

And then suddenly one finger was breaching the exquisitely tight ring of muscle, pushing up into the searing heat of her ass without hesitation, forcing its way through, demanding entrance. She came instantly, jerking with such force it shocked her that she didn't knock him to the floor. But Kieran was nothing but rock-hard muscle and savage male, and he simply moved over her, pressing her down deeper into the giving softness of his mattress, forcing her to take the pleasure for everything it was worth while he held his cock high and hard inside of her. He held it there, stretching the clenching muscles of her cunt so impossibly wide while they struggled to clamp down, and then a second large finger joined the first, the two long digits lodged completely up her backside.

Té gulped much needed blasts of air, while Kieran shuddered above her, working his fingers deeper and deeper, until his cock resumed its rhythm and continued to give her the kind of fuck she'd only ever thought to feel in her dreams. Hard and rough and brutal, as if he'd die without the feel of her soaking, cum-drenched pussy to sink into over and over.

She nearly came again as his teeth bit into her lower lip, drawing on the stinging flesh, and he whispered, "Christ, feel all that sweet cum coating me. It's so perfect it blows my mind. Fucking you," he panted, struggling to explain, his voice gruff with lust and all the raging things he felt for this woman, "being in you, it's like *nothing* I've ever had before."

He lifted his head so he could look into her passion-glazed eyes, his upper body supported by the elbow of his free arm, and smiled with a wicked promise, his cock punctuating his words as he crammed it in deeper and deeper, changing his angle of penetration with the shifting of his hips. "This is the only cunt I've ever felt come on my naked skin, Té. The only one I've ever sunk into without a rubber. The only one I'll *ever* feel again. *Only* one I'll ever — so long as I live this life and every one to follow — will want or take. And I'm going to make you come like this every damn day and night, just so I can feel this tiny cunt sucking on my dick…my fingers…my tongue, soaking me with all this rich, sweet cream."

"*More,*" she pleaded, lifting her open mouth against his, reveling in the way his mouth attacked, utterly savage in its intensity. Then just as suddenly he ripped his lips from hers. They pulled back over his teeth, and she drank in his bursts of smoky, wine-flavored breaths, feeling intoxicated by the impact his words made on her mind. Her short nails dug into his bulging biceps, and she moaned, working her pleasure-filled pussy and bottom on his powerful, talented fingers and cock, demanding even more — all of it — everything he could give her.

"Do you know how tight you squeeze me when I do this?" he grunted, twisting his fingers inside her ass, pressing the tips into the thin wall that separated them from his pounding, burgeoning cock.

She smiled beneath him, shifting so she could wrap one slender arm around his pistoning, muscled buttocks, twisting beneath him, shocking him into a sudden, violent stillness as she wriggled the tip of her index finger into the hot, taut rim of his own ass. He opened his mouth, but no sound escaped as she pushed it slightly deeper, and his cock nearly erupted into her then and there, feeling as if it tripled in size from the pounding rush of blood, the tendons in his neck defined with sleek prominence as his body jerked to a sudden, heart-jolting stop deep inside of her.

He swallowed, black eyes fixed on her own, throat working as he struggled for his voice, a small vein ticking rapidly in his temple, and she knew that she had him right on the edge. With a siren smile, she pushed her finger even deeper, nearly burying it up the searing heat of his ass, and she could have sworn his eyes nearly crossed with the look of stunned pleasure falling over his gorgeous face. She'd clearly shocked him, and it was a sinful delight to know she'd managed to do something so wonderfully new to a man as sexually experienced as her wicked Warlock.

"Bloody fucking hell," he finally grunted, just as she got her finger completely thrust up his hole, pressing the "trigger" she'd read would be there in one of her favorite erotic romances, and the impossible inches of thick cock buried up her cunt suddenly blasted her with a violent, vicious force of hot, sizzling cum.

"*Fuck, fuck, fuck,*" he panted over and over, cum continuing to jerk from the heavy head of his cock, though his erection remained rock-hard and ready. He pressed his forehead against her own, his hair falling around their faces like a thick veil of black silk while he struggled for breath…for control, and she felt his cock twitch at the exact moment he pulled back his fingers and rammed them up her ass so hard she nearly screamed with the hot burst of pleasure spearing through her.

They were soaked in the other's cum, their bodies sweat-slick and aching from pleasure—and yet, Té knew he was nowhere near done with her yet. Somehow, they were just getting started, and she couldn't help but be thrilled by the knowledge. He made her feel like an insatiable, bloodthirsty little nympho, and God help her, she loved every single decadent second of it.

Kieran stared down at her, feeling himself fall into her—body, heart, and soul—his cock throbbing at the luscious feel of being buried up her juicy cunt and his ass burning with pleasure at the sensation of her finger beginning to fuck him. She worked him with a soft, lazy pattern, pulling out a few inches and then gently thrusting back inside, giving him a little more each time. He couldn't believe what she'd done…or his reaction to the thrill of having a part of her inside of him. Not to mention the fact that he was still hard and aching, crammed up her lush little cunt, her succulent tits cushioning his chest, feeling each beat of her heart as it pulsed around him, each breath as her chest panted against his own. It hit him so hard he would have fallen on his ass if he'd been standing—the undeniable fact that his entire life now rested in the hands and heart and womb of the perfect little creature beneath him. She could cut him and kill him with a word, and the knowledge of the power she held over him was as terrifying as it was beautiful.

The words rushing up through him stuck in his throat as the fear clawed them back from his very soul, disgust swelling so thick he nearly choked on it. He'd never been afraid of anything in his entire life, and now he was so fucking frightened it made him sick. Scared shitless of losing the only thing he'd ever honestly wanted—knew he couldn't go on without.

His eyes moved over her face, marveling at the beauty of her expression as he moved within her. She looked at him with what could only be *love*—the one thing that could scare the ever-loving hell out of him, because he didn't know what he would do if he lost it…*lost her*.

His eyes found the bruised, angry bite of his monster on the tender junction of her neck and shoulder, and the knowledge of his undeniable possession filled every cell in his body, pumping with life and lust...and what he knew was nothing short of absolute devotion. The kind of love that never died. That went beyond this life, into the other. That went beyond the flesh. The kind that would always gladly bind him to this woman. He'd told her he'd never want another, and he'd known it was the truth from the very second he'd set eyes on her.

And, damn it, he *knew* there had to be a way to prove it to her—to make her understand. If he had to fuck her into submission and acceptance until she was blissfully raw, then Saephus help him, it was exactly what he'd do.

"You can't hide from it forever, Kieran."

He blinked down at her, thinking it was eerie how well she could read him, even when they were buried up one another. Her soft murmur struck a definite nerve, and his beast shifted into sudden awareness, waiting for its turn to pounce and claim—anxious for its turn to fuck the hell out of their woman. He worried that he'd lose control with her, but he didn't pull back. Instead he traced the sensuous upper curve of her lip with his tongue, nipped tenderly at her chin, nuzzling her jaw. "You fucking kill me, lass. I look at you and I canna breathe. I get inside of you and my heart stops. *I willna lose you.*" It was a snarled statement of *fact.* "Never. So dinna even bother making the threat."

She didn't say anything, simply gave him a slow, knowing smile that infuriated his Warlock's need for dominance and control—the beast's determined desire to force it from her. The little *gnach* was playing with fire, and may her god help her, he was looking forward to showing her just how serious he was in his intent to claim her for his own—for eternity.

And then his deep voice was all smooth seduction as he drawled, "But let's no' fight while we fuck, Té."

She shifted sinuously beneath him, then tightened the muscles in her cunt, squeezing him so tight his breath hissed through his teeth. "Are we still fucking, Kieran?" she asked with a husky rasp to her voice, the sound tingling down his spine, curling around the burning pleasure of his speared backside.

"You've still got your sweet little finger rammed up my ass, lass. And I've still got you packed front and back. So, aye, I'd say you'd best be expecting more fucking."

A satisfied smile spread slowly across her lush mouth, and she began thrusting her finger once more, dancing it within his tight hole, just as his dick began grinding inside the tight clasp of her cum-soaked cunt and his own fingers began screwing her ass. "I do so love how insatiable you are, Kieran," she panted, her body jolting beneath him. "Is that a Scot thing, or strictly a Warlock trait?"

He pulled his cock out to the tight mouth of her pussy, then lunged back in, forcing a hungry moan from her parted lips as all that thick, vein-ridged flesh parted her muscles, packing her with pleasure. "It's a Brontë thing, darlin'. Anytime my dick gets anywhere near you, all it wants to do is fuck you raw and feel you come."

"Mmm…lucky me," she moaned, stretching her arm to keep her finger thrust up the hot tunnel of his ass as his hips began to pound his big, beautiful cock into her, not wanting to pull out of him just yet. In fact, she wanted to push him as much as he pushed her. A carnal smile of challenge curled her lips and she quickly pushed a second finger alongside the first, twisting further to the side for better reach, gasping as his cock penetrated at a new, delicious angle. He closed tight around her slim digits, and she curled them into him, loving the way he jolted in shock at the erotic feel of her stroking penetration.

His eyes narrowed as he stared down at her, black ice glittering with fire, his cock pumping hard enough to jerk a sudden cry from her lips, the sound lost somewhere between ecstasy and pain.

"You're going to fucking pay for that, lass."

"For daring to fuck you?" she asked in a sudden breath, digging her fingers deeper, wanting to push him to lose that maddening control of his.

"No...for pushing me too far. For testing my control. For *tempting* me to give it to you exactly the way I'd love to."

"Well, don't hold back on my account," she challenged. "Have at me, beautiful."

His smile was so full of the devil that for a moment she wondered if she'd bitten off more than she could chew, but he didn't give her time to reconsider. Within seconds their fingers were free and his wet cock withdrawn, her body being turned over with such ease she could only marvel at this man's—*this Warlock's*—overpowering strength. She'd barely taken a breath before she found herself face first in the bedding, her legs spread blatantly wide as he positioned her up on her knees, ass presented high and vulnerable for his to do with as he pleased. She turned her face into the soft, sex-scented linens, breathing in huge lungfuls of their sweat and cum, finding the soft, rich scents unbearably erotic.

His stiff cock nudged her thigh as his rough palms smoothed over her cheeks, pulling them apart until she felt the pleasure pulling at her hole. Her cunt creamed like crazy, drenching her folds and the tops of her thighs, desperate to please.

"You owe me, and I'm taking payment right here, lass," he growled, and she nearly screamed at the feel of his tongue lapping at the puckered entrance. Her head turned side to side as she forgot how to breathe—forgot everything but the erotic feel of his tongue digging into her ass, pushing her open, rooting into the tight passage, fucking her with a long, lazy lick.

"*Oh hell...oh God,*" she panted, thinking she'd die as he pulled it out, then rooted deeper, ravenous in his demands, giving her a slow, delicious tongue-fuck in the last place she'd ever thought to feel one.

Then he was moving over her, mounting her, and she felt the wide, wet head of his cock teasing her ass, pressing forward, demanding entrance. "You ready to have this pretty little ass fucked, Té?"

"*Yessss*," she hissed, pushing back against him, desperate to feel him breach her opening and invade her in a way that she'd never thought she could crave with such savage abandon and hunger.

His breath touched the sensitive shell of her ear an instant before she heard him whisper, "Then beg me."

Her breath hitched. "What?"

He nipped at her lobe, teasing her with the scrape of his teeth. "You heard me, beautiful. *Beg me*."

He held her hips and pressed, stretching just inside the tight entrance, and she couldn't have stopped the words if her life depended on it. "Yes…*please*. Please, Kieran. *Fuck me*."

His tongue licked her ear, teeth nipping lightly at her neck. "Where, lass?"

"My ass," she groaned, shivering with excitement from her toes to the tops of her ears. "Please, fuck my ass. Fill me up with that huge cock. Make me take it. *Force* me to take it."

He went absolutely still behind her, muscles clenched, poised on the taut line of anticipation. "All of it?" he rasped.

"All of it. Fuck me, Kieran. *Make me scream*."

He drew a great shuddering breath, control helplessly shattered by her raw cry and the fisting heat of her tight little hole around the wide head of his cock. "I shouldna be doing this without any lube," he moaned helplessly, knowing that he damn well would anyway. "You're too bloody tight, baby."

"I don't care," she argued, husky voice muffled from the pillow. "And it's not as if I'm not—*wet*, damn it. Just use that."

He laughed a soft, strained sound at her commanding tone, then used his calloused fingertips to bring more of that sleek, sweet juice slipping from her succulent cunt back toward her gorgeous ass, covering his dick and her rosy little asshole. Every second he held back pushed him that much closer to the breaking point, until he finally couldn't hold back any longer and forced the thick head of his dick just a fraction deeper. Gritting his jaw against the impossible pleasure, Kieran worked his hips in a slow, rocking motion, the brutal width of his dick sliding in a little further with each thrusting dig, until he'd buried nearly half the length up that precious, virgin opening, her juices providing just enough lube to make it possible, though he knew it must hurt like a son-of-a-bitch. Still, you'd have never known it from the hot little moans breaking out of her, the throaty pleas jerking from her lush lips as he penetrated that tight, tender ass, inch by delicious inch.

Kieran looked down at their joined bodies with feral eyes, a crazed sense of possession reaching into his chest and squeezing painfully around his heart. Her cheeks were spread and rosy, trembling with his grinding, shallow strokes, the tiny little fissure of her ass stretched excruciatingly open around the deep reddish flush of his cock.

"Ah Té," he groaned, pushing forward, giving her yet another inch, knowing he was already packing her full. "Ah Saephus, lass, I wish you could see this. You're so beautiful, baby. This tight little ass packed so full o' me."

She moaned a hoarse sound beneath him, lifting up higher, clearly loving it, and he trembled, knowing he wouldn't last much longer. His rough palms moved over her flanks, thumbs slipping between to pull her cheeks even wider, his next stroke spearing another inch into her heated depths, jerking a startled cry of pleasure from her throat. "Yeah, I wish you could see this shiny little ass, all wet with cunt juice, just gleaming in the candlelight. You're beautiful, Té," he growled, his hips jerking faster, balls tightening as he struggled to hold back the flood. "*So fucking beautiful.*"

She wiggled against him, trying to draw in more of those incredible inches, and it was too much. With a rough, strangled shout, he fell over her, reaching beneath her jerking hips, seeking the ripe little bud of her clit. Trapping it within two fingers, he sawed at it until she screamed a raw cry of release, body clenching as another orgasm ripped through her sex-ravaged cunt, and she shoved back hard, nearly taking him to the root.

Stars exploded before his eyes at the feel of being crammed up her tight ass, the contractions rippling through her cunt pulsing against his buried shaft, and a blistering surge of sizzling cum erupted from the head of his cock, blasting into her. His mouth opened helplessly against his bite in her shoulder, harsh shouts bursting from his throat until the last drop mercifully pulsed free, draining him.

And when it was finally over and they were deliciously spent, they fell to the bed in a tangle of limbs, neither moving but for the harsh expansions of their lungs—slow, satisfied smiles curving their swollen lips.

"I'll—I'll beg for that anytime," Té wheezed over their panting breaths, and his chest shook with laughter against her back, their flesh slick, front and back glued helplessly together with sweat, his cock still packed up tight inside the warm clench of her body.

Kieran pressed his lips to the raw wound of his bite, laving it slowly with his tongue, his heart so full he didn't know how it kept from shattering. "So long as you're only beggin' *me*," he growled playfully, giving her a gentle nudge that sent nerve endings in a sudden rush of sensation that left her gasping. "I'm afraid I'm going to be as possessive of this little hole as I am of the other two."

A soft, satisfied sigh met his ears. "I'll keep that in mind, gorgeous."

He nipped softly at her earlobe, tugging purposefully at her clit, confident in the bonds that now held them together. "See that you do, angel. See that you do."

Chapter Fifteen

When Té came back from freshening up in the bathroom, after Kieran had taken his own turn, she found him propped up against the heavy mahogany of his headboard. He had several fluffy, white down pillows stuffed behind his back, one knee bent, cock hard and deliciously thick, rising as proud as the ancient oak standing just outside the bedroom window. The heavy curtains had been pulled back, allowing brilliant splashes of late afternoon sunlight to stream in through the white gauze of the inner curtains, painting his magnificent body with an incandescent light.

Rays of soft, shimmering gold bathed his dark skin, giving life to all the vivid details of his long body, so breathtaking it looked as if he actually glowed with heat. He lay there like a Renaissance masterpiece, something too beautiful for words—as if they'd captured an ancient warrior in a sensual moment of repose. The soft light lay achingly…breathtakingly erotic across the masculine lines of his body, giving life to each separate perfection. Té drank him in with her hungry eyes, feeling drunk from the wealth of beauty he so effortlessly presented.

And yet, he was too wonderfully rugged…too dangerous…to ever be called pretty. Beautiful, yes—but pretty was too delicate a word to describe the dark skin stretched taut across the corded muscles and long, powerful bones. The mapping of scars across his arms, legs, and even torso spoke of his life as a soldier. And yet, they only added to the masterpiece, rather than detracted.

She wanted hours, days…even years to explore all that strong, rugged, masculine terrain. She wanted to run her small palms over the heady power of his biceps, trail them down the lean sides of his torso, then settle them into the twin shallows at his hips and pelvis. Wanted to explore lower, across the long length of bulging thigh, strong shin, down to those big, hair-sprinkled feet. Wanted time to explore the jagged scar on his left kneecap, the dark, silky hairs of his powerful legs, working her way back up to that mouthwatering cock.

She tilted her head as she gave her total concentration to his magnificent erection, knowing that on most men it would have seemed extreme. But on Kieran's long, masculine form it was a perfect fit—the ultimate crowning perfection. Thick, dark, and long, jerking slightly beneath her avid attention as she hungrily stared, curving up and across the ripped expanse of his abdomen.

His eyes followed her with an equally hungry intent as she walked to him, for once in her life utterly comfortable in her nudity, her breasts swaying, nipples puffy and hard, cresting before her. When she reached the foot of the bed, she crawled up between his strong legs, eyeing the beautiful bulge of his balls beneath the stiff column of his purple-headed cock. Her eyes explored from there, drinking him in, until they reached the ebony brilliance of his long, devilish mane. "I love your hair," she murmured, her voice husky from all the cries of pleasure she'd sobbed throughout the long day. "It's so sinful and dark. So black it's almost blue. Beautiful."

He grimaced and she smiled, knowing she'd embarrassed him by calling him beautiful. Men were such funny creatures. You could talk about the size of their cocks all day and night, but mention a pretty feature and they went pink with discomfort.

"I thought all little girls dreamed of having a white knight," he grunted, clearly trying to cover his uneasiness. "You know—all blond curls and baby blue eyes."

Her full, kissable, *fuck-me* lips lifted in a tempting smile, and he was more *tempted* than he could've ever thought possible. He wanted to slip between their fleshy, slick surfaces—cock, tongue, *anything*—and just spill into her through that little sexy, fuckable hole. Her tongue flicked out to lick the pouting fullness of the lower one, and he actually felt the tip of his dick release a hot burst of fluid, moistening the head. He felt that burst of pre-cum like a bullet traveling the huge length of his shaft, sizzling within his flesh, then erupting from the slit in search of her moist mouth.

Oh…fuck… yesssssss.

In a second he was going to be on his knees, rubbing that burst of pre-cum into her tongue, watching her swallow that first bit of his taste, and then he was going to fuck her mouth, forcing his cock between those juicy lips until he was flooding the back of her throat and she was taking every inch of him. Every single burning, throbbing, aching inch.

She was going to eat his cock and he'd love every single second of it.

He was so unbelievably hot, burning alive as he lifted his thumb to the corner of her mouth, testing the resilience of her flesh, running the calloused pad across the lush expanse of pink. Again, he felt the animal shift, rearranging itself within his skin, and he knew with the inherent knowledge of his power that the *beithíoch* would always be there. He'd no longer be able to force him to the background, leashing him in, pretending that he wasn't an integral part of him. The animal had tasted freedom and feasted on the most amazing, incredible, mind-shattering woman Kieran had ever known—the fuck of his life—and it was now here to stay. He'd have to adjust, to learn to live with it and accept, because he wanted…needed…*had* to have Té by his side forever.

Her eyes glazed with passion as she licked the tip of his thumb with her pink tongue, bringing a rough, rumbling growl from between his lips that neither recognized as human. But she didn't even blink. If anything, her eyes went darker, as if she not only accepted that feral, primitive part of his soul, but wanted it.

Maybe even loved it.

The hunger knotted within his cock like a fist of pain and lust and something else—something so dark and needy he had no word for it—and it was all he could do not to throw her to the ground, lift that rosy little ass up in the air, and fuck her so hard she shattered around him. Hard and hungry, with sweat and growls and the heavy, pounding, hammering rhythm of a lust that he'd never be able to satisfy. Every time he looked at her, he only wanted her more.

Her teeth nipped his still stroking thumb, the only sound— the rough, uneven cadence of their breathing—and he nearly buckled, ready to fuck her until it hurt them both.

Saephus, didn't she know how much danger she was courting? Why didn't she turn away in fear and run from the risk, instead of teasing it…tempting it with that little fuckable mouth and the promise of heaven he'd find in her tender, lush, *so sweet little cunt*. The hottest, most delicious, tightest little pussy he'd ever had. The one he'd claimed as his and no other's the moment his fangs had sunk into her shoulder, marking her—her hot, sweet blood flowing into his belly like the richest, most decadent of sins.

"Faith, lass, I'm no white knight. I'm the devil and you're playing with fire again."

She lifted her brows. "Mmm…maybe that's because I like the heat."

"And I'm afraid I'll burn you so badly, you'll run. I dinna have my control with you. No' a single bloody shred of it. All I have is hunger and need and things you wouldna even understand." His hand gripped her jaw, pulling her closer. "There's so much going on inside o' me, Té. So much coming to life, and it's all centered on you, as if my heart no longer fucking beats for me, but for the both of us—for no more than the promise of seeing you and hearing you…*and touching you*. Of fucking you, Té. I canna—*willna*—get enough of sinking into you…*ever*. And instead o' getting easier, I want you more each time, as if each taste only makes me hunger to take you that much more, when I already want you so badly I ache in my bones from it. I crave you, Té, like I'm starving for just a sip of you."

She stared straight at him, not backing down an inch. "You know the thing about fairy tales, Kieran? Not all little girls dream of the white knight. Not all of them want safe, boring ol' Prince Charming and his life of tedious luxury."

A small, wry smile twisted his lips. "And what did you dream of, lil' Té?"

"I always wanted the Black Knight," she whispered, weaving a warm, intimate spell around them with her words. "The bad boy. When I lay in bed at night and touched myself between my legs, running my fingers through the warm folds of my sex, I dreamed of the one with danger in his eyes—the one with the *real* power to show me what could be between a man and a woman. The one who would know what to do with me once he got me within his castle chamber, or his carriage, or wherever the hell else he decided I needed to be *fucked*. That's what I thought about while my fingers stroked my cunt and I came all over my teenage nightgowns."

Her words, spoken so low and throaty, sent a sledgehammer of desire right through the core of his cock. It tightened his lungs, squeezed at his heart, hammering away at his promise not to take her again—too soon—even though he knew damn well that he would.

"Remember when I said I hadna wanted another woman since I met you?"

She sat back on her heels, her heart beating triple time within her chest. "Yeah?"

"I lied." In one deft movement, he rolled her beneath him, pinning her with his hard, solid weight. "I've no' wanted one since *before* I met you—because my heart already knew you were out there. The first time I saw that little picture of you in Evan's wallet, it was like a bolt of lightning shot straight through me. I almost fucking changed then and there, even though I didna really understand any of it at the time. But my beast recognized you, my power recognized you—and my *soul* recognized you."

"Soul mates?" she questioned in a breathless rush. "I never knew you were such a romantic."

"Yeah, well, the thought that you were mine was immediately followed by one that said you were mine to fuck—so I'm no' sure you should hold out much hope on the whole romance bit," he chuckled around a crooked smile.

"Oh, I don't know. You claim I'm your soul mate, you vow to kill to protect me, are stupidly willing to risk your life to do just that, and promise to always be faithful. I'd say that's pretty damn romantic, big guy."

His eyes narrowed down at her. "Yeah well, just dinna go telling anybody."

She nodded, studying him with those deep, dark eyes that he felt he could lose himself in…forever. "If you're serious, then I should probably warn you that if you were really mine, I'd most likely kill you if you ever cheated. Maim you at the least."

With tender strokes, he brushed her hair back from the smooth perfection of her brow. "Yeah, well, I'd kill myself, but it's no' something you'll ever have to worry about. And it doesna get more serious than this."

Té squeezed her eyes shut against the heady temptation of his emotion-filled gaze. "Yeah, yeah, I know—because you *promised* to be faithful, huh?"

Her voice was almost solemn—all traces of teasing vanishing as quickly as they'd appeared—and his dark head shook in exasperation. "It doesna get hard for anyone but you, lass. No' anymore. And it never will again. And someday you're going to believe that."

"Someday?" she questioned, arching one brow in perfect imitation of his own arrogant expression.

His wicked lips twisted into a sexy, knowing smile. "Aye, after we've spent the next—"

"Don't say it," she whispered, squeezing her eyes shut once more, all traces of amusement vanished from her glowing face.

"Té," he rasped, running his lips across her cheekbone, stroking the delectable little beauty mark with the soft pad of his tongue. She trembled in his arms, but she didn't give in.

"Not like this, Kieran." Her eyes opened, blinking slowly up at him, shadowed with mystery. "You can't just dictate to me what our future is going to be. It doesn't work like that."

He stared down at her with nothing short of pure, unadulterated resolve. "That's how it works in mine."

Her mouth thinned with anger, hands pushing against his warm, solid chest until he finally loosened his grip, allowing her to scoot out of his reach. She sat on the edge of the bed, looking back at him over the delicate, golden line of her shoulder, her eyes huge in her pretty face. "Not in mine."

Kieran climbed out of the bed with rough, anger-tinged movements, the air around her swirling with tints of warm, red-splashed energy. "You'll do as I say, damn it," he vowed, stepping into his jeans. "You're my mate, and that bloody well means we make it permanent."

Her head cocked to the side, expression suddenly more inquisitive than irritated. "Meaning?"

The sharp nod of his head said he already believed the matter to be settled. "Meaning we get bonded."

Té licked her lips. "You mean like Lach and Evan?"

"Aye," he murmured, narrowing his gaze...not liking her tone.

"No."

"What do you mean, no?"

She shrugged her shoulders in a calm gesture of control, as if she weren't nearly dying inside, her heart wanting to give in, though her will refused. "I mean it just like it sounded. No."

She watched as every muscle in his long, dark body hardened with tension, his disbelief and pain obvious in the way he held himself, all tight lines and rigid dignity. "You can fight it all you like," he vowed in a low, hard voice, "but nothing'll ever change the fact that you're mine, Té. What we have, it's no' going to disappear just because you think you can make it go away—ignore it or deny it or whatever the hell you think it is you're doing."

She held his glittering stare, and tried to convey with her eyes what she could not tell him with words. "Maybe I'm waiting for a better reason to bond myself to a man for all eternity than him simply saying 'it's going to happen'? Maybe I'm waiting for something *more*, Kieran."

His eyes flashed, mouth a hard line of frustration as he stared at her from across the darkening room, the growing shadows between them seeming to symbolize this rift they couldn't work their way across—not without one of them giving what they expected the other to give first. Neither willing to risk it—to make that first terrifying leap into the unknown, opening their heart and soul to the other.

Gritting his teeth, Kieran's black gaze drilled into her, as if he could use his power to make her submit, though he knew far too well her heart was something he could never control. No—the prize he wanted was one all his powerful *Magick* could never provide. It was something that would have to be given freely.

But that didn't mean the man in him was any less desperate to have it. "Damn it, Té, you *will* bloody well bond with me. Fight all you like, sweetheart, but that's my fucking bite in your shoulder and my cum in your sweet little cunt. And before this goddamn nightmare is over, you're going to admit you belong to me…forever."

She watched him from her position on the edge of the bed, letting his angry determination wash over her, fueling her own purpose and will. "We'll see about that, babe. But something tells me I don't take orders as easily as you'd like."

* * * * *

That fact was proven not thirty minutes later, as Kieran tried to convince her that leaving her in his father's cozy library for the night was the right thing to do.

"Damn it, dinna be doing this again, Té. I canna hunt when I'm worried you'll no' be staying where I've put you."

"And what makes you think I'll stay just because you've pointed your finger and told me to?"

"If you run, I'll track you down and bring you right back where you belong. I dinna care if I have to kill a fucking path to get to you—you are no' ever...*ever*...getting away from me, woman. Make sure you understand that before you do something stupid."

"As stupid as you trying to track down Maldari on your own?"

Black eyes narrowed with outraged pride. "I told you I can handle the little bastard *Gan Bhrí*. Do you really doubt me?"

Té paced before him, hands planted angrily on her slim hips. "I think you underestimate him, yes, and what he's capable of. You're so angry, you'll walk right into one of his traps just to get your hands on him. And he doesn't fight with honor, Kieran."

It was galling to know that she thought Maldari could pose any kind of threat to him. Hell, he could crush the little weasel with his bare hands, and here she thought he should be worried. "He dies for what he's done, Té. No one hurts you and lives to remember it."

"Then you should let me help. If we're really a couple, if you really believe all that you've claimed, then we're partners. We do this *together*."

"No way in hell," he grunted, shaking his dark head. "I willna let you witness his death."

And she knew that what he really meant was that he wouldn't let her see him *kill*. Everything hinged on his fear of her turning away from him—his belief that she would eventually think him a monster.

"And if you die instead?"

"Do you have so little faith in me?" he rasped.

"Don't worry, Kieran. I give as much trust as I get." And with those whispered words, she closed the library door in his face, the significant click of the lock feeling like a sharp slap across his burning face.

He stood there in the empty hallway, staring stupidly at the scuffed toes of his boots, knowing what he should do but too bloody afraid to do it.

There was still that little bit of himself that remained disgustingly afraid. Afraid of how she really felt. Terrified of what she'd say in return if he opened his veins and spilled the truth of his heart. He'd given her so much of himself…but withheld that *one part* that he knew she needed.

Knew—because he needed the same damn thing from her.

They were like two opposing warriors at a stalemate, evenly matched, neither willing to take that final, terrifying step that would lead to either mutual surrender or destruction.

He reached out to open the door, just as his father rounded the end of the hall. "The Council is waiting, Kieran."

With a deep, fortifying breath, he released the handle, promising himself he would do it tomorrow. Yeah, tomorrow, when she woke in his arms, the sun streaming across the beautiful features of her face, shining through the silken locks of her hair—*then he would tell her.*

Then he'd give her the words he already knew were true— had known for some time now, if he were completely honest with himself.

And in doing so, he would be offering her the trust—*the faith*—she so very much wanted him to give.

Yes, he sighed to himself. *Tomorrow.*

* * * * *

"She refused."

"*She what?*" Reggie shouted, nearly falling out of his chair around the great table in Iain's study.

"She bloody refused," Kieran muttered, hating that he was being forced to discuss such an intimate topic, even if it *was* with his family.

Seamus looked as if he'd faint. His hand clutched at his strong chest as he sagged against the cushioned back of his chair. "*She canna do that*," he stammered, clearly scandalized by the thought.

"Yeah?" Kieran snorted, his pride stinging as fiercely as he'd known it would when he had to present the unbelievable news to the Council. "Well, you try telling that to her."

"But…in all my years…I've never heard of such a thing. It just isna done!" Seamus ended on an outraged roar.

Kieran opened his mouth, but his father cut him off, holding a hand across his son's chest to signal it was now *his* turn to take control of the situation. "Seamus, I'll remind you that the boy's heart is involved here, and your archaic attitude is no' helping anyone. We canna simply make the lass accept a bonding that she feels we are all trying to force her into—"

"Force?" Seamus thundered, clearly livid. "Is *that* what you call our sacred traditions? *Force!*"

"That's how the lass sees it," Iain insisted, nodding his white head. "You know how those Americans are. No respect for tradition, although in this case I'm afraid I must agree. If I were in her shoes, I wouldna want to be pledging myself to a man who hadna once told me what was in that black heart of his, either."

His uncles looked equally taken aback. "Is this true, Kieran?" Donald demanded, deep voice rough with disbelief. "Have you no' told her how it is between a *Magick* and his mate?"

Kieran stepped forward to stand beside his father. "Thanks for nothing," he muttered beneath his breath, and to his irritation his father only smiled. *Wily old bastard*, he thought, sensing the trap his Da had so cleverly set before him. Saephus, when was he going to learn never to underestimate the man? It was…*embarrassing*.

"No' exactly," he said in a firm voice, addressing the Council, though now that it was here, out in the open, he suddenly couldn't understand why he'd been so bloody afraid to just say it. The gods knew it was true. Knew that he *loved* her with everything that he was—everything he would ever be. *Forever*.

And suddenly he didn't want to live a moment longer without telling her so. Without opening his heart and letting her completely in, right where she belonged. Where he knew she would always be.

"If you'll excuse me," he said in a hurried rush, bowing to the Council as he quickly made his way to the door with long, purpose-filled strides. Loud voices called out to him, but by the time he reached the hallway he was already running. There was a savage desperation in his soul to hold her in his arms, to come into her body, hard and deep and strong, and then, at that perfect point of penetration, he'd tell her *everything* that was in his heart. All of it. Every single goddamn feeling and emotion rioting to life inside of him.

His long legs carried him quickly through the ancient house, and it was with a great, rushing breath that he blasted into the library—the lock falling open beneath the force of his power, the door banging against the wall twice before coming to a stop, he'd thrown it open so swiftly—only to draw to a skidding, painful stop.

She was gone.

Fucking gone!

Kieran stalked to the table where a handwritten note lay waiting, already knowing what it would say, his heart raging at the risk she had taken, palms itching to turn her over his knee and spank her into submission for the rest of his bloody days. He scanned the neat script, feeling that tender place in his soul that she inhabited rip open, bleeding and raw with terror.

Fear clawed at the back of his throat, his feet already carrying him quickly out the door, down the hall, back to his family.

Goddamn it, he was going to need all the bloody help he could get.

He burst into the study like a furious force of rage, the wind rushing behind him in a powerful surge, scattering the Council's scrolls like snowflakes in a storm.

Iain immediately gained his feet, black eyes dark with worry. "What's happened?"

"*She's gone,*" Kieran snarled.

"What?"

"She's fucking gone, Da! Shit, you were supposed to be keeping your eye on her. I thought you had this fucking place *protected.*"

"It canna be," Iain argued. "Nothing can enter across my shields!"

"No, but they can bloody well leave," he growled, shoving Té's note toward his father, already scrolling for Blu's number on his cell.

"Donald, call Dugan. Tell him I need him at the Parkinson's Brewery on 21st — *now.* Tell him to bring Lach and Mal, too."

"I dinna believe it," Iain stammered, shaking his head as his eyes scanned the letter. "She bamboozled me, that sneaky little bitch."

Donald was already dialing Dugan's number as Kieran narrowed his eyes on his father, waiting for Blu to answer the ringing of his phone. "I'm telling her you said that when I find her," he warned on his way to the door. "Trust me, old man — that'll be punishment enough for letting her get away."

Chapter Sixteen

The taxi had delivered her to the address not ten minutes ago, but already Té was questioning her sanity. Was she crazy for doing this? What if Kieran didn't find the letter she'd left for him until it was too late? Why had she placed such faith in the *feeling* that he would check on her again before leaving—that he wouldn't leave his father's without attempting to ease the dispute between them one last time?

Hell, what if he was so angry he didn't even bother with a rescue?

Maybe it was foolish, but she hadn't had a choice. Damn it, he hadn't left her with any. She couldn't just sit by while he went out and risked his life for her, night after night, never knowing when or if he would fall into one of Lexi's deadly traps. She had no doubt that Kieran could annihilate the bastard one-on-one, but neither did she expect Lexi to fight fair. No, he was a bully, and bullies always cheated.

She'd *had* to do this—she only hoped Kieran would understand why when he found her.

And please, God, let it be in time.

Already she was treading onto some treacherous territory. The brawny blond paced before her, fists clenched at his sides, his goons standing guard just outside the brewery's private offices. She stood before him, head held high, while his gloating face stared down at her, promising all the twisted retribution of his arrogant wrath. She'd rung Lexi's service using Iain's library line and had her "urgent" call put through to his private number. But he'd known the moment she sneered away from his greeting embrace that her ploy on the phone had been a lie—known she had no intention of "discussing" their reconciliation.

He was furious at her deceit, and God only knew what his reaction would be when he finally discovered that she'd left the brewery's address for Kieran, leading the McKendricks to his hideout.

True, she could have just as simply searched Kieran out and given him the address, letting him deal with Maldari on his own—but she hadn't been able to do it. She *needed* to be here—needed to be sure of what was happening or she would have gone out of her ever-loving mind. And the blunt truth of the matter was that she deserved to be a part of this. Kieran may be a devastatingly powerful warrior, but she wasn't useless. Her role in this little scenario may be no more than as decoy and diversion, damn it, but she was going to see it through to the end.

She only prayed her duplicity didn't completely occur to the malicious ass who'd once been her lover, before her *new* lover came charging to her rescue.

If he came charging to her rescue.

No, she couldn't let herself think that way, because she *knew* that he would. She trusted him to save her—even if it was from herself—and in her heart, she knew she'd done the right thing. Her beautiful wolf was probably going to kill her for it when he finally got his hands on her, but that was a battle she'd deal with when the time came.

Right now, her only worry was keeping Lexi distracted until Kieran arrived, and the best way to do that was to attack that which he held most dear—*his insufferable ego.* Only someone as arrogant as Lexi would have given her the address to this place, never guessing that she would lead his enemies to his den. Either that, or he was simply too stupid to realize that when it came to the McKendricks, his "borrowed" powers were no match for their superior strength and abilities.

"Where's your pathetic little wand?" she laughed. "Come on, Lex, aren't you going to try to enrapture me with your beauty again?"

"Wand?" he scoffed, the smooth perfection of his brow marred by a confused frown. "Sorry, but this isn't *Harry Potter*, love."

"I'm not, nor was I ever, *your* love." Her voice was hard…cool…controlled, betraying not one ounce of her fear.

He stepped closer, dressed in a cable-knit sweater and designer jeans, looking like something out of a fashion magazine, every blond curl on his head in perfect placement. Behind the fly of his jeans, there was an obvious bulge that quite simply made her want to gag.

"You may not be my love, but you were my *fuck*, weren't you, beautiful Bronté?" He reached out and stroked her cheek, smiling when she flinched beneath his caressing touch. "Tell me, have you told your overgrown pup how loud you used to scream for me? How you used to leave scratches down my back from coming so hard beneath my pounding body?" His eyes narrowed as if in memory, one finger tracing the delicate line of her jaw. "In fact, I've still got a few of the scars to prove it, sweetheart."

Her lip curled in disgust, head jerking away from his sickening touch, though she stood her ground. "And here I thought you needed a *spell* to make a woman come." His baby blues widened at her words, clearly showing his surprise. "Yeah, I'm sure you'd be amazed at the things I've learned about your kind, Lexi. Seems that *lust spells* are the only way you *Gan Bhrí* can get it up these days, eh?"

He jerked his hand high, raising it as if to strike out, but she only laughed, no longer afraid of him and his pathetic threats. "Oh, and just in case you were wondering," she drawled with a wide grin, clucking her tongue. "Kieran makes me cream with no more than a look."

He garbled out some kind of strangled sound of fury, and her head snapped to the side as his palm smacked strongly across the right side of her face, nearly knocking her to the ground. She almost gagged from the rush of blinding pain, but choked it back with a mouthful of pride, determined not to give him the satisfaction.

Breathing deeply through her nose, Té looked up at him from beneath her brows and forced a small chuckle past the tight line of her lips. "Wow, considering your reaction to that bit of news, you probably don't want to know what that big, beautiful thing between his legs does to me." And though her face hurt like a son-of-a-bitch, she shivered, her body trembling with a delicious blend of remembered sensation. Hell, if she died, at least she'd go knowing that she'd just enjoyed the most amazing twenty-four hours of her life. "He fucks me so good—I swear I can hardly walk afterwards."

There was no warning this time, though she knew it was coming. Just a blur of movement and then his fist arcing high through the air, and the next thing she knew her head cracked so hard to the left she was amazed her neck didn't break. Within seconds there was a warm, metallic taste in her mouth and she knew he'd busted her lip with that one.

She groaned beneath her breath. Oh man, Kieran was going to be so pissed at her for this.

Lexi's hand fisted in the back of hair, jerking her face up to his, and she sneered up at him, letting the full force of her hatred blaze from her pain-dazed eyes. "Tell me, sweetheart, does he make you take it like an animal?" he snarled, spittle spraying her face as he forced his words out in a raging blast of fury. "Does he fuck you with his animal's cock while you're on your knees like his little whore?"

Aching, she struggled to push the words out, but her lips burned numb with pain. His hand suddenly cracked across the left side of her face with more force than before, her lip splitting further beneath the pressure—and from somewhere inside the blackness of her mind, she could have sworn she heard Kieran's low snarl. *Thank God.* Much more of this and she'd find herself kneeing the asshole in his nuts, which would surely bring his goons rushing to his rescue. Smiling, she raised her face to look up at the real monster before her.

"I asked you a question, bitch."

"*Yessss*," she hissed, the throbbing in her jaw making it damn near impossible to speak. "He fucks me better than you and your pathetic *spells* could've ever hoped to. And you know what, Lex?" She ran her tongue over her top lip, tasting her blood, knowing Kieran could scent it on the air. She could feel his rage, the threatening force all but knocking her over as she struggled to stay upright—and she knew he was near. "He really knows how to lick, too."

Lexi's eyes narrowed to nothing more than sinister slits. "Does he now?"

"Yeah," she whispered, her lips curling in a satisfied, blood-smeared smile. "And in *all* the right places."

In the next instant, as if on cue, she heard a deep, rumbling growl on the other side of the door, followed by a series of gargling, high-pitched screams from Lexi's men—then nothing but deadly silence. Another second passed and what once had been a solid oak door splintered into two broken pieces. And there he was, looking more terrifying than she could have ever imagined.

Jesus Christ. It was the first time she'd seen him in his full-blown wolf form, standing over seven feet tall, and Té felt her heart begin a mad little dance of awed fascination.

Lexi jerked around, eyeing Kieran, his pretty features twisted into a mask of maniacal hatred…and what was beginning to resemble a very reasonable panic. "So this is your new little lapdog, Bronté?" he snorted, though his voice quivered with uncertainty.

"Isn't he beautiful?" She flashed the blond a gloating smile. "And unless I'm mistaken, Lex, you look like his midnight snack."

Kieran set his silver gaze on the *Gan Bhrí* and curled his upper lip with a low snarl, letting the abusive bastard see the gleaming length of his deadly incisors. With all the arrogance of his kind, Maldari lifted his thick arms and began an ancient chant in a futile attempt to use his borrowed power and blast his opponent with his evil—but it was of no use.

Kieran took one long look at the battle-ready *Gan Bhrí* and then roared his outrage in a howling wave of wrath. One moment Lexi stood upon his two steady legs, prepared to fight, and in the next Kieran lifted his arm and with his power over the wind, hurled the hefty blond into the far corner of the office. The *Gan Bhrí's* body slammed into the plastered wall with crushing force, ripping a pained cry from his mouth, the air around him churning with violent intensity.

"Kieran," Té called, reaching out to steady herself against the wooden desk at her back as the air inside the cold, utilitarian room continued to rip around their bodies, scattering papers across the scarred wooden floor.

"Yes, angel?" came the deep, scratchy, entirely inhuman reply.

Lach walked to her side and handed her a clean square of linen, which she used to dab at her mouth as the other McKendricks continued to stalk into the room behind her lover, their fierce expressions battle-ready and intent. "There's something I'd like for you to do for me," she drawled, voice so casual you'd have thought she was discussing nothing more interesting than the weather.

Kieran nodded his lethal head, pointed ears back in preparation for his strike. "Anything you want, lass."

Her voice went deceptively soft, and Lexi slumped onto the floor, covering his head with his arms as he crouched down into a whimpering little ball, knowing exactly what was coming—understanding far too late that he was no match for the power of a McKendrick.

Té jerked her head toward the now sniveling ass responsible for making the recent months of her life such a living hell, and smiled with deep, telling satisfaction. "Do me a favor, gorgeous, and take out the trash."

A slow smile of understanding curled Kieran's beastly mouth. "My pleasure, love." Dropping to all fours, Kieran prowled to the pitiful ball that Maldari made in the corner, big head low and menacing. When he was crouched before the *Gan Bhrí*, he made a deep, snarling noise in the back of his throat, and Lexi let out a high-pitched cry that nearly rattled the windows within their frames—the knowledge that he'd been bested pounding through his system in a nauseating tide of terror.

"You'll pay if you hurt me!" he threatened in a low, horror-filled voice that was muffled by his shielding arms. "There are those who will not allow my death to go unanswered."

Kieran merely grunted in response, the need to rip the bastard's throat out burning in his belly, but he wouldn't— *couldn't*—kill before his woman. He threw back his beastly head and howled until the very foundation shook beneath their feet, enjoying the sheer terror he inflicted upon Maldari—a small payback for the hell he'd wrought upon Té.

The howl was followed by three sharp blasts of air through his nostrils, and then he looked over his broad shoulder, knowing Dugan would be at his back, just like the rest of his cousins.

McKendricks looked out for McKendricks…and they always would.

Looking back to Maldari, who was staring at him from between his spread fingers, blue eyes terrified, Kieran leaned closer, not stopping until his snout was touching the man's trembling hands. A sudden, acrid aroma filled the air, and he knew the bastard had actually pissed himself.

"I'd take you apart myself," he snarled, "but Té's seen enough violence, thanks to you." He leaned even closer, his fang-filled mouth right at Maldari's ear, and whispered, for the *Gan Bhrí's* ears alone, "So I'm going to let my cousin do it for me. And as an Enforcer, I'm sure you'll appreciate Dugan's skill with his blade—*but no' before you've told him everything we want to know*."

Maldari made a choked, sobbing sound, and Kieran moved back, allowing Dugan to reach down and haul the trembling *Gan Bhrí* to his feet. With a deadly gleam in his dark green gaze, Dugan said, "You're going to be sorry for raising your hand to one of our women, you useless piece of shit." A slow smile curved the wide line of his mouth, as if he were actually looking forward to what lay ahead. "But first you and I are going to have a little heart-to-heart."

And with that parting promise, the two vanished from the spot, dissolving into nothingness, though Maldari had not been aware of the spell that would deliver him to his doom, in a location of Dugan's choosing.

No—the arrogant *Gan Bhrí* had already fainted.

* * * * *

The moment they were gone, Kieran padded to Té on all fours, so much larger than she had imagined he would be in this form. She opened her arms to him, and he nudged her hand with his head, the dangerous, fanged muzzle pressing into the vulnerable, giving softness of her belly like a cat nuzzling into its owner.

He could kill her in an instant, but she felt no fear. No, her only feelings were those of undeniable love and pride, and the heady beat of knowledge that he would be hers forever.

Hers…and no other's.

For an eternity.

And then the beast began to slip away, bones popping in an unmistakably painful crackle of sound, snapping in the suddenly eerie silence of the room. A sharp hissing of skin vibrated through the air, his original shape re-forming, and the man was reborn at her feet—shaky and nude, kneeling before her, the vulnerable fear in his eyes her complete undoing.

He was so large she felt dwarfed in size, even though he was on his knees, cradling his head to her belly. So big and beautiful and achingly sexy, she just wanted to melt into him.

Just pour over him in a wave of love and lust and promises until he'd taken her in—absorbed her into his pores, the rich flood of his blood, the very air that he breathed. She wanted to be pumped into the pounding beat of his heart. To feel the erotic catch of his breath. The savage surge of his arousal. All of him. She just wanted to sink inside and fill him with life—*with love.*

Oh God…she *loved* him. Loved him so much it was almost more pain than pleasure as her heart experienced its own transformation. Feeling the world shift beneath her feet as the stars spun wildly out of control, she slid away from the woman she'd once been, slipping comfortably into her own *new* skin like a butterfly shedding its cocoon, born to a new creation. Power surged through her veins like a flash of heat, pumping heavily through her heart as she expanded with everlasting love and desire…and found a magic of her own in their indestructible power.

She smiled down at him, wondering why she didn't shine with the brilliance of everything blossoming inside of her, and he clutched at her with desperate fingers biting into her tender flesh, as if he'd restrain her from leaving.

"Dinna," he grunted, the harsh word stuck in his throat. "Dinna—"

With trembling fingers, Té smoothed his tangled hair back from his wet face, tucking it behind his ears. He was unbelievably hot, pouring off heat, his skin slick with sweat and the unmistakable splashes of blood from his earlier kills in the outer hallway. "Don't what, baby?" she asked in a gentle voice, trying to soothe the anxiety she could feel in his biting grip. The pain in his expression burned so brightly, so intensely for her that it filled her with fire, scorching her veins.

His lips parted, breath panting, voice still on the raw side of inhuman, gruff and undeniably dangerous. "*Dinna…run…from…me.*" The plea came halting and passion-filled, thick with obvious fear.

Té shook her head. *Beautiful, perfect, stupid man.* Well, Warlock, she playfully corrected herself—a soft, mysterious smile spreading across her face.

Her Warlock. Her wolf.

Hell, whatever he was, she loved him and she always would.

Did he honestly not know how much she felt for him…would do for him…even die for him?

"Do you really think I would run from my Black Knight, now that I've finally found him?" she asked, holding him to her. "No one's ever protected me before, Kieran. I don't have anything to thank you with but my body and my heart and my soul, which I offer freely for the rest of my life."

He trembled. And then the cocky arrogance that trapped her every damn time resurfaced in the sexy twist of his lips. "That's no' good enough, lass."

She arched her brow. "Yeah?"

"Aye, I'll no' be happy with just *one* life. I want them all. An eternity, and I'll no' take anything but a yes for your answer."

She smoothed his hair off his wide brow with trembling fingers of her own. "And what if I were to give you something even better?"

"Better?" he repeated.

"Aye," she drawled in imitation of his sexy burr. "How about a *yes*…and a very heartfelt *I love you*."

"Oh hell, you *would* do this to me in front of these asses." His face pressed into her middle, and she could feel the telling vibration move through his powerful frame. He was danger and violence and strength personified, and here she'd shaken him to the core with the simple declaration of her love. "The miserable bastards will never let me live this down," he muttered, deep voice muffled by her sweater.

Té tried to push his hair back from his face, a strange suspicion falling over her. "Kieran, baby, are you…*crying*?"

His cheek brushed against her midriff. "Shut up, Té," he growled.

She snorted, and it was so cute and sexy all he could do was smile against the heat of her belly while the hot wash of tears continued to fall over his face.

"I give you my love and you tell me to shut up," she giggled.

"Damn, lass, are you trying to completely unman me?" he strangled out, the clear evidence of a smile in his rough voice. "I've loved you since the moment I set eyes on you, no matter how impossible it sounds. My heart loved you before my body even knew you, and I'll love you from now until—hell, Té, not even *death* will keep me away from you, woman."

A smile of pure, wondrous joy broke across her bruised mouth, fingers unable to stop stroking him. "Forever, then, Kieran."

"Aye, Té, *forever*," he vowed, and then suddenly glared up at her. "Though I still canna believe you *didna* trust me to handle this myself," he muttered, ending the statement with a dangerous growl.

Té shook her head, blinking slowly down at him. "Don't you get it? I came here because I *do* trust you. Do you think I would've taken this risk if I hadn't thought you would be able to find me, kill the creep, and then bag the babe?" she asked with a teasing wink. "The babe being me, of course."

"I think you'd have sacrificed yourself," he snarled in a low voice, the sharp edge rough with emotion and lingering fear, "if you thought it would keep those you loved safe."

"Hmm…you're probably right. I guess it's a good thing that the *one* I love most of all is the biggest bad-ass around, huh? He can save me from my harebrained schemes and anything else that comes along."

Kieran's breath released on a long, meaningful sigh of relief, as if he was only just now starting to accept that they had won and the danger was over—at least for the moment. "Aye, that he can."

A wicked grin curled her lips. "Are you going to let me make it up to you?"

"When Blu's no longer watching you like a drooling mutt, you bet your sweet little ass I will."

Té looked over her shoulder in time to see Blu dragging his hot gaze back up to her face. She shook her head at his outrageousness, and the sexy rascal had the audacity to wink at her. Looking back to Kieran, she sighed and said, "You know you can't hurt him, Kieran. He only does it to rile you, anyway."

"No," he countered, big hands holding possessively to her waist, "he does it because you're a beautiful woman and he likes the view. So long as he's only looking, I'll let him live. But if he ever tries to touch you—"

Blu threw up his hands in surrender. "I'll no' touch what doesna belong to me, Kieran. Two banished family members are enough. I've no wish to end up like Colin, the poor bugger. Or Zach, for that matter."

"Who are Colin and Zach?" Té demanded with wide eyes. "Just how *many* of you McKendricks are there?"

"It's a long story, love," Kieran explained, rising to his feet, not a stitch of clothing covering his magnificent body as he pulled her into his side and reached for the bag of clothes a laughing Mal was handing him. "A verra long story, so I'll be tellin' ya *after*."

"After what?"

His hot eyes burned into her, smoldering with promise. "Why dinna you try to guess?"

Chapter Seventeen

"I'm too on edge right now. I willna be able to control it," Kieran rasped, his eyes wild, focused intently on the bruised bite in her shoulder, the flame of possession and desire and what was most definitely *love* igniting his gaze. They stood before a roaring fire in what had once been his bedroom, but would now be theirs.

Té stroked her greedy palms over the flat, ripped planes of his naked chest, marveling at the carnal beauty of his body. He'd already used his miraculous power to heal her wounds, easily done since Maldari had no longer been fully *Magick*, and now he'd heal her heart. "Good—I don't want you to," she whispered on a husky moan, leaning forward to nip his left nipple, his breath hissing between his lips like a rush of pain-edged pleasure. "What I want is for you to fuck me. What I *want* is for you to take me the way you need to—no matter how that might be."

"You take me any better and it'll kill me, lass. But I'll no' hurt you."

"Don't make me force you, Kieran."

He snorted, eyes bright with challenge and lust...and something remarkably beautiful, sparking in the liquid black pools of his eyes. Devil's eyes, like the wicked bastard he was. Mesmerizing and erotically seductive, bringing her to her knees...literally.

He stared down at her, his mouth opening and closing twice before he was able to form the words he needed to say to warn her. "Saephus, dinna be doing that, Té. If you fuck me with that hot little mouth, I'll lose it before we ever even make it to the bed. I'll change on you before you know what's hit you, and you'll find a wolf's cock crammed down your throat, darlin'."

She worked rapidly on the button fly of his jeans, quickly pulling them down over his hips with one great shove that included the dark gray boxers Mal had brought him as well. Immediately, his cock sprang free, so many incredibly long, thick inches of male perfection, eager to breathe now that she'd offered it freedom, one shiny drop of fluid already glistening at the heavy, plum-sized tip. Her breath caught in her throat, and she leaned closer, rubbing the hot blaze of his silken skin with her cheek, savoring his warm, delicious scent. "Why don't you just shut up," she sighed, voice breathless with anticipation, "and let the poor pup have some fun."

"Pup?" he half snarled, half laughed, the outrage he'd been trying for lost in the rough purr of arousal as he tangled his hands in her mane of red-gold silk, every muscle in his body drawing so tight with expectation that he was amazed when he didn't snap from the tension.

"Yeah, he wants to have some fun and get nasty with me, but you're cramping his style. So beat it, or learn to play along."

"I dinna understand you, woman. You should be running...screaming...no' tempting me to fuck this sweet, angel face. It'll no' be easy, Te. It's hard enough no' hurting you as a man. I'm too fucking strong and too bloody big."

"Mmm...I like you *big*," she moaned, lifting up so she could swipe her warm tongue across the wide, blunt head, loving the way it so perfectly topped off what was a perfectly beautiful, brutal cock. It tasted hot and salty, with a touch of musk, the warm skin silky against her lips while beneath he was nothing but granite-hard blood and hunger. "I'm American, remember? We live by that whole 'the bigger the better' motto. Big country. Big buildings. I just can't help it. I see this big, beautiful cock of yours and the Yank in me just turns into a bloodthirsty little nympho."

"Ah Saephus, you're too perfect to resist, you know that?"

Her lips curled in a carnal smile, clearly enjoying the power she held over him. "Then stop trying, beautiful."

"I'm no' *beautiful*," he snorted, obviously insulted.

"Oh yes, you are. I'm going to have my hands full for years to come, beating off all the little hussies who'll follow you around."

His hands tightened, pulling her hard against his groin. "Dinna do that."

Té shifted to better see his face, wondering at the sudden edge of tension in his black gaze. "What?"

"Dinna ever, for even a single second, worry yourself over that. I dinna want—" he grated, glittering eyes nearly crossing as she made her first full pass across the glistening head of his cock, twirling her pink tongue around the proud circumference before digging eagerly into the wet slit with the tip. "Oh hell…I willna ever want anyone but you," he finished raggedly, wondering if she was going to drive him crazy, sending him spewing into the air with embarrassing speed from the touch of her lips alone.

She looked up at him from beneath the thick fringe of her lashes, and he didn't care for her expression, as if she still thought he was only telling her what she wanted to hear. Hunger exploded through his system on a fierce wave of possessiveness, the need to make her understand exactly what he was getting at burning him alive.

Heat engulfed his senses, the blunt tip of his cock like a hot brand as it brushed against her cool, silken lips, and he wondered if the top of his head would come off as a knot of emotion threatened to rip through him, shattering his control. Fisting one hand in the luxurious mass of her hair, he tilted her face up to his, his cock bouncing, nudging the side of her cheek. He didn't want to scare or sicken her, but he could feel the reason of the man slipping away as the wolf's desire for dominance bled through his lust-thickened system, building a steady, thundering momentum. His lips pulled back over his elongating teeth, and he snarled, "We're mated—forever—and you carry my bloody mark. Any fucking we do *will* be done between the two of us—and it'll be done *often*. Hard and heavy, as much you can possibly take, woman. And when you beg for mercy, you best be knowing I've no stopping point when it comes to you."

Her eyes went heavy and she trembled with longing, jerking in his grip until she could run her tongue across the wet, delicious, purpled crest of his cock. "Sounds good to me," she drawled in a husky rasp, holding his brilliant stare as she scraped her teeth across the slick, bulging head, nipping him softly as his fine musky scent swam through her head, drugging her with hunger. "But I'm not taking any chances."

He looked down at her, eyes bleeding to the molten silver of the wolf, and he growled, "You'll take my bloody word on this woman—my promise--my *oath* that I willna ever want or take or fuck anyone but you till I take my last breath in this dimension, and even when we move on into the next. You've my word as a McKendrick on that, lass."

"Then prove it to me, Kieran. Prove how much I mean to you. *Change for me.*"

He shook his dark head, black hair flying, the air in the room growing turbulent, whipping the light gauze of the inner curtains against the heavy panes of glass in the windows. "You willna be able to handle it!"

She licked the wet head of his cock, holding his blistering stare, and smiled her intent. "Wanna bet?"

"*You'll run,*" he snarled.

She caught the blunt tip of his cock in her teeth and nipped, his size almost failing to fit within the circle of her lips, making her stretch them as wide as possible before pulling slowly back. "Like hell."

"The mating curse is broken, Té," he muttered, beginning to look desperate. "It's over. Leave it."

She shook her head. "No, I don't think so."

"*Damn it, woman*," he roared.

"I want this, Kieran. I want you to trust me to know what I want. Know that I want you, no matter who or what the hell you might be. It doesn't matter. It's *never* going to matter."

And then she opened her mouth over him, sucking him into the moist, hot cavern of her throat, and he threw back his head, a sharp, rumbling cry piercing the silence of the room. Her mouth tightened on him at the hungry sound, and she sucked him harder, her cheeks hollowing out as she enveloped him in lush, wet heat and struggled to draw him deeper, his cock like a burning, pumping mass of silk-covered steel within her mouth. She loved his taste, the raw-edged energy she could feel blasting against her.

His hips jerked once, nearly gagging her as his long shaft surged past her comfort point, but she relaxed her throat and was ready for the second thrust. Then he pulled back before the third.

Kieran tried to stumble away, his mind going blurry as his blood pumped with hunger and the beast stirred to life, crawling beneath his skin.

Saephus, he was going to change—right here, right now. He took another step back, struggling for control of his body, but she'd followed him, her hot little mouth capturing him again, eager tongue stroking the bulging head of his cock—and he was lost.

Throwing back his head, he let out a painful, screaming howl as the wolf broke free, feeling himself fall away, the determined strokes of her wet mouth ripping his beast to the surface with each strong, luscious pull against his cock.

He stared down at her, her deep blue eyes bright with feminine power, rosy mouth stuffed full of his dick, and watched as his body became something so foreign, and yet so much a part of him.

"Dinna be afraid" he pleaded, eyes begging for her understanding.

She pulled away from his dick with a greedy moan, licking the swollen, darkening head with her pink tongue, and laughed up at him. "Don't worry, sexy—I'm not."

And she wasn't. She craved him, starved for the feel of his power exploding into her mouth. She didn't understand the acceptance spilling warmly through her blood, blossoming to life within her soul. Didn't understand the power loving him gave her, searing through her veins, throbbing with life, anymore than he did—but she was more than woman enough to celebrate it. She felt each individual cell of her body, living and breathing—every facet of her being focused on the pleasure of being with him...giving to him...taking from him. She should've been terrified by the sheer magnificence of his power, but all she felt was love...and the burning need to blow his mind as fiercely as he'd blown hers.

They completed one another, and the gorgeous, arrogant animal was going to admit defeat one way or another.

And she'd happily fuck him into submission until he did.

Releasing his pulsing cock, Té rose to her feet and pushed him backward toward the bed, crawling over him as he fell against the white sheets. With a wicked smile, she straddled his changing cock, positioning him against the wet, pink lips of her cunt, and sank slowly down onto him. Hands which now sported deadly claws gripped her slim hips, careful not to harm her, helping to pull her down until she'd taken every impossible inch, her mouth open and panting, breasts heaving from her weighty breaths.

When she'd taken all of it, his cock packed up tight inside of her, she smiled down at him, while Kieran stared up at her in helpless wonder, completely in her thrall. Then she reached back between his spread legs and grabbed the hot, heavy weight of his balls, massaging them—squeezing—all the while working his monstrous cock into the wet, luscious heat of her cunt with the steady roll of her hips, and he threw back his head and howled with all his might, the beastly sound roaring through the room, echoing off the walls in a painful blast of sound.

Saephus help him, he could feel every silken slide of skin against skin as his thick flesh parted her tight walls, stretching her so wide, forcing the delicate slit to accept the brutal possession of his cock.

He thrust beneath her, pounding into her rhythmic movements, claws clamped possessively on her soft hips as he drilled up into the sleek, sweet suction of her cunt. And then suddenly he had her flat on her back, his hot, heavy body pressing into her, holding her down as he lunged over her, forcing her thighs to spread outrageously wide, completely open to him—to the *creature* he'd become.

"Ready to run?" he snarled, rough voice far from natural.

She shook her head against the stark white of the sheets. "No…never."

His eyes narrowed—the silver of his irises gleaming in a spiraling swirl of color. "You asked for this."

"Yeah, and I'll probably ask again," she drawled, clutching at his bulging biceps as they thickened beneath her fingers, his beast still stretching to life within his skin. "What can I say? You really do it for me."

Té thought he might have laughed, but it was hard to say for certain, with his voice so coarse and guttural.

But he was so beautiful it was breathtaking. His skin had gone a deep, dark, mesmerizing bluish-black, eyes gleaming down at her like mercury—molten silver—fascinating in their beauty. A fine pelt of soft, short fur covered his arms and legs, his chest bare, rippling with muscles as he ground into her, pulsing against her clit, killing her with the pleasure. His hair was still long, ears tipped with wicked little points, canines gleaming, though his face still retained his human shape. Those long incisors gleamed dangerously behind his parted lips, making him look like a sexy-as-sin vampire come to life. She smiled up at him, breath caught at the wonder of all that he was, and the perfection…the sheer *longing* of the smile he returned, curled her toes in savage delight.

He stared down at her, his eyes gleaming like the painful flash of metal in the hot sunlight—the animal reveling in the feel of her beneath *them*. His claws dug into the bedding, fabric ripping, and his mouth attacked hers with all the lust and feral passion of the beast, drunk on the powerful emotion of the man. He pulled her into his mouth, sucked her down his throat, as if her life were drawn through the rapacious, wicked demands of his lips and tongue and teeth.

Sharp teeth. Deadly and dangerous, piercing her lip with the utmost care so he could drink her down his throat into the aching, greedy depths of his belly. Té cried out in hunger and ecstasy, and Kieran swallowed the sound, craving more, wanting her screaming with pleasure. She was warm and sweet, like liquid lust, a heady flavor that sang to his heart, thickening his cock to the point of pain.

With a snarl, he ripped his mouth from hers, his lips red with her blood, and Té stared up at him with her mouth open, neck arched, breath panting in sharp gasps as his body continued to drive her higher and higher. The thick, plunging strokes surged ever deeper, reaching parts of her she'd never known existed, until it felt as if he lived in the fiery, sizzling liquid center of her womb.

"*Watch*," he growled in a low, rumbling rasp.

She lifted up on her elbows, taking in the intimate, erotic sight of her wolf's beautiful cock fucking her, moving in and out of her wet, pink little slit. It was intoxicating—the dark, veined flesh pushing, stretching her delicate entrance so impossibly wide, her glistening juices drenching them both, and the humid air filled with the wet, slick, slapping sounds of an incredible, powerful fuck.

Kieran looked with her, watching the pink, wet flesh of her cunt quiver as he drilled into it with his throbbing cock, giving it to her as hard as he dared. Then he fastened his avid gaze onto the pebbled tips of her lush, swaying breasts, her nipples as plump and pink as ripe little berries.

"What are you trying to tell me, beautiful?" she asked around a slow, knowing smile. "What do you want?"

A low growl rumbled in his throat, and he looked down at the sopping wetness of her penetrated cunt, then fixed his gaze hungrily upon those sweet, bouncing tits once again.

Té smiled up at him, then slipped her fingers between their bodies, down between her widespread legs, and dragged the slender digits through the rich juices spilling from her body, her cool fingers brushing the blistering heat of his cock as it pistoned in and out of her. When they were nice and slick, she brought her hand up to her chest and slowly painted the trembling tips of her breasts with her cream, his silver eyes following every soft stroke. When they were shiny and wet, she stopped, lifting her fingers to his beautiful mouth, pressing them between his silken lips.

He sucked the honeyed juices from her flesh, chest rumbling, eyes narrowed with a hunger that went beyond sex, to something deeper and erotically thrilling. "So good," he snarled, looking as if he'd like nothing more than to take a big ol' bite out of her.

But Té knew *exactly* what he wanted.

Placing her hands beneath her breasts, she palmed them, lifting the swaying mounds up in offering. "Eat, Kieran. I know you want it."

His cock slammed into her so hard it jerked another startled cry from her tender throat, and he quickly lowered his head, pulling one breast into the biting heat of his mouth, wrapping his tongue around the juice-painted tip, suckling her as if he'd draw her straight into his belly. Her back arched, carnal screams of raging pleasure ripping from her throat as he ate at her breast, his cock hammering her into a building orgasm that felt as if it would tear her apart. And when it finally came, when he latched onto the other nipple, pulling the entire breast between his jaws and allowed his teeth to pierce the firm, silky flesh, her warm blood spilling into his mouth, she exploded, her cunt squeezing down like a hot little clamp, milking his pounding cock.

He drove into her harder, intensely powerful, pounding her into the mattress, until she should have been ripped and bleeding from the force, and yet she took him, the orgasm pounding through her system so violently it felt like death. He was so blissfully hot…so wonderfully wide…the long, thick heat of his cock cramming into her clenching depths over and over — the aggressive, grinding motion of his hips working him into her suctioning depths again and again. The bed screeched against the wall and wooden floor, the scraping noise punctuated by their combined shouts and laboring struggles for air, a symphony of sound that resembled a battlefield of lust, tempered only by love. He rode her without mercy, and she took him with a craving equal to his own, reveling in the carnal bliss of being so utterly fucked with no control by the man she loved with all that she was — with everything.

The long muscles of his biceps tightened as he lifted away from her, the liquid silver of his eyes a roiling flame as he looked down at their joined bodies, watching the beautiful, erotic sight of his dark, vein-bulged cock spearing into the tight little hole of her pulsing cunt — her sweet, pink lips bare and glistening as her cum slipped free — stretched to an obscene extreme — and yet, taking everything that he had.

"Té," he cried out, his voice jagged and low, more beast than man.

"Kieran," she sobbed, the intensity of her orgasm going on and on, until she could do nothing but ride the thundering wave of pleasure with utter abandon.

"*Té…I…hell —*"

And then she smiled up at him, her beautiful face glowing, flushed with love, and Kieran felt as if he would shatter from the rush of wonder spilling through his thrusting body. "It's okay, baby," she whispered. "I love it. *I love you.*"

"Ah, Saephus, I'm going to come. I'm going to fill you so fucking full."

And he did. With one final impaling stroke that lifted her hips and back off the bed, he rammed into her and his dick exploded, a violent wave of release erupting like a burning flame from the buried head of his shaft, spurting into her womb, drenching her with his cum.

Another searing orgasm knotted her womb, caressing the pumping length of his cock, and he shouted into the pillow at her ear, grinding against her, coming and coming until the slick fluid was spilling out of her, drenching them, wetting the sheets. They bucked and jolted, her arms wrapped tight around his head as she held on for dear life, wondering if she'd pass out before it was over.

"*Baby…baby…baby,*" he grunted in her ear, his voice a low rasp, and she knew that in that moment it was true. He was giving her a child, and it was suddenly the one thing she wanted above all others—*Kieran's baby.*

Chapter Eighteen

Most Binding Ceremonies were joyous affairs, but never was one quite so crazy as Kieran and Té's. Of course it was all the doing of the groom, who could no more keep his hands off the glowing bride than he could concentrate on the ceremonial words he was supposed to say. He was too deliriously happy and preoccupied with trying to steal a taste of his radiant mate's lush lips to listen to Seamus' repeated prompting. It took three tries before he was finally able to properly recite his binding vows, while Blu and Mal snickered with mischievous glee from their places in the front row of chairs within the grand hall at Seamus' country estate.

As was custom, they were dressed in white ceremonial robes, while each member of the Council created a shimmering band of silver light to wrap around the couple as they knelt upon a raised dais fashioned of pure, intricately carved gold. The smiling couple faced one another, faces bent close together, their bodies pressed flush against the other, the spiraling bands "bonding" them, pulling tight against their legs and torsos until the couple themselves shone with glinting arcs of light, their bodies aglow with a soothing, mystical heat.

As Council Leader, Seamus recited the ceremonial chants in the lyrical language of Kieran's *Magickal* ancestors, the joyous words a celebration of everlasting love and fidelity. The packed room sat in reverent silence while the remaining four Council members joined in with the closing chants, the final blessing only moments away, when the couple suddenly vanished, the bands of light left hovering in empty space, the dais shockingly missing a bride and groom.

Seamus stared with wide eyes, his jaw hanging open in stunned surprise before he was finally able to stammer, "What? Where? Are they—*is he just going to*—"

Iain nodded his white head, an unmistakable gleam of humor blazing within his black eyes. "Aye, he is."

The Council Leader blinked slowly, his voice a hoarse rasp as he proclaimed, "He canna do this!"

"Och, now, Seamus," snorted Conrad, nodding to the empty dais, "all evidence would point to the contrary."

"It's an *outrage*," the esteemed leader grated through his teeth.

And then, almost before the words had left his lips, the couple reappeared, caught once more within their shimmering bonds, their faces flushed with apparent, visible satisfaction, mouths still intimately attached, arms entwined tight around the other's neck.

Iain cleared his throat, hoping to gain his son's attention, while Seamus gathered his ceremonial robes around him with a great, irritated flourish, preparing to conclude the event before any more "unexpected" happenings occurred.

Unfortunately, he wasn't quite fast enough. Two stanzas into the closing chant, Kieran growled into his bride's mouth, kissing her like a man possessed, and in the next instant they were gone again, vanished, the bands left empty once more.

Seamus tossed up his hands in disgust, while Lach threw back his head and roared with laughter, Evan elbowed him in his side, and Blu, Mal, and *the girls* snickered with wicked delight. Even Dugan's lips curled in a humorous smirk, dark green eyes momentarily alight with laughter.

"Damn it, Iain," Seamus roared. "Will you go get your son! The lad canna be this bloody randy. He only just *had* the lass thirty seconds ago!"

"Knowing Kieran, I dinna think he's ready to be got just yet," Blu called out from his seat. "That first one was just the teaser."

Seamus grunted in exasperation. "We've no' even had the bloody celebration yet."

"Oh, I think he's probably already started one of his own," Mal drawled from his sprawled position beside the now tearing Blu, the entire hall erupting into uncontrollable giggles over Kieran's apparent *inability* to control himself around his beautiful bride.

At the end of his patience, Seamus raised his voice to a towering bellow, loud enough to bring the ancient walls crashing down. "Kieran Lindsay McKendrick, get your blasted ass back in these bonds or I willna complete this bloody ceremony! Do you hear me, boy?"

Five. Ten. Fifteen seconds passed, with no sign of the couple, and then they finally reappeared, Té's robe slipping precariously off one shoulder, and Kieran's greedy mouth still attached to her own. With what appeared—to the avid eyes watching them—to take considerable effort, he finally managed to stop kissing her long enough to lift his dark head and address the Council. He stared at Seamus with liquid eyes shimmering from midnight black to glinting silver, control clearly hanging by a tenuous thread.

"Finish it," both man and beast ordered, rasping voice thick with lust and love. "*Now.*"

Seamus motioned the other members quickly back into place, muttering a low litany of curses beneath his breath, and then promptly had them moving forward once more. The bonds remained intact, binding the couple securely within their *Magickal* power as the final chants were recited, the deliriously happy bride and groom lost in the other's gaze. Then Seamus finally gave the closing blessing, and the bands began to spiral with a dizzying, mesmerizing speed.

Within the whirring, hypnotic spiral, Té looked up into her husband's beautiful gaze, feeling his heart within her chest, beating beside her own, knowing that the wonder of what she'd found would last for all eternity. Kieran smiled down at her, mouthing the words, "I love you," over the hissing of the bands as they moved faster and faster, creating a crackling sound of air and electricity. And then suddenly the bands erupted into a shimmering, mesmerizing blast of gleaming pinpoints of fiery light that shot high up into the air, slowly showering down upon the kissing couple and their cheering guests.

"Forever," groaned Kieran, nuzzling her smiling lips.

"Aye," laughed Té, mimicking his deep burr. "Forever."

* * * * *

"You took it too far, you know—this time—considering his circumstances," Lach remarked in his deep voice, the last of the guests making their way out while he and Seamus sat in the back garden enjoying their ales and late-night smokes. The bride and groom had already retired upstairs to one of the many lavish suites, and no one expected to see them emerge anytime soon. At least not if Kieran had his way.

Seamus nodded sagely, thinking on Lach's words while savoring a long draw from his pipe. Finally, he said, "We did what had to be done."

Lach snorted. "You couldna have just cursed his cock— same as you did mine?"

"Och," Seamus tsked, shaking his silver-threaded head of hair. "The lot o' you are too bloody clever for that. You'd have figured out a way around it by now. No, we'll keep you guessing. It's the only hope we have of making this work to its completion."

Lach's auburn brow arched, green eyes bright with humor. "You could just leave it to fate, you know."

"With the way you five run—have *always* run—from commitment!" Seamus snorted. "We were no' born yesterday, Lachlan McKendrick. And with this reappearance of the *Gan Bhrí* and that bloody list Dugan got out of Maldari, we can no longer wait for the five of you to find your mates in your own time. Who knows how many others have bartered their way back to power, as he did. No, the McKendrick Clan needs to be at full strength—our warriors complete, both in heart and soul—if we are to survive."

"And what of Colin and Zach?" Lach drawled, finishing off the last of his icy cold McEwans. He'd always found it unspeakably unfair that his cousins had been forced into exile and banishment, when their so-called crimes had been far from serious. But then—when one angered a god, one tended to pay a higher price than others. Still, it had never sat well with him that they served sentences better suited to men of Maldari's rank.

The only saving grace was that they had not been sentenced as *Gan Bhrí*. When—or rather, *if*—they were ever allowed to return to this world, their power would remain intact.

Seamus' brow furrowed at his nephew's question, bushy brows merging into one long line of worry and discontent. "Aye, we'll have to come to a decision about those two—sooner, rather than later, mind you."

"Well, you know how I feel about it—have *always* felt about it. The punishments were too harsh, and they've been gone for too damn long. They dinna deserve to be treated like criminals."

"Aye, but then—it's no' an easy world we live in, is it, boy?"

Lach leaned back in his chair and gave a crooked grin, shaking his head in amazement. "Seamus, I'm thirty-six years old and blissfully mated to the most remarkable woman in the world. Dinna you think it's time you began to refer to me as a *man*?"

Seamus snickered, thumping his purely decorative cane upon the terracotta tiling of the patio with a sharp blast of sound. "Until you've bred that beautiful little lass of yours and contributed to this clan, you'll remain a boy, Lachlan McKendrick, and not a day sooner."

The keen, shit-eating smirk that slowly spread across Lach's face gave his game away in the next instant. Seamus appeared dumbstruck, but for a moment, then let out a high-pitched wheezing of sound that Lach could only guess was some kind of cross between a joyous shout and gleeful laughter.

"May the gods bless you," the elder finally announced in a booming voice, slapping him heartily on his broad shoulder.

Just then Evan made her way through the French doors, waving to her husband as she began to weave her way through the many tables that had been set up for the party's guests. The corners of his green eyes creased as he smiled, his heart tripping, pounding with the kind of love and devotion that only grew stronger each day, filling his life with inconceivable joy. "They already have," he replied with deep satisfaction, his hot eyes glued to the gentle roll of her hips as she made her way to him. "Trust me, Uncle, they already have."

Enjoy this excerpt from
Against the Wall
© Copyright Rhyannon Byrd 2004

The first words to pop into her head were strange ones—a resurrection from the warmth of childhood in an instinctual attempt to find comfort in the decidedly uncomfortable.

I don't think we're in Kansas anymore…

How wonderfully mad to be quoting The Wizard of Oz, she mused—but standing in the doorway of Red's Bar, Shea Dresden felt a strange affinity with the displaced Dorothy and her little dog. Red's was definitely a far cry from her usual haunts. Places like the university's lecture hall and library.

Yeah, okay, so she was a geek. No one knew that better than she. But she was a determined geek, damn it, and no Wicked Witch of the West or burly looking bully was going to send her running before she got what she'd come here for!

Yeah, you go girl, her woman's pride cheered, and Shea put everything she had into focusing on the rallying war cry, rather than the flurry of nervous energy pumping through her over-excited system. Her body quaked with it, and the smoke filled air only made the nauseating exhilaration that much worse.

It wasn't that she couldn't stand a little smoke. Heck, she smoked sometimes herself, when she got too restless or tense—or just needed an excuse to sit on her balcony listening for her next-door neighbor Ryan. But this wasn't just a little smoke. The inside of Red's was dingy gray with the thickness of it, and Shea knew when she left she'd still be able to smell it on her clothes and in her hair.

Not that I'm wearing all that many clothes, she thought with a wry twist of her lips, but then she was here to meet a man.

And not just any man, honey, her incessantly complaining libido chimed in, *but Ryan McCall, the sexiest damn thing we've ever set eyes on!*

Ryan was everything Shea thought a man should be, and gorgeous to boot. Tall, tawny-headed, and ruggedly, insanely, *made you want to wrestle him to the nearest bed* handsome.

Without a doubt, the quintessential stud.

Shea wanted him unlike anything she'd ever wanted before. Wanted him enough to swallow her stupid pride and do whatever—*whatever*—it took to get him. She was done accepting his casual brush-offs. Done tiptoeing around that infuriating distance he insisted on maintaining between them.

Tonight, she was ready to get as up close and personal as two people could get. Ready to slip under his guard and batter down his defenses until she'd gotten as far into him as he'd worked his way into her. She wanted it all, every single intoxicating detail that made him so irresistible. Wanted absolute access to every breathtaking inch of skin, muscle, and bone. Wanted to know first hand how it felt to be at the mercy of all that overwhelmingly raw, masculine power.

That's why she was here.

"When he wants a woman," her best friend Hannah had told her, "Ry likes to hang out at Red's. It's not that it's really dangerous or anything, but it definitely caters to a rough and tumble kind of crowd. Let's just say it's not the kind of place where you and I would hang out, but Ry does just fine there."

Shea had wanted to know why someone as gorgeous as Ryan McCall didn't have a steady girlfriend, when he could so obviously have his choice of any woman he wanted.

And that had been Hannah's answer.

Red Mackey's Bar.

Ryan, it seemed, preferred a no-strings-attached brand of sex—and he found it at Red's.

It was hard to believe the sexy ATF agent resorted to this place for his pleasure, but Hannah had known Ryan forever. If she said he went to Red's to get laid, then Shea knew it was true. Why he would come here to look for a woman was beyond her, but here she was, ready to do her best to finally get the stud right where she wanted him.

Sure, she didn't know a whole heck of a lot about playing the part of a hot, willing, available woman, but no way in hell was she letting that hold her back. Tonight, Shea intended to be that woman—the one—*the woman*, which was why her palms were damp and her stomach was flip-flopping with sexual tension, winding her up tight enough to snap.

It wasn't that she was afraid. Not of Ryan—not of how she felt about him—and she sure as hell wasn't afraid of what she wanted from him.

The only thing she feared now was failure—but tonight it wasn't going to be an option.

She worried about going through life never craving another human being the way she craved him. But she had it now, that heady, beautiful burn of need spearing through her system, and all she wanted to do was embrace it. Celebrate it. Satisfy it. She wanted to surrender and succumb to it, drowning her senses…drenching them in the ravenous, insatiable, consuming feelings of heart-pounding lust and sexual hunger that this man inspired in her. Wanted to fill up on the dizzying rush of energy that just looking at him pumped through her veins, filling her cells, until she felt packed full of life.

And more than anything in the world, she wanted to be packed full of that beautiful bad boy.

All she had to do was find him. Of course, beneath the eerie, flickering glow of the fluorescent beer signs, that was probably going to be harder than she'd expected.

Damn, and here she'd thought this would be the easy part. It was Friday night, and despite its nitty-gritty interior, Red's was packed with people. Men and women obviously looking for a place where they could drown their sorrows and hook up with a warm body for the night.

And Shea knew Ryan wasn't much of a drinker.

She also knew he wasn't much on relationships either, but she hoped to change that. At least that was the plan. The first part of the plan, though, was to get sex. Lots and lots of hard, heavy, mind-shattering sex—with Ryan.

About the author:

Rhyannon Byrd is the wife of a Brit, mother of two amazing children, and maid to a precocious beagle named Misha. A longtime fan of romance, she finally felt at home when she read her first Romantica novel. Her love of this spicy, ever-changing genre has become an unquenchable passion—the hotter they are, the better she enjoys them!

Writing for Ellora's Cave is a dream come true for Rhyannon. Now her days (and let's face it, most nights) are spent giving life to the stories and characters running wild in her head. Whether she's writing contemporaries, paranormals…or even futuristics, there's always sure to be a strong Alpha hero featured as well as a fascinating woman to capture his heart, keeping all that wicked wildness for her own!

Rhyannon welcomes mail from readers. You can write to her c/o Ellora's Cave Publishing at 1056 Home Ave. Akron, Oh 44310-3502.

Why an electronic book?

We live in the Information Age—an exciting time in the history of human civilization in which technology rules supreme and continues to progress in leaps and bounds every minute of every hour of every day. For a multitude of reasons, more and more avid literary fans are opting to purchase e-books instead of paperbacks. The question to those not yet initiated to the world of electronic reading is simply: *why?*

1. *Price.* An electronic title at Ellora's Cave Publishing and Cerridwen Press runs anywhere from 40-75% less than the cover price of the exact same title in paperback format. Why? Cold mathematics. It is less expensive to publish an e-book than it is to publish a paperback, so the savings are passed along to the consumer.

2. *Space.* Running out of room to house your paperback books? That is one worry you will never have with electronic novels. For a low one-time cost, you can purchase a handheld computer designed specifically for e-reading purposes. Many e-readers are larger than the average handheld, giving you plenty of screen room. Better yet, hundreds of titles can be stored within your new library—a single microchip. (Please note that Ellora's Cave and Cerridwen Press does not endorse any specific brands. You can check our website at www.ellorascave.com or

www.cerridwenpress.com for customer recommendations we make available to new consumers.)

3. *Mobility.* Because your new library now consists of only a microchip, your entire cache of books can be taken with you wherever you go.

4. *Personal preferences are accounted for.* Are the words you are currently reading too small? Too large? Too...**ANNOYING**? Paperback books cannot be modified according to personal preferences, but e-books can.

5. *Instant gratification.* Is it the middle of the night and all the bookstores are closed? Are you tired of waiting days—sometimes weeks—for online and offline bookstores to ship the novels you bought? Ellora's Cave Publishing sells instantaneous downloads 24 hours a day, 7 days a week, 365 days a year. Our e-book delivery system is 100% automated, meaning your order is filled as soon as you pay for it.

Those are a few of the top reasons why electronic novels are displacing paperbacks for many an avid reader. As always, Ellora's Cave and Cerridwen Press welcomes your questions and comments. We invite you to email us at service@ellorascave.com, service@cerridwenpress.com or write to us directly at: 1056 Home Ave. Akron OH 44310-3502.

NEED A MORE EXCITING
WAY TO PLAN YOUR DAY?

ELLORA'S
CAVEMEN
2006 CALENDAR

COMING THIS FALL

THE
ELLORA'8 CAVE
LIBRARY

Stay up to date with Ellora's Cave Titles
in Print with our Quarterly Catalog.

To recieve a catalog,
send an email with your name
and mailing address to:

CATALOG@ELLORASCAVE.COM
or send a letter or postcard
with your mailing address to:
Catalog Request
c/o Ellora's Cave Publishing, Inc.
1337 Commerce Drive #13
Stow, OH 44224

Discover for yourself why readers can't get enough of the multiple award-winning publisher Ellora's Cave. Whether you prefer e-books or paperbacks, be sure to visit EC on the web at www.ellorascave.com for an erotic reading experience that will leave you breathless.

www.ellorascave.com